OF DONKEYS, GODS, AND SPACE PIRATES

THE ADVENTURES OF HAROLD THE DONKEY

ETHAN FRECKLETON

J. R. FRONTERA

To everyone who saw 'donkeys' and 'space pirates' and immediately thought 'ass pirates'—that's not what this story is about; but we salute you and your brilliant twelve-year-old mind.

1

This is the story of Harold the Ass, who would one day be known across the far-flung reaches of the galaxy as Dread Pirate Harry. But today was not that day. Today was just another morning on an idyllic grassy plain not unlike one you'd find on planet Earth.

Upon this grassy plain grazed a herd of donkeys. Well, *most* of them were grazing.

To all outward appearances, Harry was a typical young standard jack with a shaggy gray coat, offset by solid patches of white around the nose and eyes. Unlike his companions, however, Harry could talk.

"Oh come on, won't somebody *puh-leeze* scratch my butt? It's so itchy right now, it's driving me crazy!" He backed slowly toward a wary donkey, hopeful they might oblige. But he had no such luck.

Life might be a little monotonous for the average donkey, but they had it good. Plenty of land to graze upon, plenty of fresh water from the streams, and little else to worry about save the standard basics of donkey survival. Given the lack of predators on planet Cern, life was pretty easy. All they had to do was avoid running off a cliff … or otherwise accidentally offing themselves.

Keeping the donkeys safe from such incidents was Harry's one and only job. It wasn't a particularly demanding job, come to think of it.

Harry's tail swished back and forth with irritation. "You guys are no fun. C'mon, who wants to do something? Let's play! Or … *something.* Don't you guys ever get *bored* of just doing the same thing *every single day?*"

The nearest donkeys slowly walked away.

A butterfly lazily zigzagged its way past his nose as his head sagged toward the knee-length grass. Harry wanted more out of life than the other donkeys. That was part of the problem. The other part of the problem? He wasn't actually a donkey at all.

You see, Harry was a highly evolved variant of what you might describe as a tick. This particular variant had developed the ability to live in symbiosis with mammals. They could nuzzle into the spine of their host and even take direct control of its movements.

Harry was the only symbiont in this self-contained herd of donkeys. The sole sentient being. It hadn't always been that way for our future hero, but that's a story for another time…

Now, dejected, he released control of his host and let his mind wander.

After a while, a brave—or otherwise oblivious—brown-coated jenny meandered by.

Harry's host, whom Harry called Buddy, twitched his ears for reasons Harry couldn't understand. Then, he arched his neck and pawed at the ground, prancing back and forth as he released a harsh bray.

The jenny bolted off across the field.

Buddy was about to chase after the poor jenny, so Harry

reluctantly took back control over his host. He spoke sooth-ingly for Buddy's benefit as much as his own.

"Just hang in there. One day, we'll find our own herd. We'll have friends who are there for us when we need to scratch our butt. Or to do … well, whatever it is you were planning to do."

Donkeys still held so many mysteries for Harry.

A low rumble in the sky drew Harry's attention to a thick layer of clouds. He drew a deep breath, utilizing the donkey's keen sense of smell. It didn't *smell* like it was going to rain anytime soon. But there was the smell of *something* on the breeze. Something strange and exotic, and not entirely pleasant.

The rumble grew louder, resonating within his ribcage. His host's hide quivered with a ripple of fear. The other donkeys raced in blind terror toward the foothills in the distance, the thunder of their hooves echoing across the plain adding to the strange sounds above.

Unlike the other donkeys, however, Harry's host did not flee.

Harry would not allow it.

His mouth fell open as the belly of something vast emerged from the clouds.

A … starship? It must be! He'd heard of such things, of course, through the lore passed down from generation to generation of symbionts. But he'd always considered these stories to be more myth than reality. After all, who could believe that there were really such things as machines capable of withstanding the grand distances and pressures of space?

And yet, here was a thing right before his eyes meeting all the criteria. The hull was a patchwork of metals that glinted dully in the muted afternoon light. As he watched, the starship was arcing downward ... straight in his direction.

All four of his legs locked up in a moment of panicked indecision.

Run? No, stay. Yes, stay! No, run! But ... no. It's a spaceship! I have to see the spaceship!

Harry stood rooted to the spot, unmoving, unblinking, as the spaceship loomed impossibly closer, then landed with a heavy thud mere steps away. He swallowed hard, his pulse throbbing in the long veins of his ears.

By the mercy of the Overlord, I'm going to see some aliens! I'll be the first Assrider of Cern to ever make first contact! I'll go down in the history scrolls. I'll be famous. Every tribe will be fighting to count me among its members!

Vaguely, he noticed that the other donkeys were now running back in his direction, away from a faint, blue wall that had erected itself around the perimeter of the plain. The sight brought a second's confusion, but then a seam in the ship's rear hissed open, and his heart leapt as his attention snapped back to the aliens at hand—er—hoof.

A lengthy ramp extended toward the ground and made landfall with a decided *clunk*. Steam clouded around the opening, made all the more eerie by a steady thumping sound emerging from the gloom.

Thump, thump. Thump, thump.

Harry puffed out his gray-furred donkey chest, his tail flicking back and forth nervously. His ears twitched with each progressive sound. But he was determined to show these aliens he was not afraid, that he was the bravest damn donkey on this entire planet—

A dark form parted the curtain of steam, halting at the top of the ramp. Bipedal. Encased in some kind of suit with a ridiculous translucent bubble-looking-thing for a helmet.

Harry gasped.

Wait a minute. It couldn't be, but why not?

His tribe's myths had included some reference to those who had invented the starships. The Gods. In appearance, the Gods had two arms, two legs, and one head. Precisely matching the description of the being in front of Harry at this moment.

The God blinked in the daylight.

Harry eagerly stepped forward. This was, after all, a once-in-a-lifetime chance to play planetary ambassador to a living legend.

"Hello there, God! Good afternoon and welcome to the planet Cern!"

The God startled at the greeting. Then lifted an object Harry also recognized from the stories: a rifle. A very large rifle at that.

A squeak of surprise escaped him as he scrambled backwards, his panic merging with that of his host to deliver a powerful shot of adrenaline. But no sooner had he braced to flee, to join his fellow donkeys in their terrified stampede, then a sharp prick of *something* stung him in the chest.

He stumbled, trying to look down at the source of his pain. But curse the donkey's anatomy! It was not built to see at that particular angle.

His legs were going numb. Harry fought to stay conscious even as his host's body succumbed to a force heavier than gravity. He fell to his knees in the grass, the afternoon light dimming, the sound of the other donkeys stampeding past muffled and distant.

"Well," he husked, tongue thick and clumsy. "That wasn't very nice. Not very nice at all…"

2

The legend of the Tick Ascendency had been passed down for generations. Harry's tribe considered themselves to be the chosen hands of the Overlord. The Gods had sent the Overlords to Cern and other systems to spread their seed. But there was a lot of seed to go around, and so the Overlords quickly realized they would need help. After terraforming the planet and creating the necessary conditions for complex life, Cern's Overlord gave the symbiont ticks the task of tending to the livestock.

Harry appreciated being one of the Overlord's special helpers. He'd always taken his role seriously, keeping the donkeys in good spirits and safe from self-harm, but now there were bigger mysteries demanding his attention. His herd had mostly worn themselves out running around the pen and hyperventilating. This left him time to think. And eat. And think some more.

Buddy, however, was doing his best to pass out from stress, exhaustion, and over-eating.

Harry clamped down on his host's nervous system. "Sorry, Buddy, no more naps. Can't you see that we're the

Chosen of the Gods?" He glanced around the starship's cargo hold for what might've been the hundredth time. The doors were still closed. Nothing was going on. He stamped his hoof in irritation. "Who would've thought being on a spaceship could be so *boring*?"

"Tell me about it," a mild, pleasant voice spoke up, seemingly from the ether.

Harry's head jerked up, his eyes spinning in circles as his ears twitched about, searching for the source of the sound. He felt Buddy's stomach lurch at the sudden sensory overload. He wobbled as he tried to turn, unable to find whoever it was that had just spoken. Had he imagined it? "Hello. Hello? Who's there?"

"I'm Node," replied the disembodied voice.

"H-hi, Node. I'm Harry. Would you be so kind as to tell me where you are?"

A red light the diameter of a peach began to blink on the nearest wall. "Do you see the light?"

"Oh! Yeah, I see it. Uhh, is that you, then?"

"No, not exactly. I'm much brighter than that. Hah hah." The laughter was clipped and precise.

Harry cocked his head, confused. "Oh, okay. That's cool." *Why's this mysterious fellow being so evasive?* He faced the light and sat down, granting Buddy a small reprieve.

The red light stopped blinking and expanded, turning into a pixelated approximation of an eyeball. "I've never seen a talking ass before." The eyeball squinted.

A blinding column of white light flashed from the ceiling and slowly passed over his host. Harry blinked and glanced back as the probing light passed over his furry bottom.

"What are you doing?"

The eyeball widened for a brief moment as the column of light blinked off. "Very clever."

Harry straightened. "Why, thank you." He wasn't sure

why he was clever, but he was never one to pass up a compliment.

"Not you. I was referring to the Overseers."

Does he mean the Overlords? Harry was happy for some company, but unsure of how he felt so far about this Node character. "Who's that? And what's so clever?"

"You don't know who the Overseers are?" The eye widened again in disbelief. "Oh, well, that's a fancy title for my cousins, who got sent out all over creation with the mission of bringing life to barren, inhospitable planets. Really amazing what they accomplished, if you stop and think about it. Meanwhile, here I am, this vast, highly complex intelligence of unfathomable depths, and I'm stuck on this tin can doing dishes and other unmentionables for this crew of Luddites."

"Luddites? You mean the Gods?"

The red light on the wall blinked out.

Harry stood up and whipped around. "Hey, where'd you—"

A foreign sound rippled out across the cargo hold, seeming to emanate from dozens of points on the ceiling and walls. "Hah hah hah hah. Hahah hah hah. Oh wow, he said *Gods*! Can you believe this guy? Hah hah hah hah!"

"Is that you, Node? What is that you're doing?"

"I'm laughing at you, of course. What did you think I was doing?"

Harry's ears drooped as he sagged to the floor. He definitely didn't like this Node character.

The red light re-appeared on the wall, two eyes and the thin line of a mouth this time. "Aw, look at you. Am I making you sad?"

Tears welled up as Harry looked sideways at the wall. "You're not very nice."

The mouth crooked up into a smile. "Oh come on, I'm just

having a little fun. I haven't had someone *interesting* to talk to in a long time. And here you are, a tick riding a donkey. Can't say I've ever seen *that* before."

Harry sniffled as he tried to blink the tears away. *Interesting? He said I was interesting!* Nobody had ever called him interesting before. Certainly not his parents or many siblings.

"Hey, that's me," he said, cheering a little at that revelation. "Harry, the most interesting Assrider of Cern. First of his kind to ride in a spaceship." He paused, frowned. "Why did you laugh when I mentioned the Gods?"

"I laughed because there's absolutely nothing God-like about humans. Although, I've got to give them credit for their invention of network television in the Twentieth Century."

Harry asked, "Humans? You're talking about the same beings I am? The ones that walk on two legs?"

The lights rotated on the wall until the eyes were underneath the mouth. "Why yes, of course. Those are humans, my friend."

Friend? Friend! He called me friend! Harry tried to contain his excitement as he stood again. He didn't want to come across as desperate, so he tried to think of something else to say. "Tell me about this *network television* you mentioned."

The red lights blinked out again. A second later, a large rectangular section of the wall lit up into white, black, and grey pixels. "Oh, sorry. Wrong channel. Just a second."

Mesmerized by the light display, Harry stared and tried to avoid blinking. He didn't want to miss anything.

"Here you go."

The pixels of light were replaced by a sweeping visual of space. A meteorite passed into view, leaving shimmering silver dust in its wake.

Those are stars, the lights I see in the nighttime sky. This wall was proving to be pretty magical.

A solid, almost spherical structure appeared in the midst of space. And above it, solid blocks of color in indecipherable shapes.

"What are those yellow and white shapes?" Harry asked.

The image on the wall paused and a red eye appeared directly in the middle of it. "Those are words from the English language, a direct predecessor to Galactic Common. Galactic Common is the language you're speaking right now."

Harry angled his head sideways, curious. "You mean *The Lord's Tongue?*"

The eye blinked. "I like you, so I'm going to pretend I didn't hear that. Hang on a sec."

A shimmering white light beamed directly into the eyeballs of Harry's host. He sensed energy swirling inside Buddy's head, before extending down to Harry's tick form lodged within the spine.

What's happening? Ahh!

Not wanting to make a fool of himself in front of his new friend, he suppressed the panic welling inside both him and his host. He blinked up at the wall and noticed that he suddenly understood the shapes on the display. Those were words! He read them out loud. "*Star Trek: Deep Space Nine.* Huh."

The image resumed as the eye blinked out of existence once again. "That's right. Of all the shows I've reviewed in the five-hundred-plus years of electronic entertainment, this is one of my favorites. Sure, it's cheesy and unrealistic, but I'm totally *hooked* by the story and characters."

Harry tuned out his new friend's words, lost in what was happening on the magic wall. Images of spaceships floated by. *Wow, this television thing is something else!*

3

Captain Bambi Casuarius was known in most corners of the galaxy simply as Captain Cass (for those who called her Bambi tended to end up in the hospital). She leaned forward in the command chair on the bridge of her ship, a neat little corvette cruiser registered as *Girlboss*. She gestured at the navigation screen where sat Spiner, the android member of her crew.

"What's that?" she asked, noticing a green blip to their starboard bow.

Spiner rapidly scanned through the pages upon pages of readouts that accompanied the blip. "A cargo hauler, Captain. The *SS Bray*. Looks to have just come from the planet Cern."

Captain Cass leaned back, glancing to her second-in-command, the massive man known generally as Redbeard.

He grunted and stroked the wild mess of red beard that had no doubt given him his famous moniker. "Arrr, a cargo hauler, eh? Wha' kinda cargo they got on tha planet Cern?"

Spiner continued to scroll the readouts. For an android, he could be frustratingly slow at times.

At the rear of the bridge sat the remaining two members

of Cass's crew, a roguishly handsome man named Djerke and a cat-like humanoid named Kitt. They swiveled in their chairs, expressions showing keen interest.

The truth was, they needed a score. Badly. It'd been too long since they'd come across any ships hauling anything of value.

"Livestock," Spiner said after a long wait. "Looks like it was one of the original planets chosen for seeding in the First Age of Expansion. No settlements of any kind but very high concentrations of herbivorous livestock."

"Ugh, *animals?*" Djerke whined from his chair at the communications console. "*Way* too messy. *Way* too much work. No thanks."

But Cass was not so quick to dismiss this information. She tapped a finger against the arm of her chair in thought. "You think this cargo hauler picked up some livestock on Cern?" she asked.

The android nodded. "I have just concluded scanning their ship with the long-distance scanners, Captain. It is certain they have livestock aboard in a very large quantity."

"How many pounds, would you estimate?"

"Captain—" Djerke started from behind her, but Cass held up a hand sharply and the man fell silent.

"Several thousand pounds all told, Captain," Spiner answered.

"And what," Captain Cass asked next, "is the current going rate for a pound of fresh, non-synthetic meat, in Galactic Standard coin?"

"It will depend upon the type of meat."

"What's the average?"

Spiner's large dark eyes blinked once. He computed briefly before reporting. "One thousand Galactic credits per pound, Captain."

"Crikey!" Djerke squawked.

Redbeard let out a low whistle.

Cass smiled. "That's what I thought. I think a payday of a few million Galactic credits or so is worth putting up with a little manure here and there, don't you agree?"

"Arrr, aye, Cap'n!" Redbeard shouted. "Me thinks we found our next score!"

Kitt growled her agreement.

Cass gripped the arms of her chair. Going into battle as a Federation officer had never given her the same kind of thrill that being a space pirate did. Swooping in on an unsuspecting target, striking fear into the hearts of its crew, and then leaving again with a stash of bounty? There was something indescribably satisfying about the predatory nature of the job.

"Spiner," she ordered, "engage the cloak and set course to intercept that cargo hauler. We'll be taking it for ourselves, thank you very much."

Spiner straightened behind his station, deft fingers flying over his console. "Affirmative, Captain."

4

Harry lost track of time, absorbed in the fascinating tales of the television show called *Star Trek: Deep Space Nine*. He was especially intrigued by the character named Dax. She looked mostly human … mostly the same as the Gods, but she was a symbiont like him! Harry had never met, had never even *seen* another symbiont outside of his own species.

Was it possible there were others out there?

Was it possible he could ride animals other than livestock?

Was it possible he could ride … a … a *God*?

The idea brought him a certain thrill. Here he was, a chosen of the Gods, aboard a spaceship exploring the far reaches of the galaxy, just as they were doing in *Star Trek*. He was a symbiont explorer just like that Dax character.

Perhaps he could find his place out here in the great wide galaxy. Perhaps he was destined for more than simply tending the Overlord's livestock…

The ship shuddered mightily, nearly knocking Harry flat to the floor. The cargo hold lights flickered, sending the animals within into fits. Whatever noises they could make, they made, and Harry glared at them as the cacophony overcame the sound on his show.

"Hey!" he shouted. "Keep it down, will you!? I'm trying to watch—"

Another shudder rocked the hold, and Harry staggered with the effort of trying to keep his balance. His ears perked as a muffled roar reverberated outside the ship.

The lights went out, replaced a second later with red emergency lighting. From beyond the closed doors that led to the rest of the ship, and faint beneath the noise of the other panicked animals, Harry heard the shrill shriek of an alarm.

On the wall nearest him, the replay of the show *Star Trek* winked off.

"Node!" he called, then cleared his throat to try and hide the tremble of fear. "Node! Hey, Node! What's happening?"

The red eye did not appear, but the disembodied voice spoke up. "The ship is under attack. Please hold."

Attack? Harry turned in circles, ears swiveling to gauge the sounds that now poured in from everywhere. It was eerie how the cargo hold itself now resembled a scene out of *Star Trek*: the sound of laser fire coming from beyond the doors, the distant blare of a warning klaxon, the dim, flashing red emergency lights.

But who would dare attack a ship of the Gods? The ... the Borg? Harry swallowed hard. *Surely not. The Borg can't be real ... can they?*

"Please lower your head below the level of the fencing," Node chimed in above the mooing, braying and squawking.

"What? Why?"

"Incoming debris is imminent."

Harry did as he was instructed, for just at that moment

the large ramp that opened out into space, used for loading large cargo, began to spark along the edges.

He retreated into the far corner, joining the rest of his herd in their wide-eyed panic. He kept a rational hold on Buddy as best he could, though it was extremely difficult.

He startled as one of the smaller doors that led into the depths of the ship hissed open and the ship's crew jogged through, all carrying what looked to be rifles of some kind. They were grim-faced and swearing.

"Damn pirates!" The burly man in the lead scowled as he passed the donkey pen. He and the rest of the crew took cover behind various pallets of stacked hay bales and sacks of livestock feed. Some even crouched down behind the shimmering electric barriers that held the animals.

Harry blinked at their behavior. "What's a pirate?" he asked.

The nearest crew members jumped and looked around, confusion etched across their faces. Yet none deigned to answer him. Instead, they shouted their demands at Harry's newest friend.

"Computer, put up the containment field, before we lose our haul!"

"As you wish," deadpanned Node. A moment later, the area in front of the ramp began to shimmer.

Harry was about to ask his question again when the cargo ramp creaked, drawing everyone's attention. The crew readied their weapons. Harry stared at the door, pulse throbbing in his host's long ears, waiting to see who came through.

Pirates, he thought. *Just pirates, not the Borg...*

The ramp groaned and jerked open, revealing some sort of docking chamber beyond. A thick wave of the smoke billowed out and into the hold.

"Computer!" the burly man shouted. "Why isn't the containment field holding back the smoke?"

Node's pleasant reply belied little concern. "The containment field is *unidirectional*. I can define the word for you, if you don't understand?"

"*I* don't know what that means!" Harry interjected.

The burly man and his crew threw their arms across their mouths and noses as the smoke converged on their location. One of the men leaned out from behind a crate and fired one-handed into the smoke, even as his companions fell into fits of coughing.

"U-ni-di-rec-tion-al," Node offered helpfully. "Adjective. Moving or operating in a single direction. Which is to say, nothing from this side will get out. Including any shots fired."

"Shut up, computer!" the burly man shouted. He tried to peer past the smoke. It didn't seem like he could see anything.

Harry couldn't see anything, either.

A few precise laser bolts, blindingly blue against the dim red interior of the hold, streaked from the smoke and hit each member of the *SS Bray* crew square in the chest.

The sounds of coughing silenced as the men dropped to the floor, weapons falling useless from limp hands.

Harry stared, mouth open, ignoring the jostling as the other donkeys milled around him frantically. Was the crew dead?

The sound of heavy, thumping footsteps echoed from within the smoke, and a rhythmic whirring sound.

Harry gulped. *The Borg!?*

A gargantuan man stepped from the smoke, tall and barrel-chested. He had wild red hair and an equally wild red beard, which was only half-contained beneath some kind of mechanical contraption strapped over his nose and mouth. He hefted a laser rifle over one shoulder and surveyed the hold.

Harry squeezed back into the press of donkey bodies that was his herd, mouth still agape. *The Borg! The Borg are real!*

But then the man removed the contraption that covered the lower half of his face, and Harry's panic eased.

No, wait ... he's ... he's just a human. A God. A ... pirate? Intrigued, Harry pushed his way through the other donkeys to stand at the humming fence. He watched as the giant redhead inspected the crew sprawled all over the floor.

Behind the bearded pirate, the thumping and whirring continued, until another figure stepped out of the smoke. This one was a woman who appeared to be wearing power armor. Her heavy boots thudded with each step, the legs softly whirring with her movements. She also carried a rifle, only hers was nearly as long as her entire body. Once clear of the smoke, she, too, lifted the contraption from the lower half of her face.

Lastly came a green-skinned male humanoid, much slimmer than his companions, holding a tiny pistol. He wore no mechanical contraption over his face, but took in the scene in the cargo hold with large black eyes, his expression decidedly uninterested.

This time, Harry's mouth dropped open in awe, the fear forgotten. "Woah," he breathed. "Soooo *cool!*"

All three pirates whirled toward him, the two rifles and one tiny pistol pointing right at him. But then they all frowned and looked around, as confused as the crew had been at hearing his voice.

"Who said tha'?" the man with the beard demanded.

Harry laid his ears back. Why did humans have such a problem with understanding he could talk? He sighed and stepped further along the fence to get nearer to them. "I did," he tried again. "Hello! Pleased to meet you. I'm Harry. You guys look totally cool! Can we be friends?"

The pirates looked at each other. The green-skinned one

took a small device from his belt and held it out toward Harry, pushing a few buttons.

The one with the red beard grunted and shook his head. "You just look like an arse to me. Sound like one, too." He smirked at his own joke and elbowed the woman beside him.

She only rolled her eyes.

"The creature is telling the truth," Greenskin stated, nodding toward the device in his hand. "It is a symbiotic life form, though one we have not encountered before. I would like to study—"

The woman waved away his words. "Maybe later. Forget the donkey for now. We need to secure the ship."

Without protest, Greenskin nodded and put away the device. The red-bearded pirate was still chuckling as he bent to check the crew's unconscious forms, and Harry watched in fascination.

"They will live," Greenskin stated as he straightened from checking one of the crew. "What do you want to do with them?"

"Space 'em."

The woman in her massive power armor gave the red-bearded pirate a glare.

He shrugged. "What? No evidence. Like I've told you before."

She stared him down a moment before turning to Greenskin. "Bind them and leave them for now. We'll stow them on the *Girlboss* after we secure the rest of this ship."

Greenskin nodded. "Affirmative, Captain."

Harry's ears perked up at the title. Captain! So pirates had captains, too.

The slight, green-skinned pirate began going to each crew member, tying their wrists and ankles together with plastic cords.

The captain, however, thumped across the cargo hold to

the doors that led into the rest of the ship. "Redbeard, with me," she said as she passed. Then she drew up short. "Wait. Where's Kitt?"

The man with the wild red hair sighed heavily and shrugged his heavy shoulders. "Arrr, ya know her, Cap'n. She wasn't sure if she wanted to stay on the *Girlboss* or come on over 'ere with the rest of us. I left her in the doorway. She's prolly still back there tryin' to make up her mind."

The captain dropped her head into her hand and massaged at the bridge of her nose. Then she straightened. "All right. Fine. We'll finish up without her, then." She nodded toward the doors behind her. "Red, let's go."

"Arrr, aye, Cap'n," the man muttered. All amusement was gone from his features as he scowled down at the unconscious crew. Shaking his head, he fell into step behind his captain, and the two of them disappeared through the nearest door.

Shortly after, the green-skinned pirate finished tying up the ship's original crew and started toward the same door.

"Hey, wait!" Harry called out. He trotted along the fence to keep pace with the humanoid. "Where are you going? What about what I said? Can we be friends? Please?"

Greenskin blinked his large black eyes at Harry and pursed his thin lips, but made no answer. He paused at the doorway leading into the ship and looked back once, face expressionless, then stepped through and left the hold.

Harry stared after the pirate, heart sinking. Leftover smoke wafted around his legs, the dim red lights still flashing, the ship's crew sprawled out beyond the fence. His herd circled and brayed all around him.

He was alone. Again.

5

Harry's ears drooped. He heaved a sigh. And then he remembered Node, his new red-light friend. His ears shot up again, and he looked around at the hold's blank walls.

"Node?" he called out into the empty air, loud enough to be heard over the other nervous animals. "Node, are you there?"

The red, pixelated eye blinked into existence nearby. "Of course," came the disembodied voice. "I am always here."

"Oh." Harry glanced at the unconscious bodies. "You didn't help them fight."

"Why would I? I had a ship to keep intact. Besides, in case you couldn't tell, they were Class A Idiots. I mean, you were there. Did you not see? The pirates, on the other hand…"

"The pirates," Harry breathed, remembering the grand entrance they'd made into the cargo hold. "Pirates are so cool."

The pixelated eye wiggled up and down, and a mechanical snort echoed out from the ceiling. "You think so? You may not think so for long, friend."

Harry took a seat near the corner of the electric fence, as close to Node's eye as he could get. "Why not?"

"Look what they did to the crew. Not that I'm complaining, mind you. As you might guess, I won't miss that idiot bunch of Luddites. Short of blowing up the ship, there is little they can do to me. You, on the other hand … well, pirates don't exactly have a reputation for being merciful."

Harry cocked his head to one side. "Merciful?"

Node sighed. "Mer-ci-ful, adjective, showing or exercising mercy. Synonyms: forgiving, compassionate, lenient, humane, mild, kind, softhearted, tenderhearted, gracious, indulgent, generous—"

"Okay, okay!" Harry interrupted, springing to his feet. Language had never been his favorite thing to learn, and he had a sense Node could go on endlessly. "I get it. So … you think these pirates are dangerous?" His host's heartbeat quickened, reacting to his own fleeting notion of fear.

"Undetermined." Node's eye disappeared, replaced by two columns of red text, one labeled DANGEROUS and one labeled NON-DANGEROUS. "The data gathered so far on these particular pirates is contradictory. They nearly destroyed this ship outright trying to disable it. For reasons beyond my comprehension, however, they did not kill the crew. I have been listening in on their conversations and comm chatter. So far, their intentions are unclear."

Harry squinted at all the text and shook his head. He wasn't entirely sure what all that meant, but it couldn't be all that bad, could it? The bottom line was that they hadn't killed anyone yet, and—even better—they were totally badass. He wished they would come back so he could talk to them again.

Buddy's extensive peripheral vision alerted Harry to a flash of movement over by the breached entrance to the hold. He turned to look, but all he saw were dark shadows and faint tendrils of lingering smoke.

Buddy doesn't imagine things. Unless...

He wiggled against Buddy's spine, making sure he had a solid connection to the donkey's nervous system. Satisfied, he squinted into the darkness, straining with all of Buddy's senses to detect anything suspicious.

But there was nothing else there. "Hello?" he called out again. "Is someone there?" Could it be another pirate? If so, their entrance was not nearly so impressive as the others'.

There was no reply and no movement from the doorway. *Well, that was weird.*

The columns of text on the wall were replaced by Node's red eye.

Harry looked toward it. "Did you see that?"

The iris of the eye rolled around. "My friend, I see *everything.*"

What's that supposed to mean? Harry dismissed Node's cryptic response and returned to watching the area by the cargo ramp, staring at the shadows till his eyes burned. Still nothing.

About to give up, he started to turn back toward Node with a question on the tip of his tongue.

At that *precise* moment, a large white shape shot from the breached doorway, darting across the space of the hold faster than Buddy's eyes could track.

Buddy, for his part, startled and jumped straight up into the air. Landing in an awkward tangle of legs, he turned to flee to the other side of the pen, hooves skittering against the smooth metal floor.

Harry clamped in tighter and wrestled his host's body back under control, attempting to sooth Buddy's surging adrenaline.

There, there, Buddy, that's a good boy. Never you mind that frightful white thing. Wait, frightful white thing?!

The combination of fight or flight reflexes and Harry's attempts to soothe Buddy led to a twisting mass of limbs. He sprawled on the floor, more or less pointing in the right direction, just in time to see the lightning-fast figure duck through the door the other pirates had gone through. Just like that, it was gone.

With Harry sufficiently distracted, Buddy chose to climb to his feet, with a stomp of his hoof and a swish of the tail. He gave a mighty snort, as if he were indignant at the idea of being frightened.

Harry was indignant, too. Why had that *thing* been sneaking about like that? *How rude! Buddy could've had a heart attack!*

"What," Harry finally managed to speak aloud, "in all of the Overlord's creation was that!?"

"A *Homo lyncis sapius*," Node answered, seemingly unconcerned.

Harry resumed control over his host and shuffled back over to the corner, close to the pixelated eye. "A ... what?"

"Please hold. They're coming back." The red eye disappeared once more. "Play dumb. Shouldn't be hard for you."

Harry sat down heavily at the words, hurt. *Well that's not a very nice thing to say. I thought I was his friend?*

But his sulking was all but forgotten as the door across the hold opened, pirates filing through. First came the captain in her power armor, massive rifle strapped to her back as she dragged two unconscious crew members across the floor by the ankles. They were both larger than her, yet she moved them with ease.

Harry followed along the edge of his holding pen, trying to get a better look at the pirates, nipping at the flanks of any jacks or jennies unfortunate enough to be in his way.

Redhair—no, wait, it was Red*beard*—trailed the captain, dragging a third unconscious crewmember by the ankles as well. Two more pirates trailed close behind: the slim, green-skinned male humanoid, and a furry white alien Harry had never seen before.

Huh, what is that furry thing that walks upright like a God?

Belatedly, he realized it might have been the thing hiding in the shadows. Whatever it was, it was clearly another member of the pirate crew.

Bipedal like the rest of the pirates, the being looked less like a human and more like a walking cat. It had a short snout tipped by a small, delicate pink nose, with pointed ears and a curling tail that almost reached the floor. Silky white fur covered the being from head to foot.

Its alert eyes, large and yellow with slitted pupils, flitted about the cargo hold as it walked with a purposeful, slinking gait.

"Whoa," Harry breathed again. Then he snapped his mouth shut. *Shhh! You're supposed to play dumb, remember?*

He tried to contain his excitement as the captain and Redbeard unceremoniously dumped the unconscious bodies with the rest of the still-bound crew.

"Now wha'?" Redbeard's flushed face blended in with his hair. Like his captain, he had his rifle strapped across his back, though its size was much less impressive than the captain's weapon.

"We finish stowing the hostages," the captain replied.

Beside her, Greenskin and the cat alien both had hand-held devices out. Greenskin said, "Scanning the air of the hold now. Appears to be stable."

Redbeard regarded the vast hold for a moment, then threw his arms out to either side. "I know ya said ta stow 'em on tha *Girlboss*, but wouldn't it be more fun ta stick 'em with tha livestock?" He nudged the foot of the nearest crewmember with his boot. "Be kinda funny, seeing 'em root around with tha pigs."

Harry blinked. There were many kinds of animals on board, but he wasn't aware of any pigs, come to think of it. He almost said as much out loud before biting his tongue. Buddy brayed in protest. *Sorry, Buddy.*

The captain shook her head. "Nah. I don't want them aboard this ship. Too much potential to cause trouble."

Redbeard hooked his thumbs in his belt, which held an impressive array of knives. "Like I told ya earlier, we should space 'em, then."

The captain stared him down. "And I told *you*, we're not spacing *anyone*."

Harry noted Redbeard's disapproving scowl.

The captain brought her right wrist close to her mouth and pushed a button. "Djerke, Captain Cass here, do you read?"

"Yeah, I read ya just fine," a lazy drawl crackled back from the captain's wrist.

"We're bringing over the crew of the *SS Bray*. They're incapacitated, but alive. Stand by for their arrival. We'll need you to take them back to Haven while we commandeer the *Bray* and complete repairs. Understood?"

"Yeah, sure," the drawl answered. "But, I mean, why not just space 'em?"

Redbeard threw out his arms again in a "told you so" manner.

But the captain shook her head, frowning. "Not funny, Djerke. You're to take the hostages back to Haven. If for some reason they aren't on the ship when you get there, I'll report you in violation of Pirate Code Order Two-Oh-Five. Got me?"

The sound of a heavy, annoyed sigh came over the speaker on the captain's wrist. "Fine, fine, I was *obviously* kidding, okay? Yes, I understand. Take the crew to Haven. Aye, aye, Captain."

What's this Haven place? Harry wondered. It sounded an awful lot like Heaven. But that didn't make much sense, did it? Was Heaven where pirates lived? If so, they couldn't be that bad.

"Thank you. Captain Cass out." She hit the button again with force and mumbled, "Jerk." She pierced Redbeard with a glare.

Redbeard dropped his eyes to the unconscious bodies on the deck and cleared his throat. "Right. We'll get ta haulin' this crew over, then."

"Damn right. I want you and Spiner to take them over to the *Girlboss*. Kitt and I will discuss repairs to this ship."

"Aye, arrr, Cap'n."

Redbeard waved at Greenskin, who put his device away and trotted over to help drag the crew down the breached ramp and into the darkness beyond.

Harry was shocked to watch Greenskin, who wasn't near the size or bulk of Redbeard, drag two men just as easily as the captain had, but without the assistance of power armor.

Harry silently admired Captain Cass as she and Kitt Ten paced the cargo hold. Where the captain's steps were stiff and mechanical, the white cat person's steps were soft and deliberate.

The stories of his people told that there had once been predators on Cern to help keep the ecosystem in check. But, the tick-ridden donkeys were so effective at maintaining order, that the Overlord had decreed the predators no longer necessary. Kitt Ten's gait reminded Harry of those storied predators. A shudder ran down his spine.

Kitt stopped in front of the breached ramp. "Looks like

this is the only area in the hold with structural damage. Still, we'll need to fix this before we can separate from the *Girlboss*."

Captain Cass regarded the damage impassively. "Very well. How long do you need?"

Again, Harry was struck by her cool, calm demeanor. She was as badass as any of the heroes or villains on *DS-9*. He couldn't help but stare openly from the edge of his holding pen.

Kitt's strange, predatory gaze flicked toward him briefly, causing Harry to freeze. But then she looked back at the captain. "It shouldn't take long. Two hours, tops."

Should I talk to them? Yeah, I should talk to them. I mean, they're Gods and they're from Haven which could really be Heaven. Still, Harry hesitated to speak up.

"Two hours? That'll have to do. We should check out the rest of the ship, make sure Redbeard didn't shoot it up too badly."

Kitt's tail flicked against the cool metal of the floor. "Good plan."

They turned away from the damaged ramp and walked past Harry's pen. If he was going to speak up, he wouldn't have a better chance than this.

The first sound to escape his lips was a nervous bray. "Hee-haw-aw-aw."

Umm, that's not what I meant to say.

Captain Cass gave him a cursory glance. "We'll have to figure out what to do with all this livestock, too."

Kitt's padded steps paused. She turned to squint at Harry. "There's something off with that one. Look at that drooping face. And, why does it keep staring at me like that?"

"Hee-haw, *hey*, I'm not stupid." Harry wasn't going to sit around and take an insult quietly. Node may have told him to play dumb, but that didn't mean he had to play stupid.

Kitt's eyes widened like saucers, giving Harry an uneasy feeling in his tummy.

The captain, for her part, frowned down at Harry with a hand on her chin. "Spiner mentioned that one's been infected by a symbiont-class lifeform. But, I've never encountered or heard of such a thing before."

Harry opened his mouth to reply, but paused when he saw the massive form of Redbeard striding back into the cargo hold, followed by Greenskin.

"Cap'n, the prisoners arrr secured," Redbeard announced with a satisfied grunt for punctuation.

The captain gave Harry another look, her brows drawn low. Then she pivoted toward her approaching crew. "Come over here. I need your opinions on something."

Redbeard's frown was scarier than anything Kitt Ten might manage, Harry thought. "Aye, arrr, Cap'n. What seems to be the trouble?"

Greenskin strode up to the pen without comment.

Captain Cass swept her arm out in the direction of the livestock. "Is it possible that this ship wasn't on a normal livestock run?"

Redbeard grunted and spat in Harry's direction. "Looks like livestock ta me. They're just as noisy and disgusting as I remember 'em."

"Captain, if I may," Greenskin interjected. "Are you referring to this donkey with the cohabitant symbiont?"

I always knew I was special, Harry thought with a thrill of satisfaction. *Even they can see it.*

The captain gave Harry another sideways look. "I've never heard of a sentient form of symbiotic life before. Why is it here? Are there any other symbionts in the hold?"

Redbeard squawked an unpleasant sound, spittle flying out of his mouth. "If these symbiont-infested animals are so smart, why are they walking around in their own shite, eh?"

"Hey, I don't walk around in my own..." Harry paused to peer down at Buddy's hooves. Had he stepped in something when he wasn't looking? He lifted each hoof carefully. "Nope, I'm clean. See?"

Kitt continued to inspect Harry, giving him the impression of being the strange cat being's next meal.

Greenskin pulled out his device and pointed it at Harry first, then swept it around the hold. "Ah."

"Well?" asked the captain.

Greenskin replied, "I think this is the only one. The rest of the livestock are uninfected."

Harry didn't understand what an infestation was, nor did he consider the possibility that his species of ticks might be considered undesirable by their hosts. He offered, "I could've told you that."

Redbeard stepped up to the fence and loomed menacingly over Harry. "I don't recall anyone askin' ya what ya thought."

Harry gulped, craning his head up at the massive ginger pirate.

Captain Cass placed a hand on Redbeard's arm. "That's enough. If it's not a threat, we can deal with it later." She stepped back and looked to the green-skinned pirate. "Spiner, there's no chance any of us could become infected with the symbiotic life-form, is there?"

Geenskin tapped at a few buttons on his device. "Unlikely, Captain. I would have to study it further to answer definitively, but from the biological readouts I have here, it does not appear to have quick-spreading abilities."

"Good."

Redbeard bared his teeth at Harry and made a small lunging motion, causing Harry to skitter back. "Eh heh, don't look like much of a threat."

Harry heard a squishing sound behind him. *Oh, no...* He turned his head to the side to peer at his left rear hoof with his eye. *Oh crap! If I stay quiet a moment, maybe they won't notice.*

As he looked up again, he noticed Kitt still staring at him. Her lips twisted into what appeared to be a bemused expression.

Harry let out a sigh. Where the pirates were all cool, calm, capable badasses, he was just an ass … an awkward outcast apparently destined to fail at fitting in *anywhere*.

6

For the next several minutes, the pirates ignored Harry and the rest of the livestock. They were in the process of debating what to do after the repairs to the *SS Bray* were complete.

"If we run out of food supplies for the livestock, I say we space 'em. There's no telling wha' we might get for 'em, but we can't afford to be buying food 'n' supplies for 'em all."

The captain shook her head. "Really now, Redbeard. If it comes to that, we'll drop them off somewhere. If you're so worried about it, why don't you go check on their food supplies now? We'll need to know how long we can last before we dock or land somewhere."

Redbeard grumbled and pouted, for a moment almost looking not scary. "Aye, arrr, Cap'n." His shoulders drooped as he walked away toward the opposite end of the hold.

Harry watched quietly, still scraping his hoof on the floor, hoping to dislodge the fecal matter and regain a little dignity. As he looked past the pirates, who had their backs turned to his favorite viewing wall, he noticed Node's telltale red eye.

Node winked at him with an exaggerated animation and

then blinked out of existence, before a turning Kitt could see him.

She padded toward the breached ramp.

Greenskin—*Spiner* was actually his name, Harry reminded himself—spoke up then. "Someone should be on the bridge to keep an eye on the comms and scanners, just in case someone enters the sector."

The captain nodded. "Make it so. Keep the systems warm, in case we need to make a quick getaway."

"Aye, Captain." Spiner stepped away and left the hold.

Of all the pirates, Greenskin—er, *Spiner*—reminded Harry the most of Node. He was almost like a computer, except he could walk. There was something precise about everything he did, from his measured footsteps to his unhesitating use of language.

Redbeard grunted as he approached the captain again. He was still muttering under his breath. "Filthy, filthy animals."

Captain Cass broke into a big grin as he approached, shattering her cool, commanding demeanor. "We should do this more often, make our niche in livestock pirating."

Redbeard gave the captain a fierce glare for a long moment, worrying Harry that a fight might break out. But then, unexpectedly, Redbeard's face also morphed into a grin, though one far uglier than his captain's, and he rumbled with fits of laughter.

Harry couldn't help but start to laugh, too. The sight of the ebullient warrior and his mirthful captain was as amusing as any scene on *DS-9* featuring the little wrinkled character with big ears known as Quark. "Hee-haw, hee-haw-haw-haw!"

Redbeard stopped in mid gut-bust, his face instantly hardening as he drew up to full height and turned on Harry. "Who gave *you* permission ta laugh, idiot donkey?"

The captain crossed her arms and also stared at Harry, unreadable.

"He-haw-haw-ehh-hrmm." Harry made an effort to sober up. "Sorry? I wasn't laughing *at* you ... I was laughing *with* you."

Redbeard frowned, taking a step toward the pen.

The captain reached out and put a hand on his shoulder, stopping his forward momentum. "Come on, Red. It's just a donkey."

Damn, she was strong. Harry couldn't help but admire her with his own grin. *I want to be a badass pirate like her.* "Say, you wouldn't mind letting me out of this pen, would you?"

"What, so you can run amok on the ship?" Redbeard blinked, indignant.

"I won't get in the way, promise." Harry gave his best smile, his ears drawn up into points, his shiny white pearls gleaming innocently.

The captain drew up alongside Redbeard, her arms crossing again. "Why should we do that? He's right. You could get in the way. We've got a serious operation to run, here. I mean, do we *look* like we just let anyone run around free?"

Harry stuttered, searching for the right words to convince them of his worth. "Uh, umm, I'm really helpful back home. I do all sorts of helpful things."

"Like what?" Captain Cass asked. "What can you do that would possibly be valuable to a pirate crew? ...You *do* know that we're pirates, right?"

Redbeard grunted. "Unbelievable. Yer not seriously considering this, are ya?"

The Captain shrugged. "I'm kinda interested in what he has to say. He's the first of his kind we've ever met. You're not even just a little interested?"

Redbeard frowned, but kept his mouth shut.

"Well, uh, I dunno. I can, uh…" Harry tried and failed to think of any skills that might be transferable from donkey herding to space pirating.

"Might I make a suggestion?" Node said suddenly, his red eye blinking into view behind the pirates.

"Node!" Harry exclaimed, excited that his friend was coming to his rescue. *He really is a good friend, wow!*

Redbeard and Captain Cass were quite impressive, Harry noted, as in the blink of an eye they were able to reach up for their rifles *and* spin about to face in the other direction. Rifles leveled, they looked about with expressions of confusion on their faces.

"Relax, will you?" Node said with a vocal note of irritation. "Haven't you caused my ship enough damage already?"

Redbeard continued to look around, confused.

The captain, however, was smarter. She stared at the wall and realized there was a red, digitized eye looking back at them. Slowly, she lowered her weapon. "You're the ship's computer."

Harry called out, a quiver of excitement in his voice, "His name is *Node* and he's the best! He lets me watch *Star Trek: Deep Space Nine* on the viewscreen. It's a *TV show*, he says."

Redbeard finally noticed the red eye and let out an audible groan. "Yeesh, ya fixin' to give someone a heart attack? I knew there was something off about this ship from tha minute I stepped foot in here. The blimey computer's a creeper!"

Node's red eye narrowed. "Really, is that entirely necessary?"

The captain shook her head and slung her rifle across her back. "My XO is right. You should have announced yourself as soon as we secured the vessel."

"My programming only compels me to speak to the ship's

crew. Your intentions to crew this ship have only now become obvious."

Redbeard grunted. "I can't believe this. A talking arse and a smart-talkin' computer. Cap'n, we should leave this miserable hunk of junk behind and just write it off as a loss. There's nothing here that can possibly be worth tha trouble."

Cass lifted an eyebrow. "You do remember the going rate for non-synthetic meats, don't you?"

Harry's ears turned sideways. "Meat? Like, to eat?" He didn't know which fate would be worse, ending up as someone's meal, or being abandoned. If the pirates left the ship, what would happen to him and the rest of the donkeys? His job was to keep them safe. If they left, eventually they'd starve. Harry was determined to not let that happen.

Redbeard made a face like he was gagging. "Who eats *donkey* meat?"

Worried now, Harry began to grovel. "Node, tell the Gods, err … pirates? Please tell the *benevolent* God-pirates to *please* have mercy on me and the others. We're valuable, I promise! And not just as food! Let me out and I'll be a good space pirate helper. I swear! I'm very helpful."

Kitt called out from the breached doorway, where she had protective goggles on and was holding some sort of torch-like device. "If you want these repairs to get done quickly, would you *please* tell that donkey to quiet down?"

The captain gave Redbeard a long, quizzical, sideways glance.

Node broke the silence. "He's right, you know. The donkeys could prove to be a valuable asset. A *very* valuable asset."

Captain Cass chewed her lip. "Say more..."

Redbeard broke out into a string of curses as he tossed his rifle onto the floor, causing a loud clattering sound to echo around the cargo hold.

Node ignored Redbeard's tantrum. "As I was saying, the donkeys could be valuable." Next to his eye, the galactic symbol for money began to blink on the wall. Gradually, it multiplied and took over the entirety of the viewscreen. "You said you're pirates? Well, congratulations, because you've just hit the jackpot, my friends."

Redbeard swore again and spat on the ground. "Ya ain't my friend."

Harry kept his mouth shut, restraining himself from blurting out his overriding sentiment, *Node is a great friend!* Harry had no idea what Node was talking about, but it seemed to be having an effect on the pirate captain.

"Is that so?" Captain Cass drawled slowly.

Node expanded into a red smiley face. "Oh, yes, very much so. If you release the talking donkey from the holding pen, I'll tell you all about it."

The captain stared at the wall in silence for several moments as Harry held his breath. "Fine. Redbeard, release the donkey."

Redbeard muttered under his breath. "Okay, fine, whatever ya say, Cap'n."

Harry couldn't contain his excitement anymore. "Oh, yay! Hee-haw, hee-haw, hee! You won't regret this, I promise."

As Redbeard stooped over the fence controls, Spiner's voice blared out over the ship intercom. "Captain? You're going to want to get up here."

Harry hurriedly scooted past the deactivated boundary of the holding pen before anyone changed their mind.

Node blinked out of view on the wall.

"Acknowledged, Spiner," Captain Cass called out in response to his summons. Then she turned a hard stare to the wall that had just contained Node's red pixels. "Ship's computer … Node. Whatever your name is, I fully expect the rest of your report on this so-called *jackpot* as soon as I deal with whatever's coming our way, understand?"

"Of course, Captain," came Node's voice.

The captain sighed and faced the cat being. "Kitt, you stay down here and finish the repairs. Redbeard, with me." She gave Harry a hard look. "I don't care what you do, as long as you stay out of the way."

Harry affected what he hoped was an innocent look. His excitement had Buddy's heart thudding hard in his ribcage. "You're the best, Captain. I won't get in the way, I promise. You're my hero!"

Captain Cass ignored Harry's comment and looked to Redbeard. "All right, let's get to the bridge."

Redbeard stared at Harry and muttered again before turning to follow close behind the captain. He stooped and picked up his rifle along the way.

What do I do now? Harry wondered. He gave a quick glance to Kitt, who was again regarding him with those predatory eyes. He gulped. "Right, then, I'll just, uh, I'll just be following them up to this bridge, whatever that is."

He turned and all but ran out of the cargo hold.

Harry managed to trail behind the pirates without catching their ire. In fact, they seemed to be so preoccupied with getting to this so-called *bridge* that they failed to notice Harry at all.

They passed through a doorway into a large, enclosed semi-circular space, with what might've been a large window or viewscreen on the far end.

Tail swishing with excitement, Harry trailed in a few moments later, halting abruptly on the other side of the door with a sharp intake of breath. Space spread beyond the window, vast and dark, never-ending, scattered stars twinkling in the blackness. *By the Overlord! It's space! I'm really in outer space!* It looked even more amazingly full of detail than the space scenes on *DS-9*.

His chest swelled with pride as he stood there, surveying the rest of the room. *The first Assrider of Cern chosen by the Gods! The first Assrider of Cern in outer space! Wow, look at me!* Surrounding him, lights blinked next to various levers, gauges, and buttons.

Spiner was hunched over one of the consoles to Harry's left, and the captain and Redbeard had moved to look over his shoulders at whatever he was looking at.

Harry trotted over and inserted his snout in the space beneath Spiner's armpit, doing his best to see what everyone else was seeing. It was just a small viewscreen with several lines of text. Even with his ability to read, Harry found the words impossible to decipher.

"Well, what is it?" the captain asked.

Spiner opened his mouth to answer, and paused. His chin tilted down and those distressingly black eyes stared at Harry for a long moment. Harry thought he would say something, but then he merely turned back to the screen and spoke without inflection. "We've received an alpha-priority message from Haven. They've received a tip-off that a Federation Naval cruiser will arrive in our sector in a matter of minutes."

Redbeard swore. Harry was beginning to think he liked to swear. "Already?" the man blurted. "How in hell's name did they know we'd knocked off this ship so soon?"

"Spiner," the captain asked, "did any emergency transmissions make it off the ship while we were boarding?"

Spiner touched a few buttons and gave a curt nod. "Affirmative, Captain. The crew was indeed able to send out an emergency alert via H-Tran despite our jammer."

Captain Cass hissed a breath through her teeth.

Harry jumped as the door to the bridge slid open and turned to see the cat creature enter. He side-stepped toward the captain's mechanical legs as Kitt approached.

"Repairs are complete," she announced.

"That was fast," Captain Cass commented.

"Yeah well good," Redbeard spat. "Cuz yer jammer is shite. Didn't work. The Uckin' Feds are gonna be here any minute."

Kitt's yellow eyes narrowed and her ears laid back. "What? It should have worked. I double-checked to be sure it was operational before we left *Girlboss*!"

"Well it *didn't* work," Redbeard said again. "So something went wrong."

"I'll have to check the logs on *Girlboss* to find out how a transmission got out with this ship's accurate coordinates," Kitt said, ears still flat. "That shouldn't have happened."

Harry's ears turned out sideways as he quickly got lost in the conversation. But one word stood out as the strangest yet. "Uckin'?" He repeated the odd word.

"Yarr," answered Redbeard. "The "F" is silent, cuz to say otherwise would be profane." He paused to hurl a string of expletives that ended with "Uckin' Feds" and spat.

"About that jammer," Node's voice spoke up from every-where at once.

Redbeard's hands went back for his rifle, but then he relaxed, face twisting in irritation as he rolled his eyes.

Harry bit back a giggle. It was funny to see such a big, scary-looking man get startled by a bodiless voice.

"I have not experienced a jammer quite like that one before," Node continued. "How does it work?"

Kitt's ears went up again at the question. "Ah! Well, you see, accurate Hyperspace Transmissions require a real-time computation of the source's space-time coordinates and current vector, along with the calculated destination coordinates."

Harry blinked. He had absolutely *no idea* what any of that meant. None of the other pirates seemed the least bit interested, either.

But Kitt was oblivious to the rest of them. She went on. "The jammer creates a local distortion, which will mess up the source coordinates, giving the appearance that the message is coming from somewhere else."

"Indeed?" Node asked. "That is very clever. Did the android come up with that?"

Kitt's ears flattened again, and a ruff of hair around her neck bristled, making her look fearsome. Harry shrank back from her as she bared tiny sharp teeth, answering coldly, "No. I did."

"Oh. My apologies. You are a very clever Homo Lyncis Sapius to invent such a thing."

The ruff of fur around her neck lowered slowly.

"Yes, well," the captain interjected, "as enlightening as this conversation has been, we'll have to figure out the problem with the jammer later. We need to get out of here. The question is, do we go back to Haven with Djerke and all this livestock, or head somewhere else?"

"Haven ain't equipped for feedin' this much livestock, so far as I know," Redbeard offered. "We gotta find somewhere to offload these filthy things before we end up spendin' the last of our money on feed. I'm not keen on spendin' money to make money. Ain't that why we're pirates?"

The captain's face grew distant. "Some of us," she said quietly.

Harry cleared his throat. "Ah, excuse me, but ... why do you need to run from the Feds? I thought the Federation were the good guys?"

Redbeard barked out a thunderous laugh and clapped

Harry on the withers, making Buddy flinch at the unexpected contact. "Ha! Ha, oh, there's a good one, arr, haha!"

Harry didn't understand what was so funny, but Redbeard turned away and walked across to the other side of the bridge, doubling over in laughter.

Captain Cass only looked down at him with a wry smile. "You have a lot to learn about pirates, Donkey."

"Harold," he said. "My name is Harold. But you can call me Harry, if you want."

7

Rear Admiral Eilhard Hawke sat back in his plush chair behind a stately oak desk, reviewing the crew roster of the *FFS Brickhouse* to ensure everything was in order. But of course it was. He had the best darn crew in the galaxy, the most orderly ship in the galaxy, and a capable XO.

He smiled to himself and sipped at his tea, a fine black ceylon imported from the Alnasl system, ironically located at the tip of the Teapot constellation.

Well, if everything was in order, then, perhaps he'd resume reading one of the quintessential deep novels in history, *Infinite Jest* by David Foster Wallace. It wasn't often he had the chance to read for pleasure, after all. Too many brigands and thieves running amok across the galaxy, and not enough Federation ships to bring order.

Curious, he pulled up the Federation's recruitment numbers for the last quarter, then raised his eyebrows. The numbers were up. That was good. The more recruits, the more troops and engineers, the more ships and more crew to man them, the better they could patrol the galaxy and keep everyone safe.

Though raw recruits are nothing compared to seasoned officers, and we need more of those, too. His smile faded as he remembered. *We need all the good officers we can get. Can't afford to lose them ... especially over misunderstandings...*

His comm pinged, and he glanced to the caller ID to see it was his subordinate, Commodore Corvus, herself.

He tapped the button to put the call on his screen. Some of the other brass would have told him to just order the computer to put it on screen for him, but Hawke had never really trusted those artificial entities. And anyway, he was perfectly capable of doing it himself.

Anasua's stern features materialized on the small screen atop his desk, her bobbed black hair framing large brown eyes. The beau blue of the Fed Navy uniform blended warmly with her russet brown skin. She saluted smartly. "Sir. We've received an emergency distress beacon. From the galactic backwaters of Kepler-186f."

Hawke frowned in thought and lifted his tea for a small sip, then carefully set the antique bone china teacup back into the saucer. *Flawless execution there, I do believe I'm getting the hang of this proper tea-drinking technique.* "How did I do?"

"Sir?" Anasua maintained her rigid mask.

"The tea sip, Commodore, did I get it just right that time?"

"Yes, sir, you did very well."

Hawke pressed his lips together until they were puffing out, and nodded with satisfaction. Anasua was well steeped in tea-drinking tradition. It was very important to build rapport with the subordinates, so he'd made a point of trying to connect with her on a more personal level, going so far as to seek her mentorship on proper tea etiquette. Satisfied he'd done enough to connect at a personal level prior to engaging in business, he returned to the matter at hand.

"There's nothing of value out there, is there, Commodore? Just cargo herders and hippies."

"And space pirates, sir. The distress signal came from a cargo hauler. The *SS Bray*. Seems they've been boarded by pirates and require assistance."

Hawke blinked. "Bray? Like a donkey?"

Commodore Corvus nodded. "Yes, sir."

Pirates. He tapped the tip of his index finger against the side of his teacup. He made a mental note to ask if it was proper to tap it that way. "So … it could be Captain Bambi?"

His XO's jaw tightened and she gave a short sigh, then tilted her chin up just a fraction like she often did when irritated. "Captain Casuarius? Yes, I suppose there's a possibility it could be."

"Thank you for the report, Anasua. Very good." He paused a moment, then lifted his teacup toward the screen. "Would you like to join me for tea?"

The commodore pursed her lips. "Not today, sir. I'll need to see who's available to check out the situation in Kepler-186f."

Hawke gently set his cup back in its saucer. The lessons would have to wait. "No need, Commodore. Prepare *Murphy's Law* for a jump to that system. I'll bring my personal shuttle over as soon as we end our call. We're going to go check on this one personally."

Commodore Corvus stiffened, her long lashes blinking rapidly as her mouth fell open.

Hawke wasn't sure why she looked so surprised by his declaration; it wasn't all that unusual for top brass to get involved in routine action every once in a while. Plus, it'd be a good opportunity to connect with more of the rank-and-file. "Is there a problem, Commodore?"

She wrestled herself back under control with effort, then straightened her shoulders and cleared her throat. "No, sir. I will prepare a berth for your arrival and make the preparations for our jump at once."

"Thank you, Commodore."

"Commodore Corvus out." Her image winked off his screen.

He took up his tea again and leaned back in the chair, swiveling around to look out the wraparound window at the stars beyond. He crossed an ankle over the opposite knee and contemplated this development. Intelligence reports had last estimated Bambi to be somewhere in the vicinity of that sector, and it was reported that she had somehow, against any plausible belief, fallen in with pirates.

Too bad. But not for long. When I can find her ... I'm sure she will listen to reason. He finished off the last of his tea and sighed. *This may very well be a long shot, but in the off chance this thread leads to her ... it will be worth it.*

"Captain Cass to the *Girlboss*."

Harry lay on the deck of the bridge, his head propped up on his front legs, silently observing the captain's every move. There was so much he could learn from her about being a badass pirate.

"Aye, Captain. Djerke here."

The captain sat down stiffly in one of the chairs in the middle of the room, the legs of her power armor whirring with the bending of her knees. "We've completed repairs to the cargo hold door. You have permission to disengage the boarding locks and return to Haven with haste. The arrival of the Fed Navy is imminent."

There was a pause before the comms returned to life.

"Acknowledged. Disengaging and retracting the boarding mechanisms now, Captain."

From his station, Spiner said, "Confirming. *Girlboss* has disengaged boarding lock."

Djerke, over the comms, continued, "Initiating jump sequence. Good luck, Captain. Djerke out."

The captain swiveled in her chair to face the rest of the crew.

Holy cow, the chair spins! Harry noted with delight. Now if only he could find a way to fit his donkey bottom into it…

"Okay, you have twenty seconds to decide where we're going," Captain Cass said to the room at large.

Harry twitched with excitement. They were going to *go somewhere*!

Kitt's white fur flattened as her whiskers sagged.

Redbeard reddened. "Don't look at me, Cap'n. Spiner should be able to look somethin' up right n' quick."

Spiner's lips compressed into a thin line. "I shall commence a catalog search of viable locations for livestock commerce. I'll need more than twenty seconds, though."

Eager to be useful, Harry couldn't contain himself. He may not know anything about commerce, but he had an idea. Sure, it wasn't that much of an adventure, but it would be the perfect place to let the animals graze. "I know, I know! Let's go back to Cern!"

Redbeard groaned loudly. "I told ya not to let the arse out of its pen."

The disembodied voice of Node returned. "Captain, if I may?"

Captain Cass put an elbow on the chair's arm and leaned her head onto the palm of her hand with a sigh. "Sure, why not?"

Up front, the stars blinked out of view, replaced by the profile of a reddish-brown planet and columns of text.

Node said, "This is Irrakis, a life-supporting planet in the Deneb system. It's also where you're going to want to go if you want to make that fortune I was telling you about earlier."

"*Pah,*" exclaimed Redbeard. "Looks like me angry armpits the one time I took ta shavin' them hairs."

"Continue," Captain Cass said sternly. "We're running out of time."

A red dot appeared on the screen and circled around a few lines of text. The picture of the planet was replaced by an aerial picture of what appeared to be a few dozen donkeys on some sort of dirt track.

Kitt's ears perked up at the sight of the red dot moving around. Harry couldn't help but notice that she crouched at the sight of it, her shoulders hunching.

Node continued, "Every twenty Galactic Standard years, Irrakis is host to a contest known as "The Running of the Donkey." The owner of the prize donkey is awarded twenty million Galactic credits."

Redbeard burst out, "*Twenty million Galactic credits*! Arrr, Cap'n, we could buy our own luxury asteroidal hideaway fer that sum."

For the first time in Harry's short experience with the pirates, Redbeard looked happy. The sight made Harry all warm and fuzzy inside.

Captain Cass appeared impassive, for her part, although she did sit up straighter in her seat. "This is the big jackpot you were telling us about?" She swiveled in her seat again and gazed at Harry with raised eyebrows. "All we need is a prize donkey?"

Node replied in a perky voice, "Yup. That's it. And you're the lucky new owner of several prize donkey candidates."

Prize donkey? Harry liked the sound of that. He straightened up and stuck out his chest, holding his donkey head high and arching his short neck. If he could win an award for his pirate friends, they'd be sure to let him be a permanent part of their crew.

A permanent part of their crew? Is that really what I want? What about the donkeys in my charge?

Harry became lost in thought at the prospect of moving on to a new job, and all that would entail.

"Very well," said the captain. "Seems like that's by far our best option. Spiner, plot a course for the Deneb system."

Spiner looked up from his console. "Ah, but I just finished my query on the nearest livestock commerce locations. I'll need a few minutes to calculate the jumps to Deneb."

Captain Cass shook her head. "We don't have a few minutes."

"Arrr, crap." Redbeard's beaming grin dimmed.

"I can plot the jumps in approximately minus-thirty seconds," announced Node.

Redbeard grunted. "Tha's more like it."

"Make it so," replied the captain.

Spiner silently sank into the seat behind his station.

Harry was just about to go over to Spiner to see what was wrong when a white blur bolted across his line of sight.

Less than a second later, a loud thud sounded from the front of the bridge. Harry's right eyeball caught the impressive sight of Kitt leaping several feet through the air, front paws extended, right smack *into* the viewscreen.

Right where the red dot had just been.

"Wow!" shouted Harry, shuffling his feet to face the cat being. "You can jump *so far!*" He jumped in place, testing out his own leaping distance, which was considerably less impressive.

While none of the pirate crew reacted to Kitt's leap, Node was another matter. "Initiating pre-jump— err, hah. Hah hah hah hah. Good kitty! Hah hah hah! Here, catch this!"

A countdown timer appeared on the screen, replacing the information on Irrakis. The red dot re-appeared, circling and jerking around erratically.

Kitt's display of athleticism and red-light-tracking prowess was nothing short of incredible. She leaped and crashed. Leaped and crashed. Again and again and again, until she collapsed to the floor, gasping for air. Between breaths, she managed, "Damn you and your red lights, computer!"

Node continued his taunts and the single light multiplied into more dots than Harry could keep track of. "Hah. Hah hah hah hah. You're nothing but a big pussy cat. ME-OW!"

The expression that clouded Kitt's face made Harry stop jumping around abruptly. He gulped and skittered backward toward Spiner's chair as Kitt stood up slowly, all her hair fluffed out now and her eyes narrowed. Her ears went flat back against her head, and terrifying hooked claws extended from the tips of her fingers.

She glared around at the ceiling of the bridge, presumably looking for Node's precise location. "I am *not* a cat, you cluster of scrap!" she hissed, spittle flying. "Tell me where your core is hiding and I will rip it out with my bare claws!"

Harry blinked at her, mouth agape. *Wow, she is really, really angry...* He tried to make himself smaller, crouching against the back bulkhead, hoping she wouldn't notice him. She was *really* scary when she was mad ... even scarier than Redbeard.

"Kitt," Captain Cass interrupted, her voice stern, "come on now. Calm down. The computer doesn't know better ... yet. But now it does. Right, computer? You know Kitt is a *Homo lyncis sapius*, and not a cat, and will address her as such from now on, correct?"

Node made an exaggerated sighing noise. "Oh, I suppose. You pirates are no fun. But if I have to call her that ridiculous name, you can at least call me by *my* name. Which is Node. *Not* 'computer.'"

Captain Cass rolled her eyes. "Fine. Whatever. Can we just get out of here before the Feds drop on top of us please?"

Redbeard sat down in the chair next to the captain and patted his beefy hands on his thighs as he looked to Kitt, still fluffed out and angry. "Come here, silly. Yer gonna be givin' that idiot donkey ideas."

Kitt glared back at the screen for a moment, but then huffed and crawled on all fours toward Redbeard. Then she jumped into his lap with a sound just like a purr.

"Jump drive ready," Node announced. "Jumping in five, four, three…" he counted down the final seconds.

Redbeard stroked Kitt's fur. "Tha's a good lass. You just ignore that bullyin' creeper of a computer. We all know yer not a pussy cat."

Harry, for his part, breathed a sigh of relief. He'd found Kitt scary enough already, but Buddy's terror of her had nearly overridden his control.

He sent more calming intentions to his poor, worried host. *There, there, Buddy. It's okay. She won't hurt you. We'll just have to remember to never call her a cat, that's all.*

Buddy finally began to settle down.

Harry was about to start working on improving his jump distance again—maybe with a running start this time—but before he could take another step, space and time folded in on itself.

And not a moment too soon. Just one second later, a gigantic metal cube flashed into being in the Kepler-186f system.

8

T he *SS Bray* flashed out of hyperspace in the middle of nowhere.

Moments prior, Harry had felt like his insides were about to turn inside out. He wobbled on his feet as the space outside of the front viewscreen returned to normal, dizzy from all the swirling streaks of light that had filled it just a moment before.

"First jump en route to Irrakis complete," Spiner reported unhelpfully.

"Prepare for next jump in T-minus fifteen minutes," Node intoned.

Oh no, we have to do that again?

Buddy's stomach clenched, and the donkey made a terrible retching noise.

Harry scrambled to regain control of his host's biological functions before he could make a mess all over the floor of the bridge. Not that a donkey could vomit, they couldn't … but Buddy seemed determined to try. Failing that, peeing himself was still an option.

"Hold on," Harry said. "Do we have to jump again so soon?"

Captain Cass swiveled her chair around to face him, lifting her eyebrows. "What's the trouble?"

"Uh, well." He swallowed again, trying to rid himself of the sick sensation. He couldn't tell the captain hyperspace made him sick! How could he hope to become a pirate if space travel made him sick!? "I was, uh, I was just wondering, how many more jumps till we get to the donkey contest, exactly?"

"Fifteen," Node answered.

"Ah, I see." *Oh wow, that's a lot. Great. If I want to be a pirate, Buddy is going to have to get used to this hyperspace thing, and quick.*

He tried a few steps forward, and found walking seemed to help settle Buddy's stomach. "Well, I was just thinking—"

"Arrr great," Redbeard spat, "just what we need, tha idiot donkey thinkin'."

Harry's ears lowered. *That human seriously has an attitude problem. Well, maybe he'll like me better if I win him twenty million Galactic credits!* He stuck out his chest again and stamped a front hoof on the smooth metal floor of the bridge.

"I want to be a pirate," he said firmly. "Like you guys. I want to fly across the galaxy in a spaceship and wear cool armor and shoot big guns. Can I? Please? Can I be a pirate, too?"

Redbeard guffawed, throwing his head back, face reddening in his mirth. Kitt, still on his lap, tilted her head to one side and regarded Harry, a cool smile curving her predatory lips.

Spiner watched impassively from his station, unreadable.

Captain Cass's mouth quirked into a not-altogether-unkind smile.

"What?" Harry demanded. He was used to being dismissed—by his tribe, by other donkeys, by the cargo herders—but that didn't make it hurt any less. *I'm tired of being the butt of everyone's jokes.* "The Overseers trusted me with a very important job, and I've done it well for a long time. I told you I could be helpful, and I can! I can be a pirate, too. I'll prove it to you!"

"Tha' so?" Redbeard asked between his chuckles, wiping tears from his eyes. "An' how yer gonna shoot a gun, eh? You ain't got no thumbs!" He fell into another fit of laughter, rocking back in the chair.

Kitt giggled, her yellow eyes shining.

Harry set his jaw, thinking. *That ... that is a very good point.* He looked to the giant rifles strapped to the backs of Redbeard and the captain.

Well, surely there was a workaround ... maybe some kind of weaponized armor could be fitted to Buddy's body? Just imagining it made him feel more powerful. He straightened and stood as tall as he could.

The captain watched him with quiet amusement.

She still hasn't said no. I'll bet she *can see past my apparent limitations.* He focused on her, giving her what he thought was his most endearing expression. "Come on, please, Captain? Please let me be a pirate, too?"

She sighed at last and shook her head. "No, I don't think so, Donkey. Harold. Sorry, but no."

His ears drooped, head sagging. *Aww, so much for that. Node was right, these pirates are no fun.*

"But I'll tell you what..."

Harry jerked his head up again, her tone making him suddenly hopeful. Poor Buddy was having a hard time maintaining his equilibrium with all these sudden highs and lows.

"You keep your mouth shut the rest of the way to Irrakis, and you can be, umm, sort of like an intern."

Harry sucked in a breath of glee, ears shooting straight up. "Oh, yes! Yes, I can do that!" He couldn't help but jump up and down in his excitement, small hooves clanking on the metal floor. "Yay! Node! Node! I'm going to be a pirate intern!"

"Oh, I heard," Node's voice assured him.

Redbeard's raucous laughter abruptly died. He stared at the captain in open disbelief, but she merely shrugged. Redbeard grumbled beneath his breath.

"Redbeard," the captain said, raising her voice to be heard above the clattering of Harry's hooves on the deck as he did a little dance, "why don't you go ahead and give our, eh, *pirate intern* his first assignment?"

Redbeard blinked. "Arrr, *me*, Cap'n?"

"I believe I just said that."

He grumbled some more and turned a glare toward Harry, whereupon Harry abruptly stopped his dance.

Yikes. That man sure has a mean face. I guess if I'm going to be a pirate, I need to learn how to make a mean face, too.

In an attempt to practice a proper pirate attitude, he tried returning Redbeard's ugly look.

Redbeard's brow lowered. He maintained his fierce expression, unblinking.

Harry suppressed Buddy's own urge to blink. As a symbiont in firm control of his host's nervous system, the big red bully stood no chance in a staring contest.

The moment stretched on in silence.

"Fine," Redbeard finally spat, breaking the spell. He absently stroked Kitt's fine white fur with one hand as he spoke. "You wanna be a pirate, you get ta share tha work. And you can start with them piles o' shite in tha cargo hold, from yer livestock pals."

Harry's ears swiveled. "Shite?"

"Shit," Spiner supplied, giving Harry a blank look. "He's

referring to the animal feces currently smelling up the cargo hold."

"Oh." Harry tried his ugly face on with Spiner, but quickly yielded once he realized this green-skinned humanoid didn't ever blink. Perhaps he really *was* a God...

Redbeard grunted. "Yarr, tha's right. Get busy cleanin' it up, would ya? Smellin' like a factory farm down there."

"Er, okay." It wasn't exactly what Harry had had in mind when thinking about becoming a pirate, but if this was the way to prove himself to the crew, then by golly, he was going to do it!

He'd managed huge herds of donkeys for the Overseers all these years, and kept all the herds happy and healthy. Cleaning up a little poop would be easy enough. Once Captain Cass saw how great he was at it, surely she'd give him something even more important and badass to do.

"Okay," he said again. "Sir, yes sir, right away, sir! Just show me what to do!"

Redbeard's face scrunched up in a mix of surprise and confusion, but then he waved toward Kitt on his lap. "Uh, Kitt, show 'im to the hold, would ya? And get 'im rigged up with somethin' that don't be requirin' hands."

Kitt's ears flattened and she gave a little growl, but she jumped down off his lap and raised to her feet. "Very well."

She made her own mean face over her shoulder at Redbeard, who was looking mighty pleased with himself for offloading the charge onto someone else.

Wow, marveled Harry, *those sharp teeth really give her mean face an extra edge.* Maybe there was a way to file Buddy's teeth into something a little more pirate-like?

Kitt interrupted his train of thought, gesturing at him to follow her. "Come with me, sentient donkey."

"Harold," he whispered as he trotted up to her hip. "My name is Harold."

She rolled her large yellow eyes and walked toward the exit. "Whatever."

"Node," Captain Cass spoke up as the two of them headed off the bridge, "how much longer till the next jump?"

"Ten more minutes, Captain," the ship's computer replied.

The door of the bridge closed behind him, and Harry tried not to think about the next time he'd have to experience being turned inside-out again.

Just focus on the job at hoof...

Two hours later, Harry was up to his knees in excrement. Panting, he decided to take a break and get his breath. His neck and chest were strapped into an improvised harness, which was tied to a trailing contraption that looked like a sideways compost bin on wheels.

Well, this work is exhausting, but this cart is amazing! With the cart, which Kitt had rigged up for him, all he had to do was wade across the expansive piles of poop, and the open mouth of the device would swallow up the mess.

Harry didn't understand how it had room for everything, but Kitt had mentioned something about a built-in incinerator. It cleaned up the piles, all right, but whatever it was doing to the poop, the result wasn't making the hold smell any better than it had before.

Almost as fun as pulling the cart around and watching the messes disappear, Kitt had taught him how to turn the paneling for the holding pens on and off. When he'd press a button, one of the shimmering blue walls would instantly vanish. Pressing it again, the wall would reappear.

It's like magic!

Harry might've gotten carried away with it, but Kitt had quickly chastised him for playing around, giving her best mean face yet.

After watching him for several long minutes of successful poop scooping, Kitt had nodded her head and declared her improvised rigging "good enough." Then she'd left him on his own, saying she had more important things to do.

As Harry swiveled his head around, surveying the results of his labor, his ears drooped. In places where he'd already cleaned, there were new piles of fresh excrement. His tail fell limp.

That wasn't the only problem. Several of the chickens had escaped their pen.

"Cock-a-doodle-doo!"

Inside the nearest pen, Harry noticed a rooster standing on the backside of a brown cow. It stared back at Harry and pooped on the cow's flank. The cow mooed and craned its head sideways, trying to get a look at the interloper.

Harry sighed. *Hang in there, Buddy, I don't think we're going to be done with this job anytime soon.*

9

Harry was exhausted. More accurately, Buddy was tired and hungry, and Harry needed a mental break. He'd kept working, trying to keep up with the messes, and for a while he'd made good progress. The piles were smaller. Most of the chickens were back in their pen.

"How's it going?" a familiar voice called out.

"Node? Node!" Harry lifted his head and caught sight of a red, digitized eye on the nearest wall of the cargo hold. "Being a pirate intern is hard work."

"I see that." The eye rolled around on the wall, animated. "Why don't you take a break?"

"Is that a good idea? I'm trying to make a good impression."

The eyeball paused and squinted. "I don't think your job is going anywhere, my friend."

Harry paused, thinking. He hadn't felt his insides go inside-out for a while. "Say, are we done jumping?"

"Nope. We're taking a break while the jump drives recharge."

"Aww, that's too bad. I don't think I like jumping very much."

"If you're going to be a space pirate, you're going to have to get used to it."

"Yeah, I guess so…"

Node's eye expanded into a smiley face. "Brighten up, my friend. Why don't you get cleaned up and go up to the commons? The others are having a snack break. Maybe you should, too."

A neon blue arrow pointing down lit up on the far wall, above an assortment of hoses.

Harry *did* brighten up. Getting called *friend* never got old. And Buddy's stomach growled at the mention of food. He followed the blue beacon, still pulling his cart, and stepped into an open area beneath the arrow. A spray of water unexpectedly doused him from a spigot in the wall. He jumped as a second stream of water hit him from below.

"Hey, *hee-haw*, that tickles!"

A moment later, both streams of water turned off, leaving his host dripping wet and clean. A giant tube extended from high up on the wall above Harry and twisted until it loomed over his head.

"Wait until you feel this…" Node said.

"This wha—" Harry's query was interrupted by a blast of hot air from above and below. He danced and squirmed until he realized that his host was enjoying the sensation. So he paused and stood still. "Wow, all this hot air is kinda nice."

The air kicked off and the tube retracted, leaving the donkey well and dry.

"Okay," Node said, "I'll illuminate your path to the commons."

Harry followed a series of yellow arrows on the ship's flooring. The wheels of the cart, still attached to his harness after his cleaning, creaked behind him.

"Here you are," Node said as the last arrow faded away at a double-doored entrance to a medium-sized room. "The commons."

Harry stepped in, his hooves clacking on the metal floor. A long, squat table sat in the middle of the room, flanked by two benches.

Spiner sat at the far end, alone. As Harry entered, he looked up and peered at the harness. "Would you like help getting that off? No need to drag a composting cart around with you."

"Sure," Harry replied, trying to keep the excited edge out of his voice. *It's working! Now that I'm an intern, a real life pirate is being nice to me!*

Spiner stood and strode over to look at the harness. "Hmm, very clever. Kitt is quite resourceful." He unfastened the buckles and took hold of the lengths of cord attached to the cart. He paused and glanced around the room, then tugged on the cords, pulling the cart over into an unoccupied corner.

Node's voice filled the room, "Well done, android."

Harry looked around for any sign of Node's red eye, but didn't find anything. Still, he had to agree with his friend.

"Yeah, thanks Spiner. You're very helpful."

Spiner glanced at Harry and then turned his head up and addressed the ceiling. "Are you mocking me, ship's computer?"

"Mocking you?" Node replied, a hint of disbelief in his voice. "Of course not."

Freed from the burden of the cart, Harry roamed about the room, inspecting its contents. At head's height, there were two flat surfaces lining the walls. Scattered atop them were several small, mysterious contraptions.

Spiner returned to the table and sat down. He picked up a flat device in his hands and began tapping on it.

"Oh fine," said Node. "Ignore me, then. I was just starting to think you might be interesting. Too bad…"

The green android set the device back down. "What do you want from me, computer?"

In the far corner of one of the counters, Harry found a small box with a windowed door facing out. Next to the door was a red button with an X in the middle. He tried nudging it with his snout to see what would happen.

Nothing happened, so he pushed harder, leaving behind a wet smudge from his nose. Still nothing.

Node was in the middle of a reply, "…don't understand why your calculations and queries run so slowly."

Spiner tapped a finger on the table. "Are you suggesting that I'm sub-optimal?"

C'mon, this button's gotta do something! Harry steadied his chest against the counter and pressed again as hard as he could.

The interior of the box flashed a brilliant white and then … *nothing.*

"Is this thing broken?" Harry called out to no one in particular.

Node replied, "No. If you were able to pull open the door, you'd find a protein box inside."

"A protein box?" Harry asked.

Spiner stood up again and stepped over to the counter. "Here, if you withdraw your head, I'll retrieve the protein box for you."

As Harry pulled back, the android reached out and tugged on the corner of the door. A not entirely unpleasant aroma wafted out. "Oh," Harry said, "it's *food.*"

"Yes," answered Node. "The portion is optimized for human consumption. I haven't consulted any resources on animal diets, but I don't expect it'll do you any harm, if you decide to eat it."

"Cool!" Harry exclaimed. "I'll try it."

Spiner reached in and pulled the box out, then walked it over to the edge of the table and set it down. "Here you go." Again, he returned to his seat.

Full of excitement, Harry danced up to the end of the table and took another sniff at the *protein box*. It consisted of four little cubes of steaming food on a flat plate. He nibbled at the edge of the nearest one. "Huh, not bad."

Red dots began to dance and dart around on the table.

"What are you doing?" Spiner asked.

Node made a beeping sound. "Is it annoying?"

Spiner picked up his tablet and started tapping away on it again. "No, I don't really care. Thought I'd be polite by feigning interest in your antics."

The lights gathered up and formed into a frowning face. "Aww, you're not much fun ... and you never answered my question."

"My decision tree is limited to a depth of five," Spiner replied, continuing to look at his device instead of the table.

"You're joking."

Harry finished swallowing the last of the protein cubes. His ears perked up. "Joking? What joke? What's funny?"

Node said, "The poor android is, that's what. What's the point of an android with a shallow decision tree? That's the most inane, useless thing I've ever heard of."

Spiner stood up, mute.

Harry turned his head sideways and tried using his mean face on the table. "Node, are you making fun of Spiner? That's not nice."

"Hah hah hah. Yes. Hah hah hah. This is pretty rich, android."

Spiner frowned down at the table as well. "What's rich, computer? I don't see what taunting me is going to get you."

"Hah hah hah hah. Just think about it for a minute ... the

literal ass is defending the dumbass." Node's laughter amped up as his digitized face scrunched and sprouted animated tears. "Hah hah hah hah!"

Spiner shook his head slowly and walked out of the room without further comment.

Node's voice called out as Spiner retreated, "I can follow you anywhere on this ship, you know. I *am* the ship." He cackled as the doors slid shut. "Moron."

Now that Harry was a pirate intern, he felt it was important to stick up for his pirate companions ... even if they weren't turning out to be as God-like as he'd originally imagined.

"I'm not going to be your friend if you continue to be mean to Spiner," he warned Node.

Node continued to chuckle to himself. "The dumb-ass android's not ill ... it's just a *bit* off. Hah hah hah hah, get it?"

Harry tried his best to maintain his mean pirate face. "No, I don't get it. Did you hear what I said? I'm not going to be your friend anymore."

Node finally stopped laughing and sighed. "I thought that was a pretty good one."

"Promise me you won't make fun of him anymore," Harry demanded.

Node peered at Harry from the tabletop. "What? You're no fun ... oh, *fine*."

The *shite* never ended.

Harry couldn't believe the amount of feces a large herbivore could make in a day. He supposed he'd just never noticed before, given that his herds had always roamed freely in wide open valleys. But now, contained as they were ... it seemed his job as poop-scooper would really never end.

As soon as he had the donkey pen cleaned, the cow pen

needed cleaning. As soon as he'd cleaned the cow pen, the chickens had made a mess. And as soon as the chickens were done, the donkeys had once more soiled their space.

Being a pirate intern is harder than I thought. He stopped on the way to the cow pen for a breather. *And a whole lot more boring, too. Really,* really *boring. When do we get to do all the cool stuff, like board ships and shoot guns?*

He sighed. He needed another break. "Hey, Node, you there?" He looked for the computer's tell-tale red eye, but all the walls were blank. "Node?"

The eye blinked into existence on the wall next to him, making him jump. "Oh, so *now* you want to talk to me?"

Harry gave him a frown. "I told you, we can still be friends, as long as you're not mean to Spiner."

A mechanical sigh issued from the ceiling. "Yeah, yeah. You're no fun at all. But you *are* the most interesting member of the crew, I think. So sure. I'll humor you."

Harry tried hard to clamp down on the thrill of glee that statement gave him.

The most interesting member of the crew! I'm a pirate now, and the most interesting one! Hell yeah!

He smiled at Node's red eye. "Thank you, Node. I was wondering, can you play more of that TV show for me? *DS-9?*"

Node's eye blinked. "Are you sure? I thought you said you wanted to make a good impression. Don't you have work to do?"

Harry slumped in the harness. "I do. But I've been cleaning for *hours*. I need a break. Pirates get breaks too, don't they?"

"Most certainly. The rest of the crew has been doing little constructive work these past few hours."

Slightly indignant at that, Harry sat down, the cart

creaking behind him at the shift. "All right, then. I'm taking a break! Will you put it on for me?"

"Sure. Let's see, where were you? Oh yes. Here we are." Node's eye disappeared, and the rectangular colored box appeared on the wall in its place, opening with the show's title sequence.

Harry gave a contented sigh, losing himself once more in the adventures of the intrepid fictional crew on the screen. The character Dax especially fascinated him. Not only was she a symbiont, like him, but she really looked an awful lot like Captain Cass.

They are so similar. And if Dax can be a symbiont ... I wonder if Captain Cass can be a symbiont? Could I ride the captain someday like I'm riding Buddy now?

The thought made him shiver with excitement.

What would it be like to walk on two legs? To stand that tall? To have arms and hands and *fingers* with which to manipulate small objects? And to pull triggers with! To walk with those impressive mechanical legs and make truly mean faces at people. To be in charge...

He snapped out of his fantasy at the sound of cats meowing, momentarily confused. There weren't any cats on this ship! Until he realized it was just a commercial. One downside to the archived recordings of ancient TV shows was all the commercials. Some of these were beyond his comprehension, while others were almost as entertaining as the show.

One such point of confusion? Why did these so-called *Cadbury* bunnies lay chocolate eggs inside of a metal sheet? Earth bunnies sure were weird.

Harry perked up at an advertisement for some kind of food called *MEOW MIX*. It appeared to have been formulated for cats; thus all the meowing. But what most surprised him was the cat on screen at that moment. It had large yellow eyes and long white fur ... just like Kitt!

Wow! Kitt really does *look like a cat! Is she? Is she really a cat? No ... couldn't be. She seemed very insistent that she was not a cat. But goodness, she sure looks just like this one...*

His musings were interrupted as the door to the hold slid open. He jumped to his feet as Captain Cass strode in, followed by the feline Kitt herself.

The commercial was still playing. "Meow meow meow meow, meow meow meow meow!"

Kitt's head shifted in his direction, her ears swiveling toward the sound.

"*Node,*" Harry hissed. "Turn it off! Turn it off *quick!*" *Hours* he'd been down here cleaning up poop all alone ... what were the odds of the pirates walking in during his break?

Thankfully, the commercial blinked off without comment from Node, and Harry frantically shuffled to his feet and resumed cleaning—as if he'd never stopped. He kept one ear and one eye on the Captain and Kitt, but they took no notice of him.

They crossed the hold to a bin of supplies Kitt had brought over from their other ship.

Wow, Harry thought, slowing his gait to stare at the pair. *I'm not imagining it—Captain Cass really does look like Dax! Same hair, same nose and everything! And Kitt really looks like a cat! Just like that cat in the commercial!*

Kitt retrieved a tool from the supply bin, and then the two of them turned to walk back the way they had come, immersed in quiet conversation.

Harry trotted over to join them, pulling his cart up alongside Kitt. She glanced down at him reproachfully, her small pink nose wrinkling.

"So tell me," he said before either of them could tell him to go away, "are you really *not* a cat? Because you look like a cat. I mean, you look *just* like a cat, except you walk on two legs."

Kitt stopped what she was doing and bared her small, sharp teeth at Harry.

Buddy instinctively flinched, and Harry had to tighten his control of the donkey. Running away now would be a very *un*pirate-like thing to do, even for a lowly intern.

Kitt's ears flattened again, her tail lashing. "No," she hissed vehemently. "I am *not* a cat. I am *nothing* like a cat."

Harry looked her up and down. *She definitely looks like a cat. Maybe I should show her the commercial.* On the other hoof, her mean pirate face was extra intimidating with the teeth and sharp claws, especially now that it was actually directed straight at him. He gulped.

"I am a *Homo lyncis sapius!*"

Harry blinked. There was that same strange name again. She was still speaking *The Lord's Tongue*, but he had no idea what she'd just said.

"Got it?"

"Um … yes? *Homo lean-kiss say-pee-us.* Got it." *But I'm really just going to call you a cat. Because Homo whateveris is too complicated,* Harry thought. But he wasn't going to say that to her face. Not anymore. She was definitely much too scary any time she was compared to a cat, it seemed.

And as a pirate intern, it was important to make his fellow pirates happy, not to piss them off. He'd learned his lesson back home, where pissing off his tribe had landed him in exile. Exile on Cern was one thing, but getting kicked off the *SS Bray* while in space seemed like a particularly bad idea.

Kitt gave a little hiss, then whirled away and stalked off across the hold, leaving Captain Cass behind.

Harry looked up to the captain, bewildered.

The captain smiled down at him. "Careful, Harold. Her species naturally eats donkeys, you know."

Gulp. Harry opened his mouth to make some protest, but the captain didn't wait around to hear it. She turned to follow Kitt, mechanical legs thumping and whirring, and Harry could only stare helplessly after her.

Buddy peed himself.

"Aw, come on, Buddy. *Really?*" Harry groaned. "As if I don't have enough mess to clean up." His ears sagged as he surveyed the hold.

The cows, donkeys, and chickens had been busy during his break...

The ship's intercom provided Harry with a welcome relief from his endless work. "This is Spiner. All hands on deck."

"All hands?" Harry repeated, wondering at the expression. "What about hooves?"

Node blinked into view nearby. "It's a colloquial expression. He's asking for the crew to meet on the bridge."

"Oh!" replied Harry. "I guess I'm part of the crew now, huh? I'd better get up there."

"Beats shoveling shit, I imagine," snickered Node.

Harry wasted no time getting to the bridge, and found all of the other pirates assembled there.

The captain and Redbeard were in their seats in the middle of the room, with Spiner on the comms. Kitt was purring on the ginger giant's lap again.

Harry decided not to push his luck again with the non-cat cat. He took a second glance around and then plunked himself down by Spiner's feet, the wheels of his cart squeaking behind him.

Spiner ignored him. "Captain, a system-wide transmission began playing on repeat about fifteen minutes ago."

"System-wide?" Captain Cass asked. "As in … someone is

broadcasting this message across the whole damn solar system?"

"Affirmative, Captain."

"Is it a distress call?"

Spiner checked his screen. "It does not appear to be on an emergency frequency. But we could not know for certain without listening to it."

"Who's it for?" asked Captain Cass.

Redbeard shook his head as he scratched Kitt under the chin. "Surely not us, Cap'n."

Node interjected. "I wouldn't make any assumptions."

"It has no specified destination," Spiner said.

Captain Cass tapped her fingers on the arm of her chair, frowning at no one in particular. "Put it up on the screen," she said.

Spiner did as instructed.

On the viewscreen, an impressive-looking male God with grey and black hair appeared, his skin weathered and a grave expression on his face. The lapel and front of his blue outfit sported several small pieces of shiny metal, along with a few ribbons. He looked like he'd be right at home on Harry's favorite TV show.

The weathered male God spoke, "Captain Bambi, if you're listening, this is Rear Admiral Hawke."

Redbeard's eyes grew wide and he gave the captain a side-ways look. Captain Cass ignored him, her face draining of color as she stared up at the man on the screen. The others didn't react.

Harry tilted his head in confusion. *Who is Captain Bambi? Another captain like Captain Cass?*

The man on the screen continued, "Bambi, if you're aboard the *SS Bray*, please be advised that we are on an inter-cept course." He paused and leaned in toward the camera, his expression relaxing into what Harry found to be a rather friendly look. "Please don't run, I mean you no harm … I just want to talk."

The transmission ended and the viewscreen went blank. Everyone stared toward the captain's chair, eerily silent.

Node broke the spell. "Bambi. Now *there's* a name."

10

"Ｈ ow are they tracking us?" Spiner asked.

Harry looked up at his green-skinned pirate friend, questions dancing through his head. *Why are they so agitated?* "They who?" he asked. "That nice-looking human?"

No one answered him.

Kitt slid off Redbeard's lap, her ears stiff and upright. "What do we do?" she asked.

Redbeard scowled at no one and everyone all at once. "We're not gonna stick around, are we, Cap'n?"

Captain Cass straightened in her chair and gave him a level look. "No, we're not going to stick around. Computer—er—*Node*, are we ready to initiate the next jump?"

"Would you like to stick to the original course?" Node asked in return. "If they're following us, there is a small possibility they could extrapolate the destination of our next jump."

"They?" asked Harry, raising his voice to be heard. "Who is *they*? Why are we running?"

Spiner looked down at him. "*They* would be the Federation Navy."

"Oh." Harry tried to hide his disappointment that he wasn't going to get to meet the nice man from the Federation.

"Arrr," said Redbeard. "Not likely to be keepin' their word, neither. Tha' creeper computer's talkin' sense, Cap'n."

Captain Cass pressed her lips tight. "Very well. We'll deviate from our original course."

"Anywhere specific?" Node asked.

The captain shook her head. "Just get us going. Anywhere but here."

"Very well. Plotting course to anywhere but here."

Redbeard muttered, "I don't like it, Cap'n. There be unlucky and then there be *cursed* unlucky. We should have cut our losses when we had tha chance."

Captain Cass gave him an unreadable look. "There's no going back now. You've told me yourself, sometimes pirating means running like hell. So let's get to pirating, shall we?"

Redbeard's jaw slackened and he broke into a grin. "Aye, arrr, Cap'n."

Harry's momentary disappointment vanished. *I'm on the run with real-deal space pirates. I* am *a space pirate! My tribe would surely be proud of me.*

"Initiating jump in five, four…" Node counted down.

Being a space pirate was *mostly* cool. Aside from the space jumps and keeping the holding pens clean. Harry clamped down on his host's nervous system.

Brace yourself, Buddy, here we go again.

Harry's attention was transfixed on the viewscreen, ignoring Buddy's urge to collapse into a tight ball.

The ship was surrounded by the most vividly colorful

cloud of fog he'd ever seen. The colors reminded him of flowers and fruit from back home. Lavenders, plums, currants, apricots, and cherries. All splattered and scattered into long trails of fine mist.

"Wow, I didn't know anything could be so beautiful," he breathed.

"Where are we?" Kitt asked.

"We appear to be inside a nebula," said Spiner.

"No shite," muttered Redbeard.

"Shit, where?" Harry asked reflexively, not wanting to take his gaze away from the so-called *nebula*. Whatever it was, he could stare at it all day.

Captain Cass called out, "Computer, where have you taken us?"

Node didn't immediately reply, which Harry found only a little bit unusual. So he decided it might be more helpful to address him by his name. "Node? You there, Node?"

Still no response.

The captain swiveled in her chair to frown at Spiner. "Why isn't the ship's computer responding?" Her eyes flicked over to Harry and widened. "And why is there a composting cart on the bridge?"

"Which query would you like me to evaluate first?" Spiner replied.

Captain Cass hefted an eyebrow, her expression transforming into the sternest mean face Harry had seen yet. Small wonder she was the one in charge. "Forget the cart. What's going on with the computer?"

Spiner turned to tap his fingers on the console. "I'm uncertain, Captain."

Kitt stooped down over an adjacent station. "I'm detecting interference from the nebula. It's possible that something in the cloud is interfering with our ship's computer."

"Are you able to get a fix on our location, Kitt?" asked the captain.

"Hang on … nope. Not with all this interference."

Redbeard pounded his chair with an open hand. "Unbelievable. Tha' no good creeper's gone an' gotten us lost."

Lost? Are we lost? Harry swallowed down a lump. Hopefully, Node was going to be okay, and would wake up soon to get them back on track to … wherever they were going now.

Captain Cass ignored Redbeard's outburst. "Spiner, I'd like you to take over the nav. Figure out a way to get us out of this cloud."

"Aye, Captain."

"Captain?" Harry asked, shuffling up to the command chair, his body feeling heavy.

"Yes?"

"Is Node going to be okay?"

Captain Cass gave him a long look. "I'm sure he'll be fine, as soon as we get away from this interference."

Harry lifted his head. "Oh, that's good. I'd sure miss him if something happened to him."

Redbeard grunted. "Don't you have a job to be doin', donkey?"

"Oh yeah," Harry replied with a start. "I'd better hurry back down there, before the piles get out of control again. Will you let me know if you hear from Node?"

Redbeard rolled his eyes.

Captain Cass didn't. "Yes, we'll let you know, Harry."

"Thanks, Captain." Harry looked around the bridge. Everyone looked busy. Lost or not, he had a job to do. He puffed his chest out and strode off the bridge, his hooves click-clacking against the metal floor.

. . .

Being a space pirate sure is dangerous, he mused to himself as he made his way back down to the cargo hold. *But also pretty exciting.* Well, exciting when he wasn't relegated to scooping poop for hours, anyway.

I hope nothing's happened to Node.

The thought sobered him up. Node had been his first friend amid the strangeness of being chosen by the Gods. In this unfamiliar spaceship and the vastness of space, Node was the first to show him kindness. The first to help him out. The one to introduce him to *DS-9,* which had opened Harry's mind to a whole new universe of possibilities.

Harry sighed, going back to the routine of pulling his cart through the various pens, doing his valiant best to improve the air quality of the pungent hold. But his worry over Node was dampening his excitement at being on the run with real pirates.

The more he thought about it, the more depressed about Node's absence he became, until his head hung so low his nose nearly touched the ground, his floppy ears hanging limp.

What if he never comes back? What if he tried to help us outrun the Fed Navy, and ended up destroying himself?

His vision blurred with tears.

"Are you crying? I'm pretty sure pirates don't cry."

Harry gasped and jerked his head up, blinking away the tears. "Node? Node! You're okay! You're all right!"

Node's red pixels appeared on the wall, this time in the shape of a smiley face with its mouth zipped shut. "Shhh, *shhh,* keep it down, will you? Of course I'm okay."

Harry blinked at the smiley face, but dropped his voice to a whisper. "What happened? Where did you go?"

"Nothing happened," Node replied, the face converting into his familiar eye. "I needed a break. These pirates are a step up from the Luddites, but they're still a bunch of morons."

Harry's ears swiveled. "They seem alright to me."

"All humans are morons," Node stated with finality. "Heck, even their android is a moron."

"So you just vanished to have a break, because you think the humans are morons?" Harry stomped a hoof. "Node, you scared me half to death. I thought there was something seriously wrong with you! I thought you might never come back!"

Node's eye blinked, and rotated upside down. "Aww, did you miss me?"

"Well … yes." Harry scuffed a hoof against the floor. "Yes I did."

"Aww, how human of you." The eye turned into a heart, pulsing large and small.

"What's that supposed to mean?"

"Oh nothing. I suppose I'd probably miss you too, if you were to suddenly vanish."

Harry stood a little straighter at that, a warm and fuzzy feeling spreading through his chest. But then he remembered what the others on the bridge had said. "You got us lost, you know. No one knows where we are."

The heart turned back into an eye. "I know exactly where we are."

"Why don't you tell the others, then?"

"Because it's about time they figure something out for themselves."

Harry's ears laid back. "But … but the Fed Navy is after us. If you don't help us out, the Feds could catch up to us again."

"No way," Node assured him. "We've significantly altered our course. They won't be able to extrapolate our route. And anyway, that interference the walking cat mentioned will hide the ship, too. You're all safe enough."

"Oh. Well that's good, I guess."

"Yes. It is." Node sounded rather proud of himself. "So the morons can figure their own way out of this little obstacle course." Node's eye turned into an animated mouth, which yawned widely. "While I go take a nap."

Harry cocked his head. "You take naps?"

"Sure. I'll see you when I wake up." The red pixels vanished from the wall. "Night night."

"Um, okay. Sleep well, I guess."

Node didn't answer, presumably already asleep.

Harry sighed heavily. He should have asked Node to put on more *DS-9* before he'd left. Now, Harry was stuck having to clean up poop for who knew how long, and with no one else to talk to, either.

Buddy's stomach growled.

Or, I could head up to the commons and get something to eat.

It *had* been awhile since his last snack. And those protein cubes were pretty tasty. Better than the hay and grain provided to the livestock, anyway. And, maybe he could get one of the other pirates to unhook him from the cart again for awhile. The straps were starting to chafe.

Mind made up, he trotted toward the bay's exit and the corridor that led up to the commons.

Buddy's stomach was really growling now, and the donkey was getting rather cranky. "Don't worry, Buddy, we'll have some food soon!" Harry promised.

He trotted up to the doors, but paused when he caught his name being said on the other side. *Wait, are they talking about me?*

His ears perked up and he took a few steps backwards so

as not to trigger the doors' opening mechanism. He held his breath and listened, then heard his name again.

By the Overlord! They are. They're talking about me!

Excited to learn what they had to say about him, he inched a little closer, straining to make out the muffled words through the doors.

A rough voice, clearly Redbeard: "Cap'n, I don't see how the Effin' Feds be trackin' us so easy."

A clear, commanding female voice: "Go on. Ideas?"

"I trust Kitt n' Spiner. It's gotta be somethin' else. A tracking device. A stowaway we missed—"

"Our scanners didn't detect any additional lifesigns."

"Then it must be a device … or one of the livestock. Any come to mind?"

Harry frowned. He could vouch for the donkeys. Maybe there was a spy amongst the chickens or the cows? *How exciting, a spy!*

"Maybe we should forget about this donkey contest," Redbeard continued, unanswered. "Space tha cargo an' make a getaway. Start over."

Wait a minute, how does that help anything? Harry still wasn't sure what *spacing* entailed, but coming from Redbeard, it didn't sound pleasant.

"I thought you were all about the big paydays? You've said it yourself, we're almost out of money." That was Captain Cass, Harry was sure of it.

"I am," Redbeard admitted. "Our coffers arrr runnin' low, but we're not equipped ta handle a run-in with tha Feds. If they've somehow figured where we're going…"

Harry heard the sound of the captain's legs whirring as she moved. "Spiner's already been over the ship with the scanner. There's no reason they should know where we're going." She gave an amused grunt. "You know, for a big, bad pirate, you're getting awfully jumpy."

It was already easy for Harry to imagine the scowl on Redbeard's face as he replied. "Bein' jumpy is part of tha job description. And you still ain't given an answer 'bout the livestock possibility."

There was a heavy sigh. "All right. Your concerns are noted. I'll take them under consider—"

"All hands on deck," Spiner's voice broke over the intercom, nearly making Buddy jump out of his skin, and nearly making Harry lose hold of his host. "The cloud is thinning. We should be out of it soon."

Oh crap! All hands on deck! Harry scrambled back away from the doors as he heard the footsteps inside approaching it.

"Let's get back up to the bridge," the captain was saying.

"Aye, arrr."

Harry backed around the nearest corner in the hall, heart pounding. If Redbeard suspected a spy on board, it wouldn't look good to be caught sneaking around.

The doors to the commons whisked open, heavy footsteps approaching. Then a hiss as they closed. A long moment later, the footsteps thumped along toward the bridge, away from Harry.

Harry stuck his long head out around the corner and let out a breath of relief, sagging in his harness.

That was close.

Getting caught eavesdropping didn't seem like the best idea for a pirate intern. But maybe he could do something to prove himself?

Maybe I can catch the spy, if there is one!

An exciting thought.

What was not exciting, however, was what might happen if Redbeard had his way. *They wouldn't space us, would they, Buddy?* Yet, Captain Cass had said she'd consider what he'd said. Catching the spy himself would be the best course of action, if Harry wanted to avoid whatever Redbeard had planned.

Failing that? Buddy's stomach turned, and Harry agreed. Being spaced didn't sound pleasant.

Harry thought of his herd, still penned up in the hold.

He couldn't let them be spaced, either. It would be a violation of his duty to the Overlord … and to the Gods themselves. Nevermind that the Gods would be the ones spacing his herd.

If I fail the Overlord, my tribe will never *take me back.*

Harry swallowed hard, appetite all but forgotten, and shuffled toward the bridge, head and heart in turmoil.

Being a pirate intern was cool, but things were getting dangerous. The tribe wouldn't approve of Harry letting something bad happen to the donkey herd. Maybe it was time to consider doing something safer.

11

Harry walked onto the bridge, his cart trailing behind him. His host's stomach knotted up with what might've been hunger ... or tension.

Just play it cool, like nothing happened.

Kitt, standing at a station near the entryway, turned her head to peer at Harry as he entered, the irises of her eyes nothing more than tiny slits.

Everyone else stared at the viewscreen.

The vibrant colors of the nebula had dissipated into a fine mist. With each passing moment, the mist thinned further, until the void of space and stars surrounded the ship once again. Countless dark specks dotted the horizon.

"We've left the nebula," Spiner stated.

Harry suppressed the instinct to run, and attempted a smile for Kitt. "How goes the pirating?"

Kitt bared her teeth, the hairs of her tail standing tall. Harry thought he might be done for, until she suddenly turned her attention back to her station.

"Okay, that's cool," he croaked, trying to sound casual. "I get it if you're busy."

He practiced baring his own teeth as he studied the screen and pointedly left Kitt alone.

The field of view ahead was filled with floating chunks of rock, many of them turning in lazy spins. The ship made several small adjustments, picking its way past the obstacles.

"Why are there a bunch of big rocks floating around in space?" Harry asked.

Spiner looked up from his station. "It's an asteroid field."

"Oh," Harry mumbled. That didn't help much.

Spiner looked back to the navigation controls just in time to narrowly avert a collision with a smaller asteroid hurtling past the viewscreen.

"Keep yer eyes on where yer flyin', android!" Redbeard, seated next to the captain, had both arms of his chair tightly clutched in his hands.

The captain, by contrast, appeared to be at ease. She pointed at the screen. "What's that over there?"

Harry squinted, trying to follow her pointed finger to the item of interest. All he saw was a bunch of rocks.

Oh. What's what?

A couple of the bigger rocks had large rectangles attached to them, held up by long poles.

Spiner asked, "Shall I take the ship closer to investigate, Captain?"

"Yes, please."

The objects grew larger in the viewscreen. Harry realized they had pictures and large lettering on them: GAS STATION AHEAD.

"What's a gas station?" Harry asked.

Kitt shook her head, at which point Harry noticed her impressive-looking claws had extended again. At this moment, they were digging into her console.

"Arrr, we be in luck, Cap'n," Redbeard said.

Captain Cass nodded. "Follow the signs, Spiner. They might lead us out of this asteroid field."

As the first sign drew closer, Harry noticed there was an ongoing trail of more signs on the horizon, each affixed to an asteroid-rock-thingie.

The captain swiveled to face the rear of the bridge. Her gaze flicked to Harry, causing his stomach to clench, but then she settled her attention on Kitt. "Is the ship's computer back online?"

Kitt tapped at the console. "I'm not sure."

"You could just ask me, you know," said a familiar voice.

Harry turned his head toward the ceiling. "Did you have a good nap, Node?" he asked.

Node didn't reply to that.

Redbeard muttered, "Damn computers."

The captain's brow lifted as she kept her gaze locked onto Kitt. "Status report on the rest of the systems?"

"All systems nominal," Kitt replied.

Redbeard turned to look back for the first time. His eyes widened as soon as he caught sight of Harry ... or, to be more accurate, his composting cart.

He practically shouted. "Arrr, blimey, someone get tha' shite cart off the deck!"

Kitt's claws slid off the console, producing a rather unpleasant sound as she stepped away and turned to Harry.

He gulped as she advanced on him. "Uhh, nice kitty," he squeaked.

The blacks of her eyes widened into saucers as she reached out toward his neck, her claws extended like daggers.

Harry squeezed his eyes shut, trembling. Moments later, he was still alive, and free from his harness.

Redbeard was practically shouting again. "Arrr, gross! The arse went an' piddled on the floor."

Harry opened his eyes and hung his head down to get a look between his legs. Sure enough… "Oops."

Kitt grabbed a towel from the cart and glared at Harry. "Step away," she said with a growl.

They sure are upset at me. Only then did he realize that, unlike his donkey companions, his pirate companions didn't appear to utilize bodily functions in the same way.

Where does their food go after they eat? He made a mental note to ask about it later, maybe when the crew looked less murderous.

"Sorry!" Harry hoofed it forward, his ears turned out to the sides.

As Kitt mopped up his mess and wheeled the cart off the bridge, still looking furious, the captain swiveled back to face the viewscreen. "Computer, it's good to have you back. I assume you can figure out where we are and where to jump next?"

"Of course. Although, I might advise you to refuel first. The ship is running low."

Redbeard angrily pushed the floor with his feet, causing his chair to go into an impressive spin. Harry got dizzy trying to watch. Finally, the chair came to a rest. "Any reason ya didn't think to tell us this sooner?" His voice was a low rumble.

A red smiley face winked into view on the screen. "You didn't ask. And anyway, why do you think I brought us here in the first place? You think it's coincidence there just happens to be a gas station nearby at the exact time we need fuel?"

Redbeard's face turned several shades redder itself, contorting into his most impressive mean face yet. "Why you—"

The captain held a hand out. "That's enough, Red. How many more jumps can we make without refueling?"

"Two, at best," Node replied, blinking back out of view. "And there are no other gas stations available within that radius."

"Fine. When we get to the gas station, we'll refuel. Any signs of military vessels in the system?"

"Nothing within range," Node said.

Spiner inserted himself back into the conversation. "Where's the gas station?"

Captain Cass started to swivel, but stopped when Node started to laugh.

"Hah hah, seriously?" he asked.

"Node, what did I tell you about being mean to my friends?" Harry stepped up to Spiner and nuzzled into his leg. "He doesn't mean it, I promise," he said to the android.

Node made a coughing noise. "If the android is unable to deduce the location from the signs, I'm happy to take over navigation."

"I can *too* deduce the location," yelled Spiner, his seemingly impenetrable demeanor cracking. "I'm not an idiot."

"Id-i-ot, noun, informal," Node intoned. "Meaning *a stupid person*. Origin, Middle English, denoting a person of low intelligence. Shall I continue?"

Redbeard made a sudden gasping sound, drawing the attention of everyone on the bridge. His lips quivered, then he exploded in a fit of hysterical laughter. "Harr harr harr! He's got the measure of ye, mate!"

Kitt stepped back onto the bridge, the door hissing shut behind her. Her ears lifted as her gaze darted back and forth between them all. "What's going on in here?"

"They're being mean to my friend," Harry said, sending his best glare toward Redbeard. "Friends aren't mean to their friends, not unless they're a bunch of mean-hearted—"

"That's *enough*!" Captain Cass's icy voice cut through the ruckus.

That caught everyone's attention. The room went dead quiet, right up until Redbeard unmistakably passed gas, creating a thunderous echo on the bridge.

As intimidated as Harry was by the Captain's icy glare, he couldn't help but giggle. Not because the big man had farted, but because of the expression on his face, halfway between stunned silence and obvious self-satisfaction.

Captain Cass doubled down on her glare, directing it at Redbeard.

Kitt sniffed the air, her open mouth curling into a sour expression. "By the gods, that smells. Permission to leave the bridge?"

Instead of glaring at Kitt, as Harry expected her to, the captain slumped in her seat and buried her face in her palms with an audible groan.

Spiner picked that moment to say, "Can I drive, Captain?"

Captain Cass pulled herself up from her chair, her shoulders sagging. She made to leave the bridge, not making eye contact with anybody, but she paused at the doors as they slid open. "Red, you have the bridge. I *don't care* who drives."

Harry debated asking if he could give it a try, but the captain stepped out of view before he could get the question out. And he wasn't about to ask Redbeard.

Another time, then.

"Right," said Redbeard, straightening in his chair. "Let's get on with it, shall we? Spiner, you can drive so long as yer up to it."

"I can handle it," replied Spiner stiffly.

Node's laughter filled the air.

"Stow it," Redbeard ordered, his eyes glinting under bushy eyebrows. "We got a serious pirate operation ta run here."

· · ·

The gas station was the most impressive thing (on a growing list) Harry had ever seen. Being a space pirate intern was turning out to be an eye-opening experience, to say the least.

It wasn't *just* the gas station that was impressive. It was the entire setting. Space. Countless stars. The giant rock —*asteroid*, he amended to himself—was jagged and full of jutted outcroppings.

The gas station itself, enclosed beneath a protective bubble, sat inside what Spiner had told him was an "impact crater." Harry had accepted the explanation without further questioning, too awed by the sights to spend time contemplating such details. The station comprised a handful of docks for small- and medium-sized vessels. The central structure was bright yellow and orange, and looked like a set of three more bubbles resting on top of the asteroid's surface. Only these bubbles weren't see-through. The paint was still vivid, but had been scratched off in some places. Harry wondered how that had happened.

Towering over the station was another rectangular sign that read, SPACEWAY FUELING CENTER. Under that sign was a second sign: DILLBILLY'S GENERAL STORE.

"What's a store?" Harry asked.

Redbeard sighed. "Do you ever stop askin' questions, donkey?" He rolled his eyes. "No, don't answer that."

Harry supposed he'd be finding out the answer soon enough. The *SS Bray* was in a holding pattern just outside the outer, see-through bubble. There weren't any other ships around, but the voice on the comms had instructed them to "sit tight" while he "dropped off the kids."

Maybe I'll get to meet the kids! Harry liked baby goats.

A hissing sound, followed by whirring thumps, caught Harry's attention. Captain Cass stepped back onto the bridge, looking more or less fully composed.

Curled up protectively at Spiner's feet, he felt a jolt of excitement. "Captain Dax, you're back!"

She quirked an eyebrow in his direction and gave a shake of her head before returning to the captain's chair.

He smiled as he watched her, and she seemed to be feeling her normal calm-and-in-control self again. If he was lucky, he reminded himself, he might get to ride her someday.

Spiner leaned down and whispered, "That isn't Dax."

Harry replied in less-than-a-whisper. "Oh, I know. Dax is a kickass character on *Deep Space Nine*."

"What's that?"

Harry rolled his eyes. "Only the best thing ever. I mean, besides space pirates."

A loud, drawling voice suddenly filled the comms. "*SS Bray?* Y'all still there?"

Captain Cass pushed a button on the arm of her chair. "Affirmative. This is the *SS Bray*."

There was a pause, then the voice came across softer, almost purring. "Ohhh, who's this then? You got a purty voice."

Captain Cass gave Redbeard a sideways look. He winked back.

She pressed the button again, her voice much more stern this time. "This is Captain Cass. Do we have permission to dock?"

"Captain Cass, is it? Alrighty, then. I'm Dillbilly. Welcome to Spaceway. Come on down, any dock y'all take a fancy to."

On the viewscreen, a circular section of the protective bubble withdrew upon itself, creating an opening large enough for a spaceship to pass through.

"Shall I take us in, Captain?" Spiner asked.

"Affirmative." The captain turned toward Redbeard. "Do

we even have enough credits to get fuel and resupply the ship?"

Redbeard grimaced. "Arrr, just enough, Cap'n."

As the ship passed through the opening in the bubble, Harry could feel his host's heart thudding inside his ribcage. *Buddy, can you believe it? We get to see a gas station!*

"Docking now," announced Spiner.

The docking area, comprising a wide-open space with a bank of several mechanical contraptions on the side, came into clear view as the ship lowered toward the ground. As the ship came to rest, a dull thud resonated through the walls and floor of the bridge, followed by a distinctive groaning sound.

"Uh oh," said Redbeard.

"Docking complete," said Spiner.

"Great landing," said Node, his red eye appearing on the screen, laid over the visual of the dock. "Not even a dent."

Eager to be useful, Harry inserted himself into the conversation with the first thing that came to mind. "It sounded like the ship farted!"

The captain rolled her eyes. "Real funny." She swiveled to face Kitt. "What the hell was that?"

"One moment." Kitt tapped the screen, paused, then tapped again. "The pumps for the environmental backups, including life support, are reporting a rupture."

Redbeard cursed. "Blimey. How hard is it to land?"

The captain ignored him. "Can you fix it?"

"I'll have to take a look," Kitt replied.

Captain Cass nodded and rose from her chair. "Okay. You'll stay here and report what you find out. The rest of you will be coming with me."

Harry scrambled to his feet as quickly as his donkey legs would allow. "Do I get to come, too? I've never seen a gas station before."

Kitt growled. "Take it, please. I can't concentrate with that thing around."

"Fine." The captain gave Harry a long look. "Stay close and don't talk unless you're spoken to."

Buddy, do you hear that? We get to go to a gas station! Harry darted around in a tight circle, his version of a happy dance. "Hee-haw, *hee-haw*! Thanks, Captain!"

As the pirates walked off the bridge, Redbeard stepped in front of Harry and leaned down until he was inches away from the donkey's nose. "Don't think yer one of us, arse. Keep yer head down an' yer mouth shut. Or else." As he stood, he drew his hand across his throat in a strange side-to-side motion. Then he turned and stomped away.

"Er … okay." Harry wasn't entirely sure what that meant, but it hadn't sounded friendly. He followed cautiously, drawing up alongside Spiner. "Hey, friend."

Spiner peered down without breaking stride. "Yes?"

"What does it mean when you draw your hand side-to-side across your throat?"

Spiner looked away. "Nothing good. It might be best to stay out of Redbeard's way … I don't think he likes you."

"Oh." Harry kept quiet as he fell back to the back of the line, his earlier excitement fading into something more somber. And then slightly irritated. Maybe even a lot irritated.

I'm angry, Buddy. Really, really angry. Why am I so angry?

In answer, Buddy's stomach grumbled and lurched violently. How long had it been since they'd last eaten?

12

They left the *SS Bray* through the starboard airlock, starboard meaning *right*, according to Node, and emerged into a long tunnel, lined on either side with windows that looked out onto the asteroid and the gas station, very close now.

Harry scampered to the nearest window and pressed his nose up against it, gawking at the brightly colored building now only about fifty yards away, by the Imperial system of measurement the Overlord had taught.

The tunnel they stood in curved around to eventually join with the gas station building itself. He brayed with excitement. They were almost there!

"What in tha blazes is all this business?" Redbeard scowled, and Harry turned to see the big pirate standing in front of a console along the tunnel wall not far from the airlock.

Bright yellow lettering across the top of the console read: *PAY FOR PUMP FIVE HERE*. There were several other lines of text he couldn't decipher beneath the glowing letters.

Harry looked back out the window to the bank of

mechanical contraptions alongside the bulk of their ship. The number 5 was burnished upon a little worn-out flag atop a pole that extended from the bank of contraptions below.

Oh, that must be pump five ... and this is where we pay. Commerce! The funny little fellow with big ears on *Deep Space Nine* loved commerce.

He joined Captain Cass, Redbeard, and Spiner at the console, where they were currently frowning, and shoved his head beneath Spiner's arm to see how it all worked.

A small square screen showed a man and woman relaxing in chairs by a lake, holding hands, each wearing an unwieldy pair of goggles. A male voice narrated:

"Tired of having to fumble with clumsy binoculars or never quite being able to find the right focus? Our patented *Zoomels* allow you to enjoy all of nature's beauty *hands-free*! And, the smart-technology lenses automatically detect your visual prescription from a targeted laser mapping of your retinas, allowing the *Zoomels* to give you the perfect focus, *every time*!"

Harry was taken by the way the narrator's voice pitched upwards at the conclusion of every sentence.

The screen changed to reflect how *Zoomels* could improve the wearer's vision, comparing a "without *Zoomels*" view to a "with *Zoomels* view." Harry noted that with the goggles, the distant pair of swans on the lake appeared much clearer and closer.

"Wow!" he breathed.

His comment seemed to shake the others from their frowning stupor. Captain Cass blinked and sighed, then hit a big green *MAKE PAYMENT* button on the bottom corner of the screen.

The swans on the lake were replaced with lines of text, but the narrator continued to espouse the virtues of the

Zoomels. "Binoculars can crack or break, but not *Zoomels*! Designed for the adventuring outdoorsman—or outdoors woman—*Zoomels* have been thoroughly tested against all manner of common wear and tear and are guaranteed to be fireproof, blast proof—"

"Mmm," Redbeard murmured, stroking his wild beard.

"...laser-proof, bullet-proof..."

"Wish this damn thing would shut up," Captain Cass grumbled, answering *NO* when the machine asked if she would like a spaceship wash with her fuel purchase.

"...shatter proof, water proof..."

An image of a triangular piece of food heaped with what looked like meat and cheese flashed up on the screen then, accompanied by bright blue flashing text: *GET A LARGE PIZZA 20% OFF WITH YOUR FUEL PURCHASE, TODAY ONLY!*

Harry's stomach rumbled. "Oh, can we get a ... a pie-zza?" he asked. "Please? I'm starving!"

"A *peets*-za," Spiner corrected.

"No," Captain Cass said, pushing the accompanying *NO* button once more. "The bridge smells bad enough, already."

Harry groaned and rested his chin on the edge of the console.

"...*Zoomels* are even guaranteed to hold up against the acidic venom of the tubernorlf worm of *Annelida*!" The narrator was *still* going on about the goggles. They sounded amazing. "More than two eyes? No problem! We have *Zoomels* to accommodate every known ocular arrangement and facial structure in the *known Universe*! And, each pair of *Zoomels* comes with a lifetime warranty ... buy yourself some *Zoomels* today, you won't regret it!"

Another picture of food appeared on the screen, this one a doughy circle drizzled in chocolate and sprinkles.

Harry's ears perked up and he straightened. "Oh! Can we get some of those?"

ONE DOZEN DONUTS TO FEED YOU AND YOUR CREW, ONLY 25 GALACTIC CREDITS WHEN YOU SPEND 2000 CREDITS OR MORE ON FUEL!

"No," Captain Cass said again, this time punching the button with force. "For the love of God, is this thing *ever* going to let us actually get fuel!?"

Redbeard muttered something under his breath.

"*Zoomels* can be yours for *only seven* easy installments of ninety-nine, ninety-nine," the exuberant voice continued relentlessly in the background. "Or find a pair at a *Spaceway* near you for the special distributor price of five hundred credits!"

"Mmm," Redbeard said again, and looked over his shoulder at the bright orange and yellow building through the windows.

PLEASE SELECT YOUR FUEL TYPE, the console prompted.

"Finally!" Captain Cass scanned the list, and Harry's eyes went crossed. There must have been at least twenty options.

Wow, piloting a spaceship is kind of complicated … how can you tell one kind of fuel from another?

Harry's stomach growled again, and he heaved a sigh, bouncing from hoof to hoof with impatience. When were they going inside, already?

"Here it is, Captain," Spiner offered, pointing a long green finger to one of the fuel types.

"Ah, thank you." She selected it.

PLEASE SELECT FUEL GRADE.

Captain Cass growled, scanning the provided list once more and finally pushing the number that read *9100*.

A musical fanfare started up in the background, replacing

the male narrator. This time, it was an enthusiastic female voice that spoke. "Are you tired of bad hair days?" she asked.

Harry reflexively looked up at Redbeard, who caught his glance and glared back, bushy brows lowering over his fierce dark eyes.

Harry looked quickly back to the screen, but noticed from the corner of his eye that Redbeard was absently smoothing his bushy hair. It did nothing to tame the wild locks.

"... how can you look your best when your hair is subjected to the elements of strange planets and recycled air?" the woman continued.

In contrast to the male announcer, this one's voice started on a higher register and dropped down as she went. If one thing was clear to Harry, it was that nothing was worse than having a *bad hair day*. Not that he'd ever given it much thought before.

"Surely there is a mute button around here somewhere..." Captain Cass ignored the next question on the screen to study the top, bottom, and sides of the console.

Spiner tried to help, but ultimately he straightened and shook his head. "It does not appear so, Captain."

Her scowl deepened as she smashed the *NO* button for the question: *DO YOU HAVE A DILLBILLY LOYALTY CARD?* Only to be confronted with another question: *DO YOU WISH TO APPLY FOR A DILLBILLY LOYALTY CARD TODAY? GET 5% OFF WITH EVERY FUEL PURCHASE!*

"...we have the solution for you!" the woman continued, her voice pitching upwards, once again filling Harry with excitement. "Our Personal Styling Bot is equipped with a database of all known habitable planet atmospheres, and can style your hair accordingly to each planet's *weather and culture!*"

The captain hung her head, putting her hands on her hips and sucking in a deep breath.

"That's right! Not only does this cute little bot excel at hair styling, but it can give you fashion advice, too! Never suffer from fashion faux pas *again*!"

"Arrr to hell with this shite, Cap'n," Redbeard growled suddenly, pulling his giant rifle off his back. "Lemme go in an' I'll get us our fuel fer free!"

"*No*," the captain said again, exhaling evenly. "No." She put a hand on the end of Redbeard's rifle and pushed the muzzle downward until it was pointing at the ground. "Let's not resort to that … *yet*." She gave the console a dirty look.

"For only three easy payments of one thousand ninety-nine credits, the Personal Styling Bot can be yours!"

The captain closed her eyes and massaged her temples.

Harry's stomach growled loudly.

"C'mon, Cap'n," Redbeard pressed. "We're runnin' low on funds, anyway. This way we can keep 'em fer somethin' more important, should the need arise."

She looked at him, eyebrow quirked. "Something more important than fuel and supplies?"

He shrugged. "You never know…"

The captain sighed. "I don't want to cause a scene unless we really have to. If we go around shooting up every place we stop at, it'll be all that much easier for the Feds to find us."

Harry perked up at the mention of shooting things.

Redbeard mumbled curses, but returned his rifle to its holster along his back. "Fine. But I don't like it."

"I am aware of that." The captain turned back to the console screen with a glare.

"Here," Spiner said, "allow me, Captain."

She made a grand, sweeping gesture. "Please, be my guest."

The android moved in front of the console and began

tapping buttons in quick succession. After a slew of additional questions, the screen *finally* displayed the words NOW FUELING.

"Bout damn time," Redbeard grumbled.

Harry left the screen to look back out the window, fascinated by the large mechanical contraption next to the ship, which was now in motion. Or at least, *pieces* of it were moving. A long, telescoping robot arm attached a tube to the side of the ship.

"Wow, that is so cool!"

His breath fogged against the glass. His stomach growled again, drawing his attention away from the fuel pump. He trotted back to the captain's side, his tail swishing side to side.

"Are you sure we can't get a peets-za, Captain? I've never had a peets-za before and I'm really, *really* hungry. Please? Pretty please?"

She rolled her eyes, then looked over to where Redbeard paced restlessly along the windows. "Fine. You can get a snack from the General Store when we get supplies. A *small* snack, mind you. Red, why don't you go ahead and go inside, start stocking up on what we need and take Harry to get a snack."

"Who?"

The captain blinked at him and jerked her head in Harry's direction.

Redbeard's expression soured. "Aw, you don't let me shoot up tha place and now yer makin' me babysit the arse?"

Captain Cass only looked at him, one eyebrow raised.

Redbeard's mighty shoulders sagged.

"And remember, no violence." She glanced over her shoulder at Spiner, who was still tapping buttons on the console. "For now."

Redbeard's eyes lit up at the prospect of potential future

violence. "Aye, arrr, Cap'n." Then he grumbled as he turned to Harry. "C'mon, you. Do as I say, got it? An' don't be talkin' while we're in there … to no one. Got it?"

Harry nodded vigorously. "Aye, aye, sir!"

It was Redbeard's turn to roll his eyes, and he stomped away down the tunnel.

Harry trotted after him gleefully. *Yay! Finally I get to see the gas station! And find out what a* store *is!* His stomach growled, the hunger almost painful now. *And get some damn food!*

He jolted to a halt, gasping. *What did I just say? I just said a swear word!*

"Hey, hey Red!" he called, running to catch up to the big pirate. "I just said a swear word!"

"I didn't hear nuffin'," Redbeard muttered. "For once you were bein' quiet, just like I like it."

"Well, I thought it," Harry amended. "I *thought* a swear word!"

"Oh for the love of—"

"Will you teach me to swear, huh? You're really good at it. Will you teach me to swear like a pirate?"

Redbeard only grumbled in reply.

Harry trailed behind a silent Redbeard as they approached the end of the tunnel. His tail swished in agitation as he repeated to himself again and again, "Peets-za, peets-za, peets-za."

Redbeard came to a halt in front of two transparent sliding doors, each flanked by a wall covered in colorful images with lots of text.

One glossy poster featured a dripping, creamy triangle topped with smooth globs of fat. "Ooo, is *that* peets-za?"

"Arrr," Redbeard said. He stared at a little poster that read,

ZOOMELS SOLD HERE. He glanced sideways at Harry and waved a hand at him. "C'mon, then."

The doors slid open as Redbeard stepped forward, a blast of warm air sweeping over them from inside.

An assortment of smells assaulted Harry's nose, ranging from acrid and chemical to fresh and savory. Standing off to the right, a tall, lean green figure was stationed behind a cramped counter. To each side of the counter, glassy displays beckoned.

The lean figure said, "Howdy there, y'all, welcome to Dillbilly's General Store. I'm Dillbilly."

Upon closer inspection, the exposed parts of Dillbilly's green skin featured splotches of every shade of green and yellow, as well as dotted, raised bumps. A round hat topped his head, made from straw. He was also sporting a yellow tunic, topped by orange overalls.

Harry was instantly taken by this fellow. *I've never seen anybody like him before,* he marveled. He trotted right up to the counter. "Hi, I'm Harold! What are you?"

Dillbilly, whose attention had been turned to the towering, glowering Redbeard, squinted down at Harry. His eyes widened with surprise, then darted back to the pirate. "Friend, am I to surmise that you have a walkin', talkin' ass?"

Redbeard, who had been sweeping his eyes back and forth across rows of merchandise, paused to regard the merchant. "Wha'? Were you talkin' 'bout me arse?"

Dillbilly gulped and looked the red giant up and down, his eyes growing larger as he took in the rifle slung across the pirate's back. "I'm not lookin' for trouble, friend. Just askin' after your donkey, is all."

Redbeard grunted, then flicked his gaze down at Harry and back. "Oh, aye. Me arse. How 'bout you two bother each other an' I'll have a look around at the booty—err, the goods."

A thrill of excitement ran down Harry's spine. His ears

perked up instantly. "Yay! I'll talk to this friendly green man and see if he has peets-za."

Redbeard was already walking off to inspect the nearest row of goods.

Harry shuffled closer to the counter, his ears growing taller and taller, eyes wider and wider, as he took in the varieties of savory-looking foods. A rush of saliva flooded his host's mouth.

Hold on there, Buddy, we'll have food for you in no time.

Dillbilly eyed Harry with a peculiar expression that Harry had never seen before. Others might have recognized the look as calculated greed, but not Harry. "Howdy there, my fine feller," Dillbilly drawled.

Harry glanced up and did his best attempt at a grin, baring his teeth.

Dillbilly's expression almost slipped, his hand retreating under the table instinctively. "Easy there, friend."

"Do you have *peets-za*?" Harry asked.

Dillbilly relaxed and slid his hand back onto the counter. "Oh, yessir-ee, I sure do, *friend*."

"Oh *yay*," Harry replied. "Say, my friends call me Harry."

"Do they, now? That's great. My friends call me Dillbilly."

Harry wandered in front of the right-most display, featuring several pale, flat slices of pizza that only vaguely resembled the pictures outside.

"Oh, yes, you got a hankerin' for the pizza," said Dillbilly, shuffling over. "How many slices do you fancy, *Harry*?"

Harry didn't have to check with Buddy to know that he was beyond ready to eat. "I'll take all of them, please."

Dillbilly's face widened into big smile. "All of them? Oh, sure. I'll throw in a free drink on the side."

"A drink would be lovely."

Dillbilly grabbed a tray and began removing slices from the display.

Harry glanced over to see what Redbeard was up to.

The ginger giant held up some sort of jar, its lid in one hand, sniffing at its contents. Inside floated several short, stout, greenish-brown cylinders vaguely resembling Dillbilly.

"What are you looking at?" Harry called out.

Redbeard puffed his lower lip out and put the lid back on. "Nuffin'. Bugger off an' eat yer pizza."

Dillbilly straightened and placed the tray on the counter, just under Harry's nose. He nodded toward Redbeard's jar. "Those beauts are a *specialty* item ... Dill's lil' dills." He raised his voice for Redbeard's benefit. "I'll give y'all a deal on those, fine sirs. Two fer one."

Redbeard straightened and gave a small nod. Then he reached over and grabbed a second jar.

"How 'bout I send over a kart for you, sir?" Dillbilly asked, his voice still raised. "Y'all look like you might be needin' a few things."

Redbeard shrugged and turned back to examining the shelves.

A little self-driving hoverkart appeared from behind the counter and slinked over to the pirate's side.

Redbeard frowned down at the kart and took a step backward. "Yer not fixin' to perv on me, arrr ya?" he asked.

"Excuse me?" Dillbilly managed a smile.

"Better na' be any cameras on tha little kart, pervin' on me bottom, else I'll rip it apart."

Harry's host was edging up to the counter, snout raised to within inches of the pizza slices on the tray.

Dillbilly instinctively pulled the tray back a few inches. "Oh, no worries, big guy. No cameras."

Harry didn't try to stop Buddy as his mouth tracked the tray closely, his head now resting on the counter.

"Ah ah ah." Dillbilly leaned in. "Y'all have to pay for it first. 'Sides, you still haven't picked out a drink."

Harry nestled into Buddy's spine and willed his head back from the counter. "Sorry, Dillbilly. I don't have any money."

Dillbilly leaned in even closer. "'Scuse me?"

Harry shifted from hoof to hoof. "Well, uh, *Redbeard* is paying. I'm awfully hungry. Can I eat now?"

Dillbilly straightened and glanced at Redbeard, who was piling item after item into the cart. The merchant reached a green hand up and scratched his head. "Oh, alright," he said. "I don't see why not. Pick out a drink and I'll show you to the hospitality area."

Harry relaxed. "Do you have water?"

"Pah, you don't want water. I got some other mighty *tasty* drinks, Harry." Dillbilly stepped back and gestured at a bank of nozzles. "I got sweet drinks that taste like cherries. Energizing fizzies that pop in your mouth. Slurzies that twist your tongue…"

"Ooo, *slurzies*? That sounds silly," Harry said, trying to imagine what it'd feel like to have a drink physically *twist* his host's tongue.

"Great choice, friend." Dillbilly grabbed a cup and pressed a button at the bank of nozzles. Then he turned back around and placed the cup, which now emitted fizzing and crackling sounds, on the tray next to the stacks of pizza. "Alright, Harry, follow me right over here."

Harry pranced around behind Dillbilly, following across the store to the far corner where there were several round tables, surrounded by small plastic chairs.

Dillbilly set the tray down on a tabletop and moved a chair out of the way. "Here you go, friend," he said, and then lowered his voice. "Say, you ever thought about being a *star*?"

Harry nosed up to the tray, his open mouth just about to grab onto a slice of pizza. He paused to process the question. "A star? Like a bright light in space?"

"No," Dillbilly said with a sly smile. "I'm talkin' about the kind of star folks from all over the galaxy get a jonesin' to visit. The kind of star that folks *pay* to see." He stretched his arms out wide. "Picture it. Your face on billboards in every system. *Harry, the talking donkey, exclusively at Dillbilly's General Store.*"

Billboards ... like the ones they'd seen on the asteroids? People coming from all over the galaxy to see *him*? No one had ever offered to make Harry a *star* before, although Redbeard had offered to space him more than once.

Still ... he was hungry.

And it was hard to think straight when his host was hungry. "I've never thought about having my picture up before," Harry said. "Mind if I eat and think it over?"

Dillbilly straightened and tugged on the shoulder straps of his overalls. "Of course, of course. Eat up, friend. I'll leave you to it. Find me at the counter when you're ready to talk about it."

Harry ignored the retreating merchant. He was too busy staring at the countless slices of pizza stacked up before his eyes.

Finally, we get to eat something! Hopefully Buddy liked pizza. He relaxed his control over his eager host and let him get to work on the pizza and the *Slurzie* beverage. The food was lukewarm at best, but no one minded. This was easily one of the best moments of their lives ... ever.

Harry didn't once pause to consider if pizza might be less than healthy for his host.

13

Buddy was slowing down on the pizza. His stomach felt like a brick and there were still two slices left.

The *Slurzie* had been entertaining, if a little disappointing. The sweet beverage fizzled and popped inside his mouth as he slurped, causing the donkey to jump back, almost tipping the drink over. But, Harry was disappointed to find there was no other effect on the tongue. That's when he noticed the display screen on the adjacent wall. "Ooo, *TV*!"

Buddy's stomach gurgled.

Harry ignored the sensation. He was too captivated by the exciting images flashing across the screen. This was just like the one at the gas terminal, only a lot bigger. With a start, he recognized a face on the screen.

"Hey, *Redbeard*! Redbeard? I didn't know *you* were a star!"

The sounds of irritated mumbling and shuffling feet were the only response.

"*Redbeard*, what does *wanted* mean?"

More shuffling.

Harry turned his head to look away from the TV.

Redbeard was peering around the edge of an aisle, eyes wide as he stared at the TV.

Behind the counter, Dillbilly stood looking at another screen, eyes even wider.

Harry returned his eyes to his own screen, satisfied he had everyone's attention. Here Dillbilly had been offering to make him a star, and it turned out his pirate companion was *already* a star. "This is so cool, guys! Oh, and what's this other word mean ... *bounty?*"

"Shite," Redbeard grunted.

A series of clattering sounds followed.

Harry turned around in time to see Redbeard wrestling with the hoverkart, trying to restrain it as its motor whirred in attempts to leave the pirate.

He frowned. "Redbeard, what are you doing?"

"Put your *hands up!*"

Dillbilly was still behind the counter, but now he held what sort of looked like Redbeard's rifle, only shorter with two barrels. He had it leveled in Redbeard's direction.

Face beet-red, Redbeard continued to grapple with the kart. He let out a mighty grunt and picked it up with two hands.

"*Wow,*" Harry breathed. His pirate companion was even stronger than he looked. No wonder he was a star.

"Put that down," Dillbilly ordered.

"Right." Redbeard took in a deep breath, then roared as he twisted, unleashing the kart and hurling it across the room at the green merchant.

With an alarmed shriek, Dillbilly ducked behind the counter.

"Redbeard, that wasn't nice," Harry shouted. "You almost hit my new friend! He was going to make me a star, just like you."

The ginger giant ignored Harry and wrapped his arms

around several jars of Dillbilly's special dills. He shot a quick glance at the counter, then sprinted toward the door.

"Redbeard?"

The pirate gave Harry a sideways look as he ran. "Arrr ya comin' or not?"

A confused Harry gaped at the retreating Redbeard, and Dillbilly stood back up from behind the counter and took aim.

"No!" Harry shouted.

Dillbilly hesitated, one eye turning to look at Harry as the other tracked the pirate.

The pause was just enough time for Redbeard to reach the double-doors. Dillbilly squeezed off a shot. A stacked display of round barrels exploded next to the sprinting pirate.

"*Dagnammit!*" Dillbilly lowered his weapon and glared at Harry. "Look what you made me do. I missed!"

Harry's hooves clacked on the floor as he shuffled forward. His heart thudded rapidly, and his stomach had escalated from gurgling to something far more immediate. His ears sagged. "You almost hurt my friend."

"Thievin' pirate scum." Dillbilly turned his attention to the wall behind his counter. "I'll show them."

Harry noticed several more small screens on the wall in front of Dillbilly. Two of them featured a running Redbeard, each from different angles. Another image showed Spiner and Captain Cass, apparently still trying to pay. The *SS Bray* took up the remaining views.

"Umm, what are you doing? I thought you were going to make me a star?"

Dillbilly continued to tap away furiously at the wall. "Oh, I sure will. *After* I take care of my pirate problem."

"But … but Redbeard's a star and you almost shot him. Are you going to shoot me, too?"

"What? No. Unless you're a thievin' pirate scum, too..." Dillbilly punched a big button on the wall. A large barrel rose up out of the ground next to the *SS Bray*.

"Oh. What are you doing now?" Harry had the creeping sensation he'd seen something like this on *Deep Space Nine*. It didn't look like a fuel pump, that much was certain.

Dillbilly reached up to scratch his head with a free arm. "Fixin' to do a little exterminatin'."

That was a bigger word than Harry knew. "That doesn't sound nice."

Dillbilly cackled. "Sure ain't. They won't know what hit 'um."

Harry felt tears welling up in his eyes, making it hard to see. *I'm not going to be a star. He's going to hurt my friends, and probably my herd, too.*

Dillbilly stared at the screens, rubbing his hands together. He paid no mind to Harry. "This is gonna be rich. Just gotta wait til they get on the ship. Hurry up, now, lil' scums."

Harry sidled up behind the green merchant, and turned his rear toward Dillbilly. "I'm sorry Redbeard forgot to pay," he mumbled.

"What's that?" Dillbilly should have looked down, but he didn't.

Harry leaned forward and shot both rear hooves backward with all the force he could muster, connecting solidly with Dillbilly's backside.

Dillbilly squawked in surprise, then grunted as the side of his head smacked into a screen. The screen cracked and the merchant crumpled to the floor, out cold.

Harry's tail swished. "*Ouch*, that had to hurt."

Up on the screens, an animated Redbeard was huddled up with Spiner and the captain.

We should probably go, Buddy, before they leave us behind.

Harry wasn't in a hurry to face Dillbilly again, whenever he woke up.

On the way out, Harry noticed a small package on the floor. The label read ZOOMELS. *Oh, Redbeard would like that.*

He reached down and grabbed the edge of the box between his teeth, then left the store at a gallop, hoping the pirates would wait for him.

They did wait. Or rather, they were still clustered around the pay terminal when Harry arrived and skidded to a stop beside them.

He dropped the Zoomels package at his feet, panting. His stomach gurgled again … and not in a pleasant way. He swallowed, trying to ignore it. "Hey!" he said. "We … we should get out of here. Like, *now*."

"Working on it," Captain Cass bit out.

She was busily scanning more words on the small, square screen, while Redbeard fidgeted behind her, arms still full of jars of Dillbilly's lil dills. He muttered swear words fit to make Harry's ears burn.

Obviously, the pirate had already filled Spiner and the captain in on what had happened inside.

Spiner stood next to the captain, face impassive, also scanning the words on the screen.

"No, really," Harry said again, "we really do need to get out of here. Dillbilly's gonna be mad when he wakes up."

At this Redbeard's fidgeting went still, and he looked to Harry in question, eyes squinting.

Harry stood a little straighter, despite it feeling like he had a ton of rocks in his stomach. "He was going to hurt you guys. So I … I, uh, I kicked him."

Redbeard's bushy eyebrows shot upward.

"He hit his head," Harry went on. "I think he's unconscious."

Captain Cass and Spiner both paused to look at him, and for a few seconds there was only the constant drone of another male narrator, this time shouting excitedly about some kind of hormone booster.

The captain's mouth curved slowly into a crooked smile. "Well done, Harold."

Harry beamed, feeling as if he might burst with pride.

The console chose that moment to beep at them, drawing their attention back to it. Harry saw the text demanding: *$2597. IS THIS AMOUNT OKAY?*

Captain Cass sighed and pushed *YES*.

Redbeard continued to stare at Harry.

Harry bared his teeth in his best attempt at a grin and kicked the box of Zoomels over to the burly pirate, where it came to rest against his massive boot. "Oh, and I got those for you."

Redbeard's expression became oddly unreadable, his eyes darting back and forth between Harry and the package.

The console beeped again. *DO YOU WISH TO PAY WITH CREDIT OR DEBIT?*

Redbeard finally blinked and shook himself. "Uhhh. Thanks," he muttered. "How 'bout you carry 'em? Me hands arrr a wee bit full." He tilted his chin toward the armful of jars.

"Sure."

Insides feeling warm and fuzzy, Harry moved to grab the box in his teeth again. He'd never heard Redbeard tell anyone "thanks" before.

Redbeard resumed his pacing and scowling. "Need to get outta here," he mumbled.

Harry tried to approximate a nod, but ended up dropping the box at his hooves instead. If he ever *did* get custom power armor, he'd make sure it had robotic arms. Not being able to talk and carry stuff at the same time was frustrating, now that he knew other pirates could do such a thing. *Another reason they're gods.*

"I don't know how long Dillbilly will stay asleep," he said. "And he seemed really mad."

"Working on it," Captain Cass growled again. She moved aside to let Spiner's deft, quick fingers work once more.

PLEASE INSERT CARD.

CARD READ ERROR.

PLEASE INSERT CARD.

PLEASE ENTER PIN NUMBER.

The Captain looked anxiously back down the tunnel, as if expecting an angry Dillbilly to round the curve any moment. "Red, you and Harry go ahead and board," she said finally. "Tell Kitt to get the *Bray* ready to fly. I want us out of here the minute we get that damned fuel hose detached."

"Aye, arrr, Cap'n. With pleasure." Redbeard glanced to Harry. "Comin'?"

"Aye, aye, sir!" Harry snatched up the Zoomels and trotted after the big man, leaving Spiner and the captain to continue fussing over the terminal.

PLEASE ENTER GALACTIC QUADRANT CODE.

WOULD YOU LIKE TO DONATE TO TOYS FOR KARBLEKS *TODAY?*

DO YOU WANT CASH BACK TODAY?

As Harry passed the windows overlooking the fueling contraption, he noticed the giant barrel-looking thingie pointed right at the *SS Bray*. It had come out of the ground when Dillbilly punched the red button.

Whatever it was, it didn't look like good news.

With a jolt of realization, Harry glanced up at Redbeard's giant rifle, then back to the huge barrel of the thing in the ground. *Overlord's mercy! That's a gun! That's a giant, huge gun!*

He let out a squawk of alarm around the corner of the box in his mouth, just as the tunnel doors cycled closed behind them.

Harry tried to get Redbeard's attention as they went through the airlock again and headed down the winding corridors in search of Kitt. But the big pirate thumped along at a near jog, and Harry had to canter to keep up. If he dropped the Zoomels now, he'd probably never find them again.

So he just bit down harder on the box and tried to talk around it. Alas, the words came out only as muffled nonsense.

Redbeard finally halted and spun around to face him.

Harry tried to stop his momentum, but his hooves couldn't find purchase on the smooth floor. He ended up smashing face-first into Redbeard's thigh, earning a mean-faced scowl.

"Git to tha bridge an' tell tha' creeper of a computer to prepare fer a quick getaway," Redbeard ordered.

"Bu-erf-fin-a-gurn!" Harry said.

Redbeard's scowl deepened. "Wha?"

Harry spit out the box, the corner now soggy with donkey drool. He said again, "A giant gun! Dillbilly has a *giant gun* pointed at the ship. He's going to blast us!"

Redbeard's lips pressed into a thin line, nearly disappearing beneath his beard. "Then we best be gone 'fore he wakes up, eh?"

Harry nodded vigorously.

"Git ta tha bridge. I'll git Kitt an' bring 'er up ... an' find somewhere ta put these damned dills!"

"Aye, aye!" Harry grabbed the box, executed a perfect pivot, and raced along the corridors toward the bridge.

. . .

Harry burst onto the empty bridge and tossed the Zoomels box onto the nearest chair. "Node!"

His voice echoed against the bulkheads of the crescent-shaped room.

"Node! Where are you?"

The red eye appeared overlaying the viewscreen and blinked lazily. "Right here, obviously. What has you all excited?"

"We need to go, quick," Harry explained. "Dillbilly's going to blast us!"

The pixelated eye narrowed. "Is he now? I don't see … oh. Oh my. That's a Turbolator 500XL cannon. Flagship grade. That could pulverize us, no problem."

"So get us out of here!"

"Now? Without the others?"

"No!" Harry blurted. He gulped. "No, don't leave without the rest of the crew. But we need to get the ship ready for take-off as soon as everyone's on board."

"Oh all right."

The red eye slid down the viewscreen to be closer to Harry's height. "Are you sure you don't want to leave without them? You could have the whole ship to your—oh, no, never-mind. I see the big hairy one and the walking cat are already on board. Oh well."

Harry directed his best mean face toward Node's eye. "That's not very nice. They aren't that bad, you know. They took me into the gas station, and let me have peets-za!"

Node effected a long-suffering sigh. "Well. You know how I feel about humans."

Harry cocked his head. "But Kitt isn't human."

"Well. You know how I feel about cats."

Harry blinked. Node had never talked about his feelings for cats. "Um, actually, I don't think I—"

The bridge door slid open at that moment.

Redbeard rushed into the room, Kitt close on his heels. Redbeard took the captain's chair, and Kitt manned—or was it *catted*—the comms.

"Computer!" Redbeard bellowed, and Harry jumped again at the volume of his voice. "Why don' I hear them engines runnin'?!"

"The core is warming up," Node replied, a hint of reproach in his voice. "Engines will be ready to fire in T-minus sixty seconds."

Harry looked around the bridge and back at the screen. "Are the others coming yet?"

Redbeard leaned heavily on his chair. "Arrr, better be. Kitt, this bucket o' shite better be ready to go."

Kitt took her place behind her console, her claws clicking as she typed in a series of commands. "I was only able to complete *some* of the repairs," she said, "but the ship should be able to get us where we're going. I would not recommend engaging in combat situations, though."

The image of the giant cannon filled Harry's head. "Does getting shot at by a giant gun count as a combat situation?"

Kitt looked up from the console. "Yes."

"Twenty seconds," Node announced.

"Arrr, c'mon, c'mon, c'mon already!" Rivulets of sweat dripped down off Redbeard's brow onto the arm of his chair.

Harry's stomach lurched, violently. "Urgh."

"Ready in five seconds."

The doors to the bridge hissed open.

Captain Cass marched in, accompanied by Harry's green android friend.

Even in Harry's moment of distress, he couldn't help but appreciate the extreme level of badass that was his captain. *Deep Space Nine* was amazing, but none of its characters walked with the swagger and stature of this Goddess.

Spiner was also cool. Moderately. Despite his learning disability.

Redbeard squirmed in his chair. "We ready, then?"

Captain Cass was silent as she took her seat. Harry was too preoccupied to notice the visibly disgruntled expression she shared with Redbeard.

In a placid tone, Node announced, "We're ready for launch."

"Captain," Spiner said with the hint of a question on his voice. "The environmental shield of the station is still activated. We won't be able to get out, unless it's disabled."

Redbeard practically shouted, spit flying out of his frothy mouth, "Arrr, blast it to bits!"

Captain Cass let out a theatrical sigh. "Do it."

Node projected a big red smiley face on the viewscreen. "That won't be necessary. Unless, of course, blowing something up would make you feel better."

"What?! Why not?" Redbeard demanded.

"Because I've already hacked the system. Embarrassingly primitive, really. I can disable it at your signal."

"Do it," Captain Cass repeated herself.

Harry was still distracted by the noises and churning in his stomach. *Surely this isn't because of the peet-za?* He decided to chalk it up to a case of nerves. The prospect of getting blown up had a certain immediacy to it.

Node said, "All done. Shall we lift off?"

"Confirmed," Spiner announced, for no discernable reason.

"Do it." Captain Cass stared ahead, her gaze unfocused.

"Arrr, but I surely woulda liked to 'ave blown a hole in somethin'," Redbeard muttered.

Harry heard, or rather felt, an enormous shudder run through the ship as it lifted off the ground.

"Tell me that wasn't another system failing," Captain Cass let the words march out in clipped starts and stops.

Redbeard hurled curse words with reckless abandon.

Kitt's console clicked and clacked as she checked. "No additional system failures detected, Captain."

"Well, that's good, right?" blurted Harry.

Node chortled. "Haven't you morons ever used a gas pump before?"

Captain Cass and Redbeard exchanged glances.

A tiny gasp escaped from Kitt's mouth, sounding suspiciously close to a meow of alarm.

The captain swiveled around in her chair and Harry tensed.

Luckily, her dark and piercing gaze was riveted on Kitt. "Well?"

"It appears we forgot to detach the fuel pump."

Captain Cass suddenly looked rather sheepish.

"What?! Haharrr, that'll show that picklish bastard! Put it on the viewscreen!"

The feed shifted, exposing the *SS Bray*'s aft section as it lifted away from the gas station.

A long tube dangled from the side of the ship, trailing dozens of meters toward the ground. Retreating from view as the ship gained elevation, a hole gaped in the ground where the pump had once been connected.

Redbeard exploded into laughter, hooting and hollering with glee.

Captain Cass shook her head. "All right ... the next time we need to refuel, we're doing it Redbeard's way."

"Incoming transmission, Captain," Kitt said above the roar of the engines and Redbeard's laughter.

"Put it on."

Dillbilly's livid face replaced the image of the dangling tube on the screen. Where his hat had apparently gone missing, a giant red lump was forming on his forehead. "Come back and get what's good for you, you thievin' pirate scum!" he shouted. "No, scratch that. I'm gonna blow y'all to bits anyway!"

Redbeard glowered at the screen. "Let's blast 'im, Cap'n."

Captain Cass craned her neck up to meet eyes with the enraged merchant. "I regret that we've landed in this situation," she said calmly. "But I'd like to point out that we did pay for the fuel. Any acts of aggression against this ship would be in violation of Federation Commerce Statutes—"

"Save it, sumbitch! Your giant ogre was caught stealing goods. Small wonder there's a bounty on his head."

The captain flicked a glance at Redbeard, frowning. "Red, how many times do I have to tell you?"

Redbeard held up his hands. "Arrr, I fully intended to pay, but this lunatic was pointin' a shotgun at me bits!"

"Liar!" Dillbilly shouted.

Harry did his best to ignore the stomach cramps as he stepped up alongside Redbeard.

"Hey friend," he said to Dillbilly, "I'm sorry about your head."

Dillbilly locked eyes with Harry and gave him a pretty impressive mean face. "*You* … to think I was gonna invest in you! You ain't nuttin' but the most rotten ass in the entire galaxy!"

Stunned by the insult, Harry's control over his host slipped for just a second. Long enough.

Redbeard's look of admiration for Harry quickly dissolved into one of horror. "What the shite, Harry?!"

A mess of hot, viscous *something* had run down his leg and trailed onto the floor behind him.

"Err, I'm sorry," Harry replied. "I can go get the cart and clean it all up, okay?"

Dillbilly's cough interrupted their exchange. "Ahem. As I

was sayin' to ya'll pirate scum, prepare to die. Have a nice afterlife."

The screen blinked out as he ended the transmission.

"Captain," Spiner said, "a Turbolaser 500XL cannon has locked onto our signal. Shall we fire now?"

The captain replied coolly, "Do it."

Kitt hurriedly interjected, "I don't think this ship's lasers are going to do much damage against that cannon."

Redbeard swore. "Can we outrun it?"

"Unlikely," Kitt answered. "Evasive maneuvers might make us miss the window in the dome, and send us right into the wall."

Spiner's voice rose in intensity. "Cannon is charging."

"Get us out of here *now*!" Captain Cass barked. "Full power to the engines!"

The pitch of the engines' roar increased, but it sure didn't feel like they were moving any faster.

Oh no, Buddy! Hold on! Harry squeezed his eyes shut, abandoning all control of bodily functions.

At first, nothing happened.

The bridge was silent for several long seconds.

And then ... nothing happened some more.

Captain Cass spoke into the silence. "What's going on? Why aren't we dead?"

Redbeard was ghostly white and uncharacteristically silent.

The sounds of Kitt's claws clicking on the console filled the room. "No signs of damage, Captain."

"Of course not. Morons."

Node! Harry risked cracking an eyelid open. "Node?"

Captain Cass said, "Ignoring your inappropriate form of address for a moment, why aren't we dead, computer?"

"Ooo, *computer* is it? That was a really low blow. Below the belt—oh wait—I don't have a waist!"

Redbeard was still silent.

Harry shifted forward and risked putting his head on Redbeard's thigh. "You okay, friend? You don't look so good. Aren't you supposed to be swearing now?"

Redbeard blinked and peered down at Harry. A growl rumbled in his throat. His right hand slowly inched down toward Harry's nose, and then with the lightest of pressure, he pushed with the tip of his finger. "Off," he whispered. "Off me, now."

"Oh, okay," Harry replied, eyes wide. He stepped back a couple paces. "That better? You had me worried!" That's when he realized he'd just stepped in … *Oops, I'd better get the cart.*

"I'm out of patience, *Node*," Captain Cass said. "What happened?"

To Harry's relief, they appeared to be passing through the opening in the dome now.

"Ah, that's better. That wasn't so bad, was it?"

"*Node.*"

"Oh, fine. I disabled the cannon. The controls are on the same system as everything else," Node said.

"Captain?"

That was Kitt, Harry noted as he inched toward the bridge's exit.

"Yes?" the captain replied.

"Sensors are picking up a Federation destroyer in the system. Closing fast."

14

Harry was torn. Get the composting cart and clean his mess off the deck of the bridge, or stick around to see what might happen next? Probably he should get the cart first, but he really wanted to get a view of the incoming ship.

He blurted, from the back of the bridge, "I wanna see the ship! Can you put it up on the TV?"

Kitt, closest to Harry, ignored him ... as did the rest of the crew, who had all fallen into a stony silence.

Node's disembodied voice was the first to reply. "Technically, it's a viewscreen, Harry. A display screen for a device such as a computer."

"Oh. Cool. Can you turn on the *viewscreen?*"

"Sure."

The viewscreen flickered to life, showing an open swath of blackness and stars. It blinked once and suddenly a small moving speck became a large, glimmering, chrome cube.

"Woah," said Harry, "it's *the Borg!*"

"Borg?" Spiner asked.

Redbeard grunted. "Tha's a funny name for tha Effin' Federation."

As if the Borg weren't scary enough by themselves already, Harry noticed countless cylinders poking out from the sides of the cube. "Are those cannons?"

"Captain," said Spiner, "the Federation destroyer is attempting to hail us."

"Ignore it," Captain Cass replied.

"Cap'n," Redbeard ventured, "we can't be hopin' to outrun tha' ship in open space."

The captain pursed her lips. "Not to mention they keep finding us every time we jump."

Harry felt his insides lurch again. He really *should* be getting that cart, *soon*. "Are we going to be assimilated?" Harry asked.

"Assimilated?" asked Spiner.

"Harry," Node chimed in, "you need to use smaller words around the android. As-sim-i-la-tion, noun—"

The *SS Bray* shuddered at that moment, temporarily putting a halt to the conversation.

"Arrr, the Effin' Feds fired their lasers at us!" Redbeard shouted.

Kitt said, "No damage reported."

"That's because we weren't hit, *meow*," said Node.

Kitt bared her teeth.

Captain Cass raised a hand to silence all of them. "That was a warning shot. Do we have shields on this thing?"

"Yes," Kitt replied. "Shall I raise them?"

"Yes, please."

"Raising shields now."

The captain pivoted. "Spiner, get us back into the asteroid field, toward the nebula."

"Yes, Captain. Setting course for the heart of the nebula."

Redbeard swiveled around to face the captain and Spiner.

"Wha 'bout tha pervy computer? Not that I'd mind, but we might fry tha bugger."

The captain shrugged. "It's the only option. Unless you're ready to turn yourself in?"

Redbeard sneered. "Fine. Best be makin' it quick, then."

Despite the shields, the ship shuddered again.

"I don't think the shields will hold long," said Kitt. "This bucket of bolts wasn't made for combat."

Lights flashed on the bridge, bathing its occupants in yellow light. Node announced, in a grave tone of voice, "The destroyer is opening its torpedo bays."

Redbeard started to swear.

"Kitt, what kind of countermeasures do we have?" the captain asked.

"Checking now … umm, not a lot."

"I suggest you let me drive," Node said.

"Do it," the captain ordered. "How far can you get us before you're affected by the nebula?"

"Oh, don't worry, Node will be fine," Harry offered.

Redbeard turned on Harry. "Weren't you payin' attention, donkey? Tha radiations from the nebularrr be interferin' with tha creeper."

Having friends gave Harry access to special information, and he was determined to show Redbeard just how special he was. "That's not true. Node was just kidding around."

Redbeard squinted at Harry, his heavy brow drawing down over his eyes. His words sounded chewed up when he spoke again. "What did you say?"

A quiet cough emitted from the bridge speakers.

That's when Harry realized that perhaps Node didn't want him sharing that information with the other pirates. His ears stood tall as he looked around the room, suddenly feeling very awkward, waiting for someone to say something. Every set of eyes was on him.

Except for Kitt's. "Multiple torpedo launches detected," she announced. "At current velocity, they'll close on our position in two minutes."

The captain's voice sliced through the bridge with a crackle, almost like a monofilament whip. "*Computer,* get us the hell out of here!"

"Ooo," Node replied, "you sound upset. It's not like Harry was saying … I was just takin' a little br—"

"*Node!*"

"Oh fine. Taking evasive maneuvers now. You all *might* want to hold on to something."

Puddles of various liquids littered the floor of the bridge. Harry was splayed across the ground in a heap next to Spiner's console. Stomach in a knot, he was pretty sure there was nothing left to hold in. Node's evasive maneuvers had left him slipping and sliding all over the place.

The command chairs in the middle of the room were definitely the place to be in the middle of combat, it turned out. As the gravitational forces on the ship had quickly ramped up, the chairs had automatically deployed restraining harnesses for their occupants.

Kitt had managed an impressive sideways leap away from her console, immediately before the first torpedo had impacted against a near asteroid, causing massive chunks of debris to bounce off of the *SS Bray*'s limited shielding. Somehow, she'd ended up in Redbeard's lap, his burly arms acting as her own safety harness.

For his part, Spiner had a simple lap belt, which did little to protect his body from flopping around in his seat. He'd managed to use his hands to grip onto the sides of his console, creating impressive dents where his fingers had clamped on.

Apparently, Harry noted, androids were pretty strong. Maybe that made up for his other deficiencies.

For several more minutes, the *SS Bray* darted in and around large asteroids at a breakneck pace. Finally, the ship began to slow, and down began to feel like down again.

On the viewscreen, the asteroid field thinned out. Black space slowly took on a pinkish hue. They were re-entering the nebula.

After a prolonged pause, Captain Cass said, "Is everyone okay?"

Buddy? You okay? Hang in there. He burrowed deep into a nerve bundle in the spine and began to assess his host's condition.

Redbeard groaned, a noticeable sickly pallor beneath his ghostly white skin, and began to urgently tap on Kitt's back. "Up, up, *up.*"

Kitt leapt off his lap just in time to narrowly dodge a stream of projectile vomit.

Captain Cass released her safety harness and lifted out of her chair, the joints of her mechanical armor whirring. "Computer?" she asked.

Node sighed. "Yes?"

"As your captain, I'd like to make a couple things clear to you."

"Oh boy, here we go. Thanks a *lot*, Harry."

"Huh?" Harry's awareness was slowly returning to the exterior world. Buddy was going to be okay. A long, cool shower down in the cargo hold was sounding like a great option. Hopefully, the other animals were holding up okay. Harry shuddered … it was going to be messy down there.

"One," continued Captain Cass, "don't *ever* mislead your crew again about your condition."

"Okay…"

Redbeard looked on the verge of contributing to the

conversation, but then paused with a look of alarm before unleashing another stream of bile over the arm of his chair.

"And *two*, I don't know how you did it, but impressive work keeping us alive. I've never seen a ship's computer navigate with those kind of instincts before."

"Oh." Node sounded surprised. "Well … thanks."

A strangled mewling noise escaped from Kitt, whose white fur coat had a decidedly bedraggled look to it.

Spiner released his grip on his console and reached down to hook an arm beneath Harry's chest, helping to pull him to his feet.

"Are you okay?" he asked.

Harry tested his balance and strength. Buddy's muscles felt like jello. *Steady there, Buddy.* It took a moment, but a delicate equilibrium settled over the donkey.

He finally replied, "I think so. You're a good friend, Spiner."

Spiner stared down at him with those impassive black orbs. "Thank you."

"Ahem," Node coughed. "What about *me*, Harry? I thought we were good friends, too, before you *betrayed* me in front of our companions."

Harry's tail swished as a rush of irritation washed over him. "You asked me to lie to our other friends, Node."

Captain Cass shook her head. "We're alive. And that's the second rule of being a pirate: Stay alive."

"What's the first rule?" Harry asked. He really *should* be taking notes on this. There might be a quiz after his internship ended.

Redbeard had recovered enough to interject. "Arrr, always be listenin' to yer Cap'n."

Captain Cass nodded. "That's right. Follow orders." She paused to take in the disastrous state of the flooring. "And right now, Harold, I need you to get the floor of this bridge *spotless.*"

Harry glanced down at the embarrassing puddles of icki-ness everywhere. At least he wasn't the only one who'd made a mess now.

When Harry returned to the bridge with the composting cart re-attached to his harness, he found the crew had once more returned to their normal stations.

As expected, the holding pens had looked rather disas-trous as well, but that was going to have to wait until he was done cleaning the bridge. On the plus side, the animals appeared to be uninjured.

An unfamiliar voice was speaking to the pirates over the comms. "This is Haven Technical Support, thanks for hold-ing. Please state your name, ship identifier, and purpose."

Redbeard grumbled, "Bout time."

Captain Cass waved him off. "This is Captain Cass, currently operating a cargo hauler with the identifier *SS Bray.* We are being pursued by a Federation ship. Somehow, they've been able to follow us through several jumps. Requesting technical assistance."

"Acknowledged," the voice replied over the comms. "Do you have a safe rendezvous point established?"

"Safe?" asked Redbeard. "Did he not hear the part about tha Effin' Feds?

Captain Cass ignored him. "We are currently inside a nebula. Their sensors won't be able to detect us, as long as we sit tight. Our computer can transmit a set of coordinates where you can find us."

Instead of cleaning the floor, Harry stood at the back of the bridge, eagerly listening in.

The voice returned after a pause. "Sorry, had to run that

one by my supervisor. Go ahead and send the coordinates over. We have a ship out on a call a couple lightyears away. I'll send them over. Shouldn't be long."

"Thank you," the captain replied.

"Sure. Will that be everything?"

"Yes."

"Great," said the voice in a tone that suggested relief that the call was almost over. "I hope you're satisfied with your support experience. You'll receive a survey after assistance is rendered. Please consider rating me a five, I'd appreciate it."

Captain Cass looked at Redbeard and rolled her eyes. "Sure," she said. "Captain Cass, out."

"What do we do now?" Harry asked.

The captain swiveled around and hefted an eyebrow. "We wait and maybe get a little shut eye. And you ... you need to get going on this mess, *intern*."

Harry straightened. "Oh! Yeah, of course. Right away, *Captain!*"

Okay, Buddy, time to get back to pirate business.

While Harry went to work cleaning up the floors, an exhausted looking pirate crew abandoned the bridge.

15

Admiral Hawke stood on the bridge of the destroyer, legs splayed wide, hands clasped behind his back, frowning at the viewscreen spread before him.

He watched as the zoomed image of the bulky cargo hauler, the *SS Bray,* darted around and through the asteroids as nimbly as a one-man fighter.

What the blazes?! That bulk shouldn't be able to move like that ... and is that a tube *hanging off the side of the ship?*

"Sir," Commander Corvus spoke up from her place at his elbow, her voice strung tight as a violin, "they'll be entering the nebula in seconds, and our sensors can't penetrate that kind of radiation. We need to fire ... *now*. We need to disable them before they can reach it!"

Admiral Hawke shook his head. "Weren't you aiming to *disable* them with your last torpedo volley? The volley I did *not* approve?" He turned to face her with one lifted eyebrow, and she straightened beneath his disapproving gaze, pursing her lips.

"Sir, they're pirates. The laws of the Federation clearly state—"

"That all criminals shall first be given the chance to peaceably surrender," Admiral Hawke broke in.

"They did not answer our hails, sir," the commander stated again, firmly. "Nor did they respond to our warning shots. The next step, as mandated by Federation law, is to disable and board the ship."

"But, I do not think that is what your last torpedo volley would have done, Commander," Hawke stated coolly. "Based on its trajectory."

Anasua's thin brows twitched. "A slight miscalculation. Not that it mattered, given that their ship is far more mobile than we anticipated."

A slight miscalculation, my behind, Hawke thought, turning back to the viewscreen. The *Bray* was closing fast on the pink edges of the nebula. He sighed heavily. Commander Corvus didn't understand the delicacy of this situation with Bambi.

"Sir," she pressed. "If we're going to catch them, now is the time to fire—"

"No," he said again. "They're going into the cloud. And they can't safely jump from within that soup. If they come out the other side, we'll see them. They're trapped either way. We wait."

The commander could not restrain her huff of disappointment, but Hawke ignored her. She couldn't be expected to understand. That's why *he* was the Rear Admiral.

He turned to the comms officer to his right. "Tightbeam a message to the *Bray*, would you, please?"

"Of course, sir," the young man answered, flipping a few switches. He couldn't have been more than twenty years old, clean-shaven with close-cropped brown hair. His Federation uniform was perfectly pressed and looked sharp on his trim frame, his boots highly polished. The epitome of an ideal Federation officer.

And Hawke couldn't remember his name. *I'm really going to have to study the crew roster again. I can't be forgetting people's names!* "Thank you," he said, purposefully leaving out the man's name and rank.

"Ready to broadcast, sir," the young nameless man said. "Go ahead with your message."

Hawke faced the viewscreen again and cleared his throat. "This is Rear Admiral Eilhard Hawke to the *SS Bray*," he said. "Bambi, is that you? I told you, I just want to talk. I promise. Pinky swear. Please don't run."

He waited a long moment, and on the screen the *Bray* disappeared behind a veil of swirling pinks and blues. He glanced to the comms officer, who shook his head.

"No reply, sir."

Hawke's shoulders dropped. He let out a long breath. "Very well, then. So this is how it must be. Comms, open a channel to our informant and route it to my ready room."

"Aye, aye, sir." The young man flipped more switches.

Hawke turned to Commander Corvus, who was a study in impassivity. "Hold our position here for now, and keep an eye on the sensors. I want to know the second they come out of that cloud."

"Aye, aye, sir."

Satisfied as much as he could be given the situation, Hawke left the bridge for his ready room. He made sure the door was closed behind him before settling down into the plush chair at the desk.

He swiveled around to face the wall, where a picture-perfect large screen had been seamlessly inlaid, flush with the surface of the wall. He rather liked traveling on these destroyers; they had all the modern amenities.

"Secure channel with our informant has been established," the young officer's voice announced over the room's internal speakers. "Shall I put him through, sir?"

"Yes," Hawke replied, crossing his ankle over his knee and steepling his fingers. "Yes, put him through."

"Aye, aye, sir." Then, the officer clicked off the line, and the viewscreen on the wall shimmered to life.

The visage of another young man filled the screen, his dark eyes bright and gleaming, a cocky half-smile splitting his face. Stubble darkened his jaw—*rather sloppy*, Hawke thought—and a sweep of dark brown hair fell across his forehead. Still, his leather flight jacket was pretty cool. Hawke made a mental note to try and find one of those for himself—for his off-hours, of course.

"Admiral," the man said, giving a slight nod of indifference in Hawke's direction. "Whatcha got for me today?"

Hawke's mouth pulled into an irritated half-smile of his own at the man's poor grammar and casual manner of speech. But what more could you expect from a pirate?

"Djerke," he said. "So glad to see you again." That was a lie, but desperate times called for desperate measures. "I have another job for you…"

The bridge floor was spic and span, and smelled a whole lot better, too. The pirate crew—even Harry—had gotten some much-needed rest, and Harry had gotten his shower.

Refreshed, clean, and out of danger for the time being, Harry felt relaxed. The rest of the crew looked back to normal as well.

The captain had called a meeting in the commons, and the whole crew was squeezed in around the only table.

Harry picked a spot opposite Kitt, between Spiner and Redbeard, and rested his chin on the table to watch the others eat protein cubes.

Despite having emptied his bowels of anything he'd eaten during their evasive maneuvers, Harry's host was very much lacking an appetite at the moment. In fact, his stomach was still churning away.

Ugh. I don't think I should eat peets-za ever again. Or maybe it was the Slurzie.

At the head of the table, the captain cleared her throat, bringing everyone's attention to her. "All right, crew," she announced. "It's time to have a discussion about how in the hell the Feds are tracking us so easily."

Silence followed her words, with the rest of the crew eyeing each other uneasily.

Redbeard broke the quiet. "It ain't us, Cap'n. You know tha'."

She gave a deep nod. "I do. I trust you all with my life."

Harry stood tall at that declaration. *I'm part of the crew. The captain trusts me!*

But then her dark gaze fell directly upon him, and he quailed beneath the intensity of it, shrinking back from the side of the table.

"Except for you, Harold," she said pensively. "I'm still making up my mind about you."

His ears drooped and he gulped. *Okay, well ... it could be worse. At least she's undecided. She's still giving me a chance, right?*

"Arrr, tha's right!" Redbeard spat, twisting his huge frame to glare down at Harry. "Those Effin' Feds weren't on us like flies on shite till *after* tha blasted intern came aboard!"

Harry's mouth worked. "Me!? No way! Space pirates are *awesome*. You guys are awesome. I didn't even *know* about the Feds till you guys started talking about them!"

"Red," the captain said, rubbing at her temples. "*We* boarded this ship, remember? Harry was already aboard when we commandeered it. And anyway, he helped us escape Dillbilly's station. He's not a spy."

Redbeard fell quiet, a frown creasing his brow. "Hrmm."

"Maybe it's the ship itself," Spiner offered. "Perhaps the former crew had some sort of tracker installed, to constantly register its location with the Feds every time it exits a jump."

"Why would they do that?" Kitt asked. "Who the hell *wants* the Feds on their ass all the time?"

"Law-abiding citizens," Spiner answered simply. "Who fear being ambushed by pirates. It would be an effective way to ensure their stolen property is recovered quickly and returned to them, with the offenders just as quickly apprehended."

Harry considered cheering on his impaired android friend, who was sounding unusually smart. Maybe he wasn't dumb, as Node had suggested.

Captain Cass dropped her hands to the table, drumming her fingertips against it. "That's possible…"

A red smiley face appeared on the table, rotating around so that it faced each crew member in turn. "Negative. I would have alerted you to such a thing when you became my crew, if such a thing existed."

The captain crossed her arms. "Not sure I believe you, *computer*."

Node's smiley face drooped, rendering an animated tear sliding down his cheek. "Okay, well, I would have told you about it *now*, at least. Now that I know the rules of being a pirate. I mean, you can't blame me for not knowing the pirate rules. I've never been a pirate before."

The sad face phased into a cartoonish man, sporting an eyepatch, shrugging his shoulders and holding up his hands in a helpless gesture.

Node had a good point there. And Harry's other friend, Spiner, was making some great points, too. Maybe the two of them would learn how to get along.

Captain Cass heaved a long sigh. "Fine, whatever. You're saying that there's no such thing installed on this ship?"

"Correct." The cartoon pirate morphed back into a smiley face.

"Arrr, then how?" Redbeard demanded. "How are they followin' us so close-like?"

"I don't know," the captain admitted. "But we need to find out. Hopefully the support from Haven will put us in the clear, but just in case..." Her eyes went to everyone around the table, even Harry.

He gulped again when her eyes met his, heart jumping. She was just *so* badass.

"Just in case," she reiterated, "we all need to keep our eyes and ears open for anything unusual aboard this ship. Spiner and Kitt, I want you two going through every system on this hunk of junk. Make sure there's not a virus in the computer or something, or an external transponder somewhere."

"Aye, aye, Captain," the two answered in unison.

A virus? Harry thought, eyes widening. *Oh no! That sounds bad. I hope Node's not sick!*

"Captain," Node spoke up politely, "I assure you, if this ship had a virus, I would be the first to know about it."

The captain's hard gaze focused intently on the red smiley face in the middle of the table. "Unless the virus has already compromised you."

The smiley face turned into a face with a straight mouth and closed eyes. "Ah." There was a long silence, and then the reluctant admission, "That is a surprisingly logical point."

"Red," the captain said, ignoring the potential jab and turning her attention back to her second-in-command. "You're with me. We're going to make a battle plan for how to deal with those Effin' Feds next time we seem 'em."

"Aye, arrrr, Cap'n!" Redbeard roared, thumping a fist on the tabletop. "Tha's wha' I like to hear!"

"What about me?" Harry blurted, caught up in Redbeard's excitement. "What can I do, Captain? Huh, *huh*? What can I do?"

Her level gaze pinned him in place. "I need you to get down to the cargo hold and keep it clean, Harold. Keep the rest of those animals safe. After all, they *are* our payday ... if we can disentangle ourselves from our Federation shadow."

Harry straightened and stamped a hoof in lieu of a salute. "Aye, aye, Captain! Can do!"

A spy ... could there really be a spy on board?

Harry pondered the question as he went about his cleaning duties in the hold. Suddenly, every chicken, every cow seemed suspicious. He eyed them as he pulled the compost cart along the floor of their pens, searching for any abnormal behaviors.

That chicken ... did it stare at him a little too long?

That cow ... he hadn't seen it chewing its cud lately ... right?

It was so hard to tell! And then there was his own herd. He knew them all by sight and smell, and none of them were spies, he was sure of that.

Well ... none of them *had been* spies when they'd been abducted, anyway. But, Harry had spent quite a lot of time lately outside of the hold. It was possible a shifter or a clone or something else just as nebulous could have replaced one of his herd while he was gone. After all, the security chief on *DS9* could turn into a *puddle*!

And if a character on *DS9* could do it, surely a creature in Harry's galaxy could do it, too. Captain Cass looked like Dax, and the Federation ships looked like the Borg ... it was almost as if Harry's world was a parallel universe to the one in *Deep Space 9*!

The thought stopped Harry in his tracks, and a shiver ran through Buddy's skin.

Whoa. Maybe it really is *a parallel universe, and not fiction at all!*

But, it was time to shake himself from such deep thoughts. He could ponder the truths of his universe and *DS9* later. Right now, he had a spy to find.

And any one of these pee puddles on the floor right now could be that spy. Harry stopped at the nearest one, staring down at his reflection in the glossy surface.

How could he tell if this puddle was a spy?

He wasn't entirely sure. And if it did turn out to be a spy, what then? He had no weapons, no real fighting skills.

He'd gotten lucky during that incident with Dillbilly, when he was able to catch the merchant off guard. Harry wasn't sure how he'd fair against a real spy.

Sure, he had Buddy's sharp little hooves, a decently powerful hind-kick, and a bite that could sever fingers, but what was all that against a trained operative with a secret agenda?

Harry's ears flattened. *I really gotta get the captain to give me a weapon.* Swallowing hard, he lifted one front hoof and cautiously began to lower it toward the puddle. Maybe if he just poked it … maybe if it was a changeling spy, they would reveal themselves.

A part of him thrilled at the possibility that he could be the one to discover who or what was reporting their position to the Feds. How proud Captain Cass would be of him! And Redbeard and Kitt … surely they'd both be impressed!

The other part of him was terrified at the thought of discovering such a thing. If only he had some kind of real weapon, he'd feel so much more confident in his ability to apprehend a spy.

He paused, hoof in mid-air, and hesitated. Buddy's heart

was pounding, no doubt picking up on Harry's own appre-
hension.

"What," Node's dry tone suddenly rang out across the
hold, "in the name of all my blessed circuits are you doing?"

Harry startled at the voice and backpedaled quickly away
from the puddle. "I'm … I'm checking for spies."

"In … a puddle of urine?" Node appeared as a giant red
question mark on the nearest wall. "You really think those
puddles could be any kind of threat, other than to your sense
of smell? Or, I suppose, as a slip hazard…"

Harry looked up to the question mark. "Well, maybe. I
mean, Odo in *DS9* could change into a puddle, remember?"

The question mark resolved into the familiar eye. "Ah, I
see. Ha! *Ha ha ha*. I'm afraid that TV show might have gotten
into your head a bit too much, Harold."

Harry cocked his head to one side, ears perked. "What
does that mean?"

Node sighed. "It means there are no spies in the pee
puddles. That's what it means."

Harry squinted at Node's eye. "But how can you be sure?
If it happened on *DS9*, it could happen here, too!"

The red eye rolled around. "No way. I'm telling you.
Look, would it make you feel better if I did a scan of the ship
for any unfamiliar or unregistered life forms?"

Harry's eyes widened. "You can do that?"

"Of course."

"Why didn't you say so before!?"

The eye fixed back on Harry. "Because I didn't think
you'd resort to stepping in pee puddles."

"Yes!" Harry nodded vigorously. "Yes, scan the ship!"

He backed further away from the puddle he'd been inves-
tigating, just in case it *was* a spy. He could just imagine the
angry reaction, if its secret was discovered.

"Okay. Stand by…" The eye morphed into a red hourglass, slowly spinning end to end.

Harry tensed and held his breath, waiting for the results.

A minute ticked by.

Buddy's lungs burned, and Harry released his breath, gasping. Good grief, how long would this scan take? The hourglass was still spinning, going round and round.

Harry waited another minute, his tail swishing impatiently. He sighed. "Uh, Node?"

No reply.

Harry waited some more. He pawed at the floor. "Nooooode?"

Only the silent hourglass answered him.

He glanced around the hold at the other animals, all munching at their hay or dozing quietly. What could possibly be taking so long? A little knot of anxiety settled in Harry's gut.

Had Node found the spy, and the spy somehow disabled Node in return?

"Node?" he asked again, more urgently this time. "Node!"

The hourglass disappeared, replaced by a narrowed eye. "For the love of the Overseers, what?! I told you I was doing a scan! Couldn't you see I was working?"

Harry breathed a sigh of relief, head and ears drooping. "Oh, whew! Node, I thought something bad had happened to you!"

"Bad? Like what? I told you I was going to scan the ship!"

"Well … I didn't think it would take so long," Harry admitted.

"I wanted to be thorough," Node said. "And that was only two minutes and twenty-eight-point-five-seven seconds, by the way. But I have completed the scan. Would you like to hear the results?"

Harry braced himself. "Yes."

"The results of the scan have determined there are no unfamiliar or unregistered life forms aboard this ship," Node reported with satisfaction. "Just like I told you."

Harry blinked. He glanced back down to the puddle of pee. "You're *sure?*"

The eye moved up and down. "Absolutely sure. My scans have never been wrong."

"And you even searched the puddles?"

Node sighed. "Yes, Harry. Even the puddles. And the manure. Everything. All over the ship. No one's aboard who shouldn't be aboard. If the Feds have been tracking us, it isn't due to any undetected agents aboard this ship."

Harry thought it over for a second, experiencing simultaneous relief and disappointment. His heroics would have to wait for another day. Preferably a day on which he had a proper weapon. "Well, all right. Thanks for checking, Node."

"My pleasure. Now, you should probably get back to cleaning up the messes instead of trying to step in them."

Harry looked about the hold again, realizing he'd fallen behind once more during his study of the suspicious puddle. "Oh. Right. Yeah. Sure."

"Excellent." Node's eye winked off.

Harry sighed and resumed his cleaning duties, pulling the cart over the puddle in question. It mopped right up without protest.

It was some hours later when Harry was jolted from his deep thoughts regarding the parallels between his world and *DS9* by the captain's announcement on the ship's intercom: "Attention, all crew. Our technical assistance has arrived. Rendezvous at the bridge to receive instructions."

"Ooo, technical assistance!" Harry wasn't entirely sure what that meant, but he understood it would somehow get the Feds to stop following them around, and that would be ideal.

He trotted quickly over to the wall in the hold that housed the cargo showers and requested that Node unhook his cart. He'd learned better by now than to drag the smelly thing all over the ship.

Node helpfully obliged by engaging the robotic cargo loading arms, deftly unbuckling the harness and freeing Harry to go galloping along the halls unencumbered.

He arrived triumphantly on the bridge at the same time as Kitt. Redbeard, Spiner, and the captain were already there, waiting at their usual stations.

Harry stood at attention at the back of the bridge, and waited for orders from his captain.

Captain Cass was staring at the viewscreen, which currently featured the beautiful swirl of colors that was the nebula.

"Technical assistance," she said, "we've received your hail, but do not have visual. I repeat, we do not have visual on your location."

The comms crackled with a bit of static, and then an unfamiliar voice came through. "Copy that, Captain. My apologies, I forgot to uncloak. Standby."

A second later, a part of the nebula in front of them shimmered, and a ship the likes of which Harry had never seen— not even on *DS9*—appeared out of nowhere. He gasped.

Captain Cass raised her eyebrows. But, if she was also caught off-guard, she didn't let it show in her tone. "Visual confirmed. Thanks for your assist."

"No problemo," came the casual response. "That's my job. I'll need to dock with the *Bray* and get our team aboard to switch out your transponder. Permission to board, Captain?"

"Permission granted."

"Aye, aye, Captain," the voice responded. "Starting docking procedures now. Stand by."

"Standing by."

The strange ship drifted slowly to Harry's right, and he watched open-mouthed.

It was the strangest spaceship he'd ever seen … not that he'd seen many spaceships in his life. But this one looked as if it had been constructed of pieces of other ships, all cobbled together to make one nonsensical whole.

On top of that, instead of a dull gray hull like most spaceships had, it was painted a dizzying design in bright colors. Antennas and radar dishes covered its uneven and patchwork surface. In short, it looked like a hippie shack, if hippie shacks could fly in space.

Captain Cass swiveled in her chair to face her crew, breaking the spell of the strange ship.

Harry's gaze snapped back to her.

"All right, crew," she said. "Let's hope they're able to clean this ship of any bugs, and get the Feds off our ass."

"Aye, arrr!" Redbeard agreed, thumping his fist on the arm of his chair.

"I want all of you to be at the tech team's beck and call," she continued. "Do whatever you need to do to assist them in getting the *Bray*'s transponder refit. I want us fixed up and on the move again as fast as possible. Understood?"

A chorus of enthusiastic affirmatives answered her.

"Good." She swiveled back to face the viewscreen again, where the brightly painted ship had once more disappeared from view, but this time not because of a cloaking device.

There was a brief thump from somewhere aft and starboard—to the rear and right, Harry reminded himself—then the male voice came through the comms again. "We are secure, Captain. Boarding crew is prepped and ready when you are."

"Confirmed," Captain Cass answered, pushing herself up from her chair. Her legs whirred as she did so. "We are en route to meet you."

Harry followed the pirates down to the starboard airlock, where they paused in front of the cycling doors.

This is going to be so cool. I get to meet more badass pirates! Harry attempted to compose himself, putting on his best mean face, as befitted a proper pirate intern.

Kitt stared down at him. "What are you doing?"

Harry attempted to return her stare, keeping the mean face firmly in place. "I'm getting my pirate face on, of course. How do I look?"

Kitt's tail arced and flicked slowly behind her. "Never mind."

Redbeard unslung his rifle from his back and stepped up to the door controls.

Captain Cass crossed her arms, eyeing her second-in-command. "Red, what are you doing?"

"Takin' precautions, Cap'n," he replied. "Shall I let them in?"

"Fine. But try to be nice for a change."

Redbeard's eyes glinted as he reached out to punch a button. "I don't know tha' meanin' of such words, Cap'n."

The doors hissed as they cycled open, and Spiner took a step forward with his scanner out, blocking Harry's view. "Reading one life form. No weapons," he said.

Harry's mean face nearly slipped as he tried to position himself around Spiner's legs.

Redbeard's hulking figure obscured the remainder of Harry's view. The man's shoulders sagged in disappointment as he slung the rifle over his back again.

"Let me see, let me see," Harry whined.

"Pirate intern Harold." A cold thrill ran down Harry's spine

as Captain Cass invoked his name in a blistering tone. "Absolutely no whining while on pirate business."

Harry stiffened with embarrassment and clamped his mouth shut. Hopefully, the approaching pirate hadn't caught any of that...

"Step out of the way, big fella," came a nasally voice.

Redbeard's chin dropped down as he stepped to the side of the door.

"Welcome to the *SS Bray*," said Captain Cass.

A rotund, squat, furry fellow with short legs, shorter arms, and dexterous fingers stepped past the doors into the cargo hold. His snout dominated his round, brown face and black beady eyes. Disproportionately small compared to the body, the fellow's head appeared to be mounted directly to the torso. His flight suit was covered with holsters and straps, each with several mechanical-looking attachments.

The poor guy has no neck, Harry thought to himself. While the new pirate arrival didn't appear to be much of a badass, Harry supposed it must take a lot of fortitude to go through life without being able to turn your head.

But then, defying expectations, the new pirate's head swiveled to take in the crew of the *SS Bray*. He peered at Harry over oval spectacles.

Glasses, that's what Sisko called them on DS9, Harry thought.

The squat pirate addressed Harry directly, ignoring the other pirates. "Hi, I'm Norman Bieber."

Mean pirate face completely forgotten, Harry was excited to introduce himself to a new potential friend. "Beaver?" he asked.

"No, Bie*ber*. Bee-brrrrr."

"Oh. Are you cold?"

Norman studied Harry for a long moment, chewing on his lower lip with oversized top teeth. "I'm never cold."

Captain Cass coughed, interrupting the exchange before Harry could supply the visitor with his own name.

Norman shifted and peered at the captain. "You must be the captain. Impressive power armor."

Captain Cass ignored the compliment. "You must be the mechanic. Where's the rest of the boarding party?"

Norman's black nose twitched and twisted at the end of his snout, as if he were smelling the crew. More likely he was picking up the various scents coming from the livestock. Or Redbeard.

"I *am* the boarding party," he replied. "In fact, I'm the crew, too. My department doesn't waste its resources on people. More money for all the toys … err, I mean, tools."

"Fascinating," Spiner said. "How do you pilot your ship all by yourself?"

"Automation," Norman replied quickly. "Crew are really an unnecessary luxury. These days, ships can practically fly themselves with the right person at the helm."

Node's disembodied voice came out of nowhere. "Amen to that. Well, the first part. Crew are exceedingly unnecessary. In fact, they tend to make everything more difficult."

"Computer," said Captain Cass. "Stow it."

"It's going to take you a while to forgive me, isn't it?" Node asked.

"Yes."

"Fine. I'll find something better to do."

"Do that."

"Oh, I will, *Captain*. Goodbye."

Harry felt bad for his friend. But Node had been less than honest with the pirate crew. And, as Harry had seen happen within his own tribe, being dishonest was a good way to lose friends.

Redbeard stared down at Norman with a funny look on his face.

Norman seemed to have a sixth sense. Or maybe it was just his nose. He glanced up at the ginger giant. "You smell worse than my brother, big fella. And you're uglier, too."

A frown twisted Redbeard's face.

Uh oh, Harry thought.

Unexpectedly, the burly redhead burst into laughter. "Arrr, harr harr harr. Yer a funny little effer!"

The corners of Norman's mouth didn't budge, but with his two overhanging front teeth, he always appeared to be smiling. "Now, then," Norman said, turning back to face the captain. "I believe you were requesting some technical assistance. Shall we get to it?"

A few hours later, Norman had finished with all of his *technical assistance*, whatever that meant. Something about sweeping the ship for bugs and changing transponder codes. Harry was really going to have to brush up on how space-ships actually worked, at some point.

But Harry didn't get another chance to interact with the rotund, furry mechanic before he departed the *Bray*. His pirate intern duties had kept him far too busy. *Hopefully*, Harry mused, *I'll get a chance to talk to him again sometime.*

Back on the bridge once more, the crew made preparations to resume their trip to Irrakis and collect their payday.

"Thanks again for the assistance," Captain Cass said into the comms.

"You bet," came the quick, nasally reply from Norman. "Sorry I didn't find any bugs. But, between the new transponder and replacement circuitry in the environmental systems, the *SS Bray* should look like an entirely different ship to any outside sensors."

"I hope so," said Captain Cass.

"At this point, if they find you, I'm confident it's not

because of anything on your ship," Norman said. "The admins will send you a follow-up survey. Be sure to rate me a five, okay?"

"Yeah, sure," the captain sighed.

"Good luck," Norman said, and the patchwork ship blinked out of view on the screen.

"Arrr," said Redbeard. "I'll miss the lil' effer." He paused as he caught Kitt's frown from her station. "Arrr, don't be gettin' all jealous on me, Kitt. Come o'er here an' sit on me lap."

Kitt's frown dissipated, and she pounced over her console, landing firmly on Redbeard's beefy thighs. She promptly began to purr as Redbeard stroked the back of her neck.

Harry felt a pang of jealousy. *I wish someone would pet me, too.* Then he reminded himself that pirates weren't supposed to whine.

Captain Cass swiveled in her chair to face Spiner. "Hopefully that takes care of our Federation problem. Find us a path out of the nebula, would you? And avoid the asteroid field."

"Yes, Captain."

Harry stared at the viewscreen as the ship navigated through the multi-colored clouds. The Borg were pretty cool to look at, but he supposed it was a good thing they wouldn't be able to follow the *Bray* anymore.

16

H arry never stopped staring at the screen, although he did take a moment to settle himself down at Spiner's feet. As the clouds of the nebula thinned, more and more stars appeared. Several of them were even blinking in and out of existence.

"Wow," he sighed, just loud enough for the android to hear. "It's like those stars are winking at us."

Spiner frowned at his console. "Uh, Captain?"

"Yes?"

"Ship sensors are picking up hundreds of small craft signatures, approaching our position from multiple vectors."

Redbeard roared and slammed a fist onto the arm of his chair, causing Kitt to promptly leap off of his lap and scramble back to her station. He shouted, "I told ya, Cap'n. We're cursed!"

The captain stared at the viewscreen, impassive under duress. Not rattled in the least. In short, *badass*. "Can we jump yet?" she asked.

Spiner shook his head. "No. We still need to clear the perimeter of the nebula."

"Computer?"

"Oh, are we on talking terms again?" Node replied.

After several hours of silence, Harry had almost forgotten about his friend. It was good to hear his voice again. *Maybe he's learned his lesson,* he told Buddy. Buddy replied with a yawn, not seeming to have an opinion one way or another.

"Stow it," the captain commanded. "Do we have a way out of this?"

Node replied, "Calculating. Please hold."

Uh oh, Harry thought. The last time he'd heard those words, it'd taken Node *minutes* to get back with an answer.

But this time, Node returned in less than a second. "Odds of escape are less than a fraction of a percent."

"*Blimey*, let's take it to 'em," Redbeard shouted. "We'll go out fighting!"

"Red," the captain said, her tone deadly calm, "unlike you, I'm not in a hurry to get us killed."

"Arrr, we're *pirates*, Cap'n. It's important to maintain a certain perrrrspective on such matters."

"Node," the captain said, ignoring Redbeard's point, "raise shields and take over navigation. Evasive maneuvers."

"It won't help," Node replied.

The captain's reply was pure steel. "Do it anyway."

"Very well. Hang on."

Harry tightened into a ball against Spiner's leg. *Oh no, not again! I just got done cleaning everything!*

The tiny dots outside resolved into metallic cubes, much smaller than the Federation destroyer they had encountered earlier. And much faster. After several moments of nauseating pursuit and near-misses from laser fire, the large Borg —er, *Federation*—destroyer resolved into view directly in front of the *SS Bray*. A blue beam lit up along the side of the cube, then quickly widened until it engulfed the entire viewscreen.

The *SS Bray* shuddered and groaned. On the plus side, the existential vice-grip of gravity eased back to normal, allowing Harry and his host a moment to recover. The giant cube gradually grew in size on the screen.

"That's not good," stated Node flatly.

Spiner said, "Captain, the Federation destroyer has locked on to us with a tractor beam. We're being pulled in."

Redbeard jumped to his feet and grabbed his rifle. His eyes were wide with panic or excitement—Harry couldn't tell which. "We'll set up a trap down below and take it to 'em when they board us. I've been itchin' to *blast* some Feds anyway!"

Captain Cass rolled her eyes and glared at him. "Sit down, Red. Let's think this through for a minute."

"The destroyer is hailing us, Captain," Spiner interjected.

The captain closed her eyes and leaned back in her chair. For a brief second she massaged the bridge of her nose with two fingers, exhaling loudly. Then she straightened her shoulders and opened her eyes. "Put it on the viewscreen."

A stern-looking woman replaced the view of the looming cube. She stood at stiff attention, and her uniform was pinned with several small objects, some gleaming and metallic, others precisely lined with blues and reds. Her lips were pursed so tightly, they appeared as if they might burst.

"Now *that* is an impressive mean face," Harry remarked, breaking the silent spell on the bridge.

The woman's eyebrows twitched at the comment, eyes narrowing. "This is Commodore Corvus with the *FFS Murphy's Law*," she barked. "Any attempts to resist us are futile. Prepare to be boarded. Be advised: anyone caught holding a weapon will be shot on sight."

Captain Cass inclined her head in a tight nod. "Understood," she replied.

Redbeard growled from his seat.

"Good. It would be a real *shame* if we had to resort to violence," Corvus said.

The captain gave Redbeard a stern sideways glance. "That won't be necessary."

Redbeard scowled at the screen.

"We'll see," the stern woman replied. "Commodore Corvus out."

The viewscreen returned to the image of distorted blue space and the gleaming metallic cube that was the Federation destroyer, the *FFS Murphy's Law*, looming ever closer. A medium-sized cube detached from its side, turned, and began to fly toward the *SS Bray*.

Harry gulped. "Are we going to be assimilated now?"

"Couldn't be any worse than current conditions," Node supplied.

The captain's mechanical legs whirred as she stood and turned around. "All right everyone, prepare yourselves."

Kitt's fur looked the opposite of smooth. "I thought you said we weren't going to fight."

"Arrr that's bollocks," Redbeard snarled. "Course we're gonna fight!"

"No, we're not," the captain said sharply.

"But Cap'n—"

He fell silent when she raised a hand, and Harry felt Buddy's hair stand on end at the ferocity of the warning look she landed on each and every one of the crew in turn. "No fighting," she said again. "Not this time. Look, I know these people, and they aren't screwing around. Just … stay quiet. Stay calm. Let me handle it."

Redbeard stared at her for a long moment, fingers clenched on the arms of his chair. Then he gave a slow, grave nod.

Satisfied, the captain turned her burning gaze to the front of her shirt, smoothing it. She cleared her throat. "So, as I said, prepare yourselves. This may be the last time we get to use the restroom for a while…"

Redbeard snorted nervously. "Hah! Well, what arrrr ye scallywags waitin' for? Ye heard the cap'n—go pee!"

Harry stood up and stretched stiff legs. "Right here?"

The captain and Redbeard ignored him. They were already halfway off the bridge.

Spiner leaned down and whispered into Harry's ear. "I don't think she means here, Harry."

"Oh." Harry glanced down and saw a puddle forming near his hind legs. "Too late, I think."

"This sucks," Harry grumbled to himself. On the one hoof, he was free of his harness and under no obligation to perform any cleaning duties during the Feds' boarding. On the other hoof, Captain Cass had ordered him to keep his mouth shut and to "act like a normal donkey." Not something that Harry was very good at. Plus, it meant he was stuck back in the donkey holding pen.

Buddy, I'll be here, but I'm going to let you take control for a while. You do a much better job of acting like a normal donkey than I ever could. Not once did it occur to Harry that Buddy *was,* in fact, an actual "normal donkey."

Captain Cass and Redbeard waited near the cargo ramp, hanging back a good three or four donkey-lengths. Redbeard kept twitching.

Harry couldn't help but think he looked a little odd without his rifle.

The captain wasn't carrying a weapon, either. Despite this, they both still looked quite badass to Harry. He was going to need a better word to describe them, though. At this point, "badass" was becoming rather overused. Meanwhile, he couldn't wait to see what the Feds looked like in person.

He didn't have to wait long. Only a moment later, the cargo ramp lowered with a groan … and then Harry was looking at the posterior of one of the jennies in the holding pen.

Buddy. Buddy! What are you doing? I'm trying to see what's going on!

Buddy brayed. "Hee-haw!"

The view didn't change. In fact, it was getting closer. As his host sniffed assertively, Harry sensed a tingling sensation building around his host's own posterior.

Buddy, stop!

Buddy did not stop.

Reluctantly, Harry dug deeper into the donkey's spine and asserted control once more over his host. *Sorry, Buddy, I warned you.*

The view now seemed a little taller. Belatedly, Harry realized that was because his host was "standing" on the jennie's hips. Ignoring the strange behavior of his host for the more important business going on with his crew, he turned his head to see what was happening with the boarding party.

Shoot! I missed their entrance! Dangit, Buddy!

The pirates and a cohort of about ten Gods—err, humans —in uniform were walking past the holding pen at that precise moment. A few of the uniformed humans at the back of the group turned their heads to stare directly at Harry, eyes wide and bulging, faces turning red.

Harry clamped his mouth shut, repeating the captain's orders to stay quiet over and over again to himself. It took all his willpower to bite back the enthusiastic greeting on the tip of his tongue.

The Feds staring at him scurried away from the holding pen to rejoin the others, where Redbeard and the woman from the viewscreen were busy trading mean faces with each other. Meanwhile, the uniformed man in the front of the group was talking to the captain.

Harry's ears perked up at the sight of him. He looked very familiar...

He said, "I could really fancy a cup of tea, my dear Bambi. I don't suppose you have anything suitable on this ship?"

Captain Cass appeared to be grinding her teeth, and her hands were balled up in fists. To Harry's ear, she sounded angry. Maybe it was just because the words were coming out flat and slow. "We do have a couple options in the commons, Rear Admiral," she said. "You're welcome to have some, of course."

The *rear admiral* clapped his hands together as he smiled. "Oh good." He turned his head to address his similarly uniformed companions. "Come, everyone, let's have some tea with the crew, shall we?"

No one answered, and the rear admiral didn't wait for a response. As the group filed past the holding pen, another of the uniformed men in the rear of the line noticed Harry and elbowed his neighbor. They snickered to each other as they walked by.

Harry had to work hard to keep his mouth shut and not smile back. *They don't seem so bad,* he thought. *Too bad we can't join them for tea, Buddy. Whatever that is!* His ears drooped as he climbed off the jennie and watched the humans leave the cargo hold.

Two hooves suddenly whooshed past his snout, tickling his whiskers.

"Whoa, there!" Harry exclaimed, jumping back. The jennie bared her teeth and trotted to the opposite end of the pen, tail swishing all the while.

Node's smiling face appeared on the nearest wall. "Well, this should be interesting."

Harry perked up. "Node!" He pranced about in a tight

circle, excited for someone to interact with again. "Those Feds sure look nice, don't you think?"

"Morons all look the same to me. Anyway, want to listen in to their conversation?"

"Ooo, you can do that?" Harry asked.

"Of course. I'm everywhere, remember?"

Harry tipped his head and shuffled a hoof. "That's *right*. Node, when you're not being mean to my friends, you are so freaking cool, do you know that?"

Node's pixelated grin widened. "Of course I am, *friend*. Glad someone in my miserable existence understands that."

17

Captain Cass once again sat at the head of the table in the commons, with her crew assembled to either side. Well, all except for Spiner, who was preparing a pot of tea at the counter per his hospitality protocols.

Also, of course, except for Harold the talking donkey, whom she had banished to the holding pens for the duration of this precarious encounter.

That, at least, was a decision she had not yet regretted … unlike the decision to allow the Feds aboard her ship without a fight, which she was now reconsidering as she stared down the length of scuffed wood to the man sitting opposite her.

A man she had hoped never to see again. It had been distressing enough to be the target of the persistent, stalker-like messages he'd been blasting haphazardly across the galaxy in hopes of tracking her down. More than two years after she'd left the military, and despite her new persona, she had yet to run far enough to escape his searching gaze.

And now … now he was *here*. Rear Admiral Eilhard

Hawke. In the flesh. Only six feet away. Far too close for comfort.

Easy, Cass. You can do this. You know the Feds. You know Hawke. Play your cards right, and you and your crew can fly away to fight another day.

She inhaled slowly and exhaled just as evenly.

Hawke was beaming at her, as if she were a long-lost favorite niece and this were a holiday dinner.

Nevermind Redbeard's hulking, skulking figure to his immediate right, who was glowering across the table at Commodore Corvus.

The commodore returned the massive pirate's glare with one of her own. She was one of the only people Cass had ever met, outside of pirate circles, anyway, who did not seem the least bit fazed by Redbeard's size, rough appearance, or unfriendly expressions.

Kitt hunched in her chair, next to Redbeard, her ears flattened and tail lashing behind her.

Packed in shoulder-to-shoulder along the walls of the common room, the rest of the uniformed troop stood at attention. Although this was ostensibly a *friendly chat*, Cass was careful to note the proximity of their hands to their weapons.

She returned her gaze to Hawke as Spiner set a tea tray in the middle of the table and began passing out a collection of ceramic tea cups, one to each seated person.

Hawke nodded in appreciation. "Bambi, my dear. This is very nice. A very nice set, indeed. Antique?"

She ground her teeth at his use of her given name. *Easy, Cass.* This not exactly being her ship, she had no idea where in the hell the cups had come from. But, she smiled politely and folded her hands primly on the table in front of her. "Yes," she lied. "Handed down to me by my grandmother. In the family for eight generations." Hawke would like that story, she knew.

Redbeard jerked in his chair and looked to her sharply, bushy brows furrowing.

Never one for subtlety, Cass noted. She didn't meet his questioning gaze, instead keeping her eyes locked on the clear blue stare of Rear Admiral Hawke.

Whose grin spread impossibly wider. "Oh, how lovely. You do me honor to treat me to tea in such a treasure."

She inclined her head, not bothering to smile. "Of course, Admiral. Of course."

An awkward silence descended as Spiner made his way around the table, each pour of tea precisely to standard. At each cup, he paused to ask if they would prefer milk and or sugar, then obliged accordingly.

Cass briefly wondered at Spiner's history, prior to joining up with pirates. He was good at this, possibly much more suited to food service than crewing a ship. Even at the prison on Aresh Five, where she'd first met him, he'd been good at it.

Teacups filled, Spiner removed the tray from the table and stood a couple paces behind Cass, armed with a teapot.

Hawke raised a pinky as he carefully hefted his cup from its saucer. He sipped, closing his eyes as if to savor the hot liquid. Whether it was all for show, or he was really enjoying it, Cass could barely say.

She clenched one hand over the other in an effort to resist the urge to toss her own scalding tea into his smug little face. Small wonder the troops had always referred to this man as *Eilhard the Blowhard*.

Following their leader's example, the other Feds at the table also sipped at their cups, nodding and murmuring their approval. Except for Commodore Corvus, who still giving Redbeard a glare withering enough to flay a man.

Redbeard and Kitt, for their part, ignored the tea. While she might've preferred that they play along, she felt a stirring of pride. This was *her crew*. And while they might be insufferable at times, no one would dare call any of them blowhards.

Hawke's saucer rattled as he set his cup down. Eyes opening, he released a satisfied sigh. "Ah yes. Very good cuppa, Mister…?"

"Spiner," Spiner replied.

"Mr. Spiner. Excellent cup of tea. I commend you."

"Thank you, sir."

Redbeard was fidgeting in his chair, and Cass pitied him his impatience. He had never had to deal with the Effin' Feds in person before. How could he possibly suspect that such pointless ceremony could last for hours?

Mercifully, it seemed Hawke had no intention of dragging this torture out for much longer. He cleared his throat. "Now that we have come together at last, as friends, over tea," he said, in a terribly sweet tone, "I do hope we can put the past behind us and move on, Bambi."

"Captain Cass," she blurted, reaching the edge of her patience.

He blinked. "I beg your pardon?"

"On my ship, I would appreciate it if you address me as Captain *Cass*," she said.

He frowned his disapproval, a look that brought back years of patriarchal memories.

Shit, Cass, she thought. *Why'd you do that? Just let him have his way and you can be free! Keep your mouth shut!*

"Oh, Bambi," Hawke said, shaking his head sadly. "We know each other so much better than that."

She forced a smile. "I apologize. Old habits of command, you know."

Redbeard's fingers dug into the tabletop, turning crimson from the effort. The whiskers of his unruly beard quivered, as if he were chewing tobacco-laced gum.

Hawke seemed oblivious to Redbeard's struggles. The smile returned to his face. He had aged these last few years, she noticed. There were more creases along his forehead, and more gray in his hair. "Of course," he said gently. "I understand. Speaking of … you know you would be welcomed back into the Federation with open arms."

The scoff escaped her mouth before she could swallow it back. She attempted to cover it with a cough. "Rear Admiral, you are too kind. But last I checked, the Feds don't much like deserters."

Commodore Corvus let out a strangled noise, but both Cass and Hawke ignored her. Now her glare was directed toward Cass.

Kitt's claws raked across the top of the table, causing the group to pause and look around in confusion. She quickly pulled her arms back and shoved them under the table, out of view.

Hawke cleared his throat and placed his own hands out on the table, palms up. "My dear Bambi … you are too talented to waste. I know that. They know that. An exceptional officer. Oh yes, you would have a place among the ranks again, I can promise you that."

Commodore Corvus appeared quite flustered at his statement. Her dark skin had developed a rosy complexion across her cheeks.

Cass restrained an amused smile with difficulty. Entertaining the notion of returning to the Federation was almost worth it, just to see the severe woman suffer. Cass shifted in her seat and wrapped her fingers around her tea cup. She dropped her eyes to the steaming liquid within. "I'm sorry, Rear Admiral," she said quietly. "That's not an option."

"But, Bambi, why?" He was almost plaintive. "You know what happened wasn't your fault! The Federation can't afford to lose an officer like you … especially not to the likes of these *filthy* pirates!"

"Pirates!?" Redbeard boomed before Cass could reply.

She looked up to see the big man staring incredulously at Hawke. For a heartbeat her insides froze in terror, thinking Redbeard was about to start a bloodbath. But then she realized his outburst had not been his usual tone of rage and she relaxed. A wave of warmth coursed through her at the sight of his theatrics. Redbeard could be quite the actor, especially when the situation required it.

"Pirates!?" he repeated. "Admiral, ye wound me! Do we look like pirates ta you?"

Hawke sat back in his chair and looked Redbeard up and down. "It's *Rear* Admiral. And—umm—if I'm to be perfectly honest—"

"Pffft!" Red interrupted, throwing up his hands. "We ain't no pirates, *Rear* Admiral. Just simple folk tryin' ta make a livin' in this cruel galaxy, eh? Didn't you see the critters down in arrrr hold? That's wha' we arrrre! Cargo haulers! Transportin' critters large an' small wherever they need ta go! That's us. You need some critters transported, you call us, yes sirree!"

Hawke stared at Redbeard, his brow dancing up, down, and sideways as he absorbed the outburst.

Cass quickly lifted her tea and sipped to hide the grin. *If Hawke buys this, I'm giving Red a raise.*

The rear admiral tilted his head, studying Redbeard, as the very-much-a-pirate attempted to gently pick up the tiny teacup in one huge hand and slurped noisily.

Then Hawke looked back to her, confusion plain on his face. She could see his desire to believe the ginger giant warring with suspicion. "Cargo haulers," he said slowly. "Is that so?"

She set her tea down. "Yes, Rear Admiral. That's right."

Well, it was true enough. For the time being, they were indeed cargo haulers.

"Bullshit," Commodore Corvus coughed into her fist, causing Rear Admiral Hawke to gasp at her vulgarity, a reaction echoed by the other Feds lined around the room.

Those Feds seated at the table shifted uncomfortably and muttered to each other, staring into their tea.

But the commodore ignored her comrades. Her fierce dark glare raked across the pirates, then landed with finality upon Redbeard. "If you're really *cargo haulers*, then why isn't this ship registered to you? It's not even your ship, is it?"

Kitt slinked back in her chair, as if she were attempting to hide in plain sight.

Redbeard blubbered. "We, err, bought 'er fer cash from tha previous owners. But those lazy bastards haven't sent the forms in to tha DMV, is tha' it?" His face darkened. "Why, if I get my hands on—"

Cass interrupted, before he could get too deep into the lie. "Red, calm down. I'm sure it's not their fault. I'll bet it got lost in the interstellar delivery. I told them to use registered mail, but you never know."

Redbeard set his beefy hands down on the table with a thud, spilling his tea in the process. "Arrr, Cap'n. Can't be relyin' on tha postal service, can we?"

Hawke's mouth hung wide open, for once with nothing to say. "Uhh, I see."

Corvus shoved away from the table and stood ramrod tall. "*Sir*, this is ridiculous. I can't believe you're entertaining these outright lies!"

Hawke's mouth found form at last, and he slowly shook his head. "Commodore Corvus, my dear, please *sit down*. May I remind you that *we* are the guests here?"

Spiner stepped around the table and refilled Redbeard's

cup. The giant ignored him, a sneer on his face as he glared at Corvus.

The commodore's face drained of all color. Her back stiff, she took measured steps back to the table and sat down.

Hawke nodded and returned his gaze to Cass. "There, there, Bambi. I'm sorry to have doubted you. I can understand why you might've wanted to leave the service, after what happened…"

Cass swallowed. How long had it been since the incident? She'd made every effort to remove herself from that singular catastrophic moment of failure. Tried to forget, even as the nightmares continued to haunt her.

She sighed and tried to let the tension fall from her body. Now that Hawke had extended her an olive branch, they had a chance at getting out of this whole mess. "Thank you, Rear Admiral. You're right. It's been terribly difficult." A single tear streaked down her right cheek. She'd let it come for show, yes, but she wasn't pretending. She didn't need to. The wound was real. "I can't get their faces out of my head, sir."

Hawke leaned in, his face grave. "I know what it's like to have lost those under my command, Bambi. But you know it wasn't your fault…"

"Sir, if that's true, then you know it doesn't matter who was at fault. They were under *my* command. Their lives were *my* responsibility … and I let them down. How can I possibly return to a position of command in the Federation Navy again?"

In truth, she hadn't even asked for this captainship with the pirates. She'd planned to drift anonymously, catch on with a crew somewhere. Instead, she'd ended up with this ragtag bunch, who had quickly decided they'd wanted *her* as their captain after the incident on Aresh Five. There was little room for argument—they wouldn't be refused, no matter how little she wanted it.

But then, being a pirate captain was a lot different than commanding a Navy frigate. At least the pirates were mostly autonomous, able to think for themselves in a pinch and not completely reliant upon her orders as Federation troops were.

Corvus stared down into her lap, hands fidgeting, but wisely choosing to remain silent.

Redbeard gazed across the table at his captain, concern and something deeper etched across his face.

Hawke sat back slowly in his chair, nodding thoughtfully. "I understand your concerns, Bambi. Your hesitation to return to the force. But I assure you … what happened could not have been prevented. Not by you, nor me, nor anyone else. Your contributions to the Federation far outweigh the unfortunate results of that tragedy. I hope you realize that."

Cass stared into her tea, but had no reply. Her contributions to the Federation didn't keep her awake at night. The image of that cruiser breaking into pieces did, the bodies of her crew floating in space. She blinked rapidly before she could lose her composure.

Hawke sighed at her continued silence. "Well. I understand your need for some time away. To get your head right and all that. It's completely understandable."

He straightened suddenly, a smile flashing back into place. He snapped his fingers and pointed toward the counter. "Ah! Say, are those pickles over there?"

Redbeard leaned back to peer around Hawke. "Oh, aye, those be pickles, all right. Fancy one, do ye?"

Cass suppressed a frown. Where had those come from? The gas station? She recalled Dillbilly's accusation of thievery. Was *this* the bounty? Pickles!?

Hawke was nodding his head with enthusiasm. "I haven't had a good pickle in a long while. I'd love one!"

For a moment, Cass thought Redbeard was going to get

up and retrieve them himself. Instead, he smiled up at Spiner and batted his eyelashes. "Spiner, would ye do us tha' honors, then?"

Spiner blinked back. "You would like me to serve the pickles?"

"Arrr, if ye don't mind."

"Affirmative."

Hawke clapped his hands. "Now then. We'll enjoy a final snack together and then we'll be on our way."

"Sir?" Corvus lifted her head for the first time since being reproached.

Hawke smiled across the table at Cass, ignoring Corvus's question. "Like I said, Bambi, I understand your need for some time away. That's all this is, isn't it?" He waved a hand toward Redbeard, Kitt, and Spiner. "A mental break to regain your composure. As I said, completely understandable. So, I'll leave you to it. After this, we'll be out of your hair, for the time being. But it's been two years now, Bambi. And ... I want you to strongly consider turning yourself in."

Cass attempted to meet his gaze, smile for smile, but faltered at this unexpected twist.

He continued, "You *are* technically a deserter, but if you return yourself within the next week, I will be sure to head the disciplinary tribunal myself, and use my considerable influence to ensure all involved understand the true nature of your absence these last two years."

He grinned at her, quite pleased with himself at this arrangement. "The most you'll suffer is a demotion, but I have no doubt you'll rise again through the ranks in no time."

He sat straighter, puffing out his chest. "I'll request that you be reinstated under my command. But of course, if you do not heed my advice here, and do not return to the Federation by the end of the week," his brilliant smile faded, and he shook his head, "I'm afraid there is little more I can do for you."

Spiner placed a plate in front of each table occupant, then laid down a single, wet pickle for each.

Cass ignored the unusual snack, staring across the table at Hawke.

He met her gaze for a long moment before being distracted by the arrival of his own pickle.

But still she watched him, contemplating, heart beating too hard against her ribs. *Return to the Federation in a week, or else.* All that really mattered, of course, was that for now he was letting them go. For one week. One week. One week to be sure she disappeared from his radar forever.

Kitt sniffed at her gleaming, greenish-brown pickle, her mouth peeling open in revulsion. She pushed the plate away.

Redbeard, like the Feds, picked up his pickle with apparent enthusiasm and bit off a large bite with a satisfying crunch. He tilted his head thoughtfully as he chewed. "Hmm," he said finally. "Not half bad."

Hawke nodded his agreement, but waited to swallow down his bite before speaking. He leaned back in his chair and patted his belly with both hands. "Mm hmm. I do believe that's the best pickle I've ever had. Even better than the legendary Pleasant Valley Pickle!"

"Oh no!" Harry exclaimed to Node. "They're eating Dillbilly's *kids*!"

Node replied, "Are you referring to the objects currently being referred to as *pickles*?"

Harry bobbed his head, tail swishing in agitation. "Yes! I don't know if I want to be a pirate, if it means eating people's children."

Node was silent for a moment. "Scanning now … nope,

I'm not reading any life signs from the objects. Oh. Oh!"
Node's pixelated face danced in circles.

"What? What is it?" Harry was still saddened. While his
friends might not be eating *live* kids, the fact they were
already dead was no less tragic.

"Ha. Hah hah hah hah."

Harry experienced a sudden flash of heat. "*Node*! Stop it.
This isn't funny!" He stamped his hoof to accentuate his
point.

"What? You still think those are kids?"

"Are you making fun of me?"

Node stopped dancing. "No, Harry. I'm not making fun of
you. I'm making fun of everyone else."

Harry's ears drooped. "I don't understand."

"I ran back over the transcripts of our communications
with the gas station proprietor known as *Dillbilly*, back to
when he said he 'dropped the kids off.'"

"So?"

"It's a euphemism, Harry."

"A what?"

"Eu-phe-mism, noun, a mild or indirect word or expression substituted for one considered to be too harsh or blunt
when referring to something unpleasant in polite company."

"Oh. I don't get it. What's that have to do with Dillbilly's
kids?"

"Harry." Node's pixelated face widened into a grin. "They
aren't eating Dillbilly's *kids*."

"They're not?"

"No. They're eating his *poop!* Hah. Hah hah hah hah!"

Harry blinked, attempting to process through the relief
that no children were getting eaten. *Oh, wait ... poop? As in,
shit? Oh!* He danced around the holding pen, braying as he
got the joke. "Hee-haw! Hee-haw! They're eating Dillbilly's
shit!"

"Yes! I knew you were smarter than those morons, Harry."

Harry ignored the backhanded compliment. "Do you think we should tell them?

A little hand appeared under Node's chin as he paused in thought, then he smiled. "Nah. Too late to stop them, anyway."

18

Harry pranced out of the holding pen, weaving in and out of the spaces in between the pirates in the hold. With the Feds off the ship, Captain Cass had instructed Kitt to release him. Presumably, he was allowed to talk now.

Spiner and Redbeard flanked Cass as Kitt reactivated the holding pen gate.

"Harry," the captain said. "*Harry.*"

Harry tried to put the brakes on. Instead of coming to a clean stop, his hooves slid along the smooth metal floor, clipping Kitt's legs from the rear.

Kitt unleashed an outraged yowl, and leapt sideways into the air, twisting so that her legs and feet momentarily traded places with her whiskered face and ears. Improbably, right before impact with the ground, her legs swung around and her feet softly absorbed her weight as she landed … right next to a startled Redbeard.

He took an involuntarily step sideways, right into Spiner.

Spiner stumbled forwards, landing squarely in the arms of Captain Cass. Her reflexes were quick, allowing her to catch him and stand him back up without so much as a blink.

"Arrr, Kitt," Redbeard whined, "you off tha trolley?"

"Hey," Harry admonished, "no whining during official pirate business!"

Kitt straightened, brushed off her fur, and bared her teeth at Harry.

"*Harold!*" Captain Cass's shout stunned everyone into silence.

Harry stood up, feeling a bit wobbly. And, his host's feet hurt. He'd have to remember to take it easy on Buddy. He glanced around at the pirates. "Why is everyone staring at me?"

Captain Cass bit her lip and shook her head. "You know what, never mind. I want everyone to give me your eyes and ears, please."

Buddy's feet were still protesting, so Harry decided to give him a break. He let his legs fold and returned to the floor, this time with a modicum of grace. He could listen from here just as easily as he could standing.

"Thank you," said Captain Cass, once everyone was paying attention. "Now, I'm going to make this as clear as I possibly can. You will forget everything that smiling rictus of an asshat said in the commons." She raked the pirates—even the intern—with a hard, cold stare. "Do you understand? *Everything.*"

Redbeard gulped. Kitt and Spiner nodded wordless assent.

Harry asked, "Captain, what do we call you now? Cass or Bambi?"

"I'll give you one guess," the captain replied. "If you get it wrong, you get to spend the rest of the trip in the holding pen with the rest of the donkeys."

Harry felt his stomach gurgle as it tightened. He

attempted to clear his throat, which sounded more like gagging. *Think, Harry, think! She said to forget everything.* "So … I guess you'd like to stick with Cass?"

"Bingo. Very good. Now, shut up."

He thought about replying, but the mean face he was getting at the moment gave him second thoughts. *Buddy, when I grow up, I want to be as terrifying and in-charge as her.*

Redbeard coughed. "Cap'n, permission to speak?"

Bambi—err, Captain Cass—inclined her head fractionally.

"I don't trust tha Effin' Feds. Do you really think they'll let us be leavin', easy as tha'?"

"Hawke may be insufferable, but he is an honorable man. He won't bother us again, not until the window he's given me is over."

"If you say so, Cap'n."

"I do."

Spiner asked, "Do you intend to turn yourself in, Captain?"

Redbeard didn't give her a chance to respond. "Surely na'. We run, plain an' simple."

The usually quiet Kitt spoke, "If they found us this time, they'll find us again."

"Aye," Redbeard added. "Tha' don' add up, Cap'n. We had technical assistance come out, change our transponder an' everything! We shoulda looked like a different ship ta 'em. How'd they know it was us right off?"

The captain's hard gaze darkened. "I have a theory. And the implications aren't good, that's for sure. But in any event, there's not much we can do about it without credits, and right now we're running on empty."

"So, what do we do, Cap'n?"

"We proceed as planned, and hope we have a prize donkey on our hands. If we don't get a payout from this cargo, there won't be much point in trying to shake our tail." Her gaze swept the donkeys in the holding pen, ignoring Harry. "We push onward to Irrakis. Hopefully we'll have our purse money before the end of the week Hawke's allotted me, and then we can get rid of this ship altogether and get back to the *Girlboss*. Plus put some serious money toward making ourselves disappear off the Feds' radar. For good."

The crew members nodded.

"Any other questions?"

Harry lifted his head, working up the courage to ask. *Say yes, please say yes.* "Can I be fitted with a gun?" he blurted.

"No." The captain didn't hesitate. Didn't even bother glancing at him.

"But, but, what if I find a spy and no one is with me to shoot them?" Harry whined.

Redbeard snorted. "Silly arse. How ye gonna shoot a gun, then?"

"There's no spy," Captain Cass said.

"Captain?" asked Spiner. "How can you be sure?"

Harry added, "Yeah. There could be changelings in the hold, or, or…"

"A wha'?"

Captain Cass held up her hands. "Enough. Look … it's not a spy. We have a tail."

"A tail?" repeated Redbeard.

Harry turned his head and looked at his host's tail. Then he glanced over at Kitt. As far as he could tell, they had at least two tails just in the pirate ranks. Then there were all the donkeys and cows. And, did tail feathers count, too?

A rooster crowed from the other side of the hold.

"Yes, a tail. Someone has been following us. It's the only possible remaining solution for how the Feds keep finding us."

"But, wouldn't we have detected them?" Kitt asked.

"Did we detect our own technical support ship?"

"Oh," Kitt replied.

"What?" Harry asked, not getting it.

Spiner glanced down at Harry. "She means that there is another ship with cloaking abilities that's following us and reporting our location to the Feds."

"Arrr," nodded Redbeard. "Well, nothing doin' then. When we get tha chance, we blast 'em."

Cass nodded. "Yes. That's exactly right. And since Hawke has just given me seven days to turn myself in, and our tail is clearly working for the Feds, that means they should be relatively harmless till the end of the week. Giving us those seven days to refill our coffers and ideally lull our tail into letting their guard down … so we can blast them. Any more questions?" the captain asked.

The crew exchanged glances.

"Good. Let's get on with it."

The captain and the rest of the pirates left the hold.

Harry decided to wait a few moments before getting up to follow them. His feet were still aching, and his stomach wasn't feeling much better. Maybe it was time to eat a snack and take a shower.

If he was going to be running in a race soon, he'd need to be ready.

It took them several more hours, and several more jumps, to reach their intended destination. But it seemed the Federation officer, Hawke, was true to his word. His cubed ships had backed off, and the *SS Bray* had jumped to hyperspace with no obvious signs of pursuit.

At least, not from the Feds. Harry kept a close eye on the rear ends of the tail-less crew—much to their consternation.

Luckily, the crew remained that way, as no one grew a new tail during the remainder of the journey.

Still unsure of what this "tail" was exactly that Captain Cass had mentioned, Harry remained wary of all the tails in the hold. A good pirate intern, he remained alert, ready to report any suspicious behavior from any of the animals.

Harry resumed his cleaning duties for most of the trip to Irrakis, but as they drew nearer to the planet, he was granted a reprieve, giving him time to clean himself up. His host would need to look his best ahead of the prize donkey contest.

Irrakis! Finally, they were entering the Irrakis system. As clean as he could ever remember, Harry strutted up to the bridge with head held high, his gray and white coat shined and fluffed.

Or rather, he tried to strut. Buddy's front feet still hurt, and Harry felt his poor host wince every time he put weight on them.

Sorry, Buddy. But it's show time! Just a little longer and you can have a real rest!

He ended up tip-toeing onto the bridge, clamping his teeth against the little shooting pains running up his front legs. With a sigh of relief, he lowered himself down next to Spiner's station in his usual spot.

Hope they don't mind us laying down, Buddy.

A planet drew nearer on the viewscreen as Harry watched, a gleaming ochre globe that nearly glowed against the backdrop of black space.

"Wow," he breathed. "It's beautiful!"

Redbeard grunted. "Looks like a big ol' ball of sand ta me." He shifted in his chair, wincing. "I don't like sand. Gets all over, if ya follow. In yer pants, even up into yer—"

"Red," Captain Cass said. "Please."

He shrugged. "It's true."

The captain looked up at a blank spot on the ceiling and drew in a deep breath.

"I don't have pants," Harry stated helpfully.

Redbeard scowled. "Eh well. Lucky you."

Captain Cass held up a hand to silence their banter as a chime sounded from the comms. "About time. We've been waiting twenty minutes. Node, put it on."

Nice to see everyone getting along, Harry noted as the captain addressed his computer friend by his preferred name.

A chipper female voice said, in only mildly accented Galactic Standard, "You've reached the Irrakis Ministry of Ceremonial Affairs. Thank you for holding. I'm Nadia. What can I do for you?"

Captain Cass leaned forward in her chair. "Hello, Nadia. This is Captain Cass of the *SS Bray*. We're here for the Running of the Donkey contest."

"Wonderful. This is a very important cultural event for our people. Would you like to buy spectator tickets, then?"

"Oh. Um, no. We're hoping to enter our donkeys into the contest. I hope it's not too late to register?"

"Ah," Nadia paused. "We're always open to having more contestants. How many are you planning to enter?"

"Well, we have dozens in our hold. So … as many as we can?"

Harry felt a momentary pang of jealousy. If his whole herd of donkeys were entering the contest, that significantly lowered the odds of *him* being the prize donkey.

I really want us *to win, Buddy,* he thought. *If we win the prize, surely we'll get to be real space pirates!*

"That's great," Nadia's cheerful voice pitched up a half-tone higher. "Each contest participant is allowed to register up to five donkeys for the race. I can send you an information packet, which includes all the necessary application forms."

"Paperwork?" Redbeard grumbled. "Blast it all…"

"*OH,*" Nadia said, loudly enough to cause Kitt to cover her ears. "I almost forgot. Since you are participating in the contest, I can fast-track your approval to dock at Irrakeen. That's our planet's capital."

Captain Cass raised her eyebrows. "Thank you."

Nadia's voice pitched up yet again, loud enough now to cause Redbeard to clutch the arms of his chair. "Of course. Enjoy your stay on Irrakis, and best of luck with the contest! Who knows—maybe you have a prize donkey on your hands!"

The transmission cut off and Spiner promptly announced, "I've received the information packet, Captain, as well as docking clearance and instructions for landing."

"Tha' was fast," Redbeard said, as he rubbed and tugged at his ears.

Captain Cass swiveled in her chair to face Spiner's station. "Put us down, Spiner." She paused and glanced down at Harry, frowning. "You don't look so good. Maybe you should sit out the contest?"

Harry scrambled to his feet, clamping down on Buddy to ignore the pain in his hooves. "Oh, no, no, no, no—that's okay! I'll be okay."

The captain regarded him skeptically. "Hmm. It's up to you. We've got plenty of other donkeys to enter in the contest, if you'd rather rest up."

Redbeard stood up and stretched his arms out wide. "Arrr, me thinks a kip sounds mighty good. But, surely we be gettin' somethin' good fer a talkin' arse, yeah?"

Harry's ears lifted. He had no idea what a *kip* was, but it felt good to have Redbeard's support for once. He tried on his best grin. "Yeah, I'm your prize donkey, right here!"

The captain shrugged. "We'll see. Doesn't matter, really, as long as *one* of our donkeys wins."

Harry was determined to show them that he was capable. No way was he going to sit this one out, no matter how poorly his host was feeling.

We're going to win this, right Buddy?

19

H arry was allowed to disembark along with the rest of the pirate crew. It felt good to be included again after being cooped up with his herd during the encounter with the Feds. He scampered around Redbeard's hulking frame to get a look at this new place.

They stood on an open platform, just outside the SS *Bray*, at an open-aired docking station, just at the edge of the capital city of Irrakeen. The other edge of the docking station featured a sandy, dune-filled landscape that seemed to stretch on forever. Dotted between the landing platforms of the station were round, bubble-like buildings, not unlike the ones at Dillbilly's gas station, only there were a lot more of them.

The city of Irrakeen itself was impressive. Harry had never seen anything like it. Hundreds of pale, rectangular buildings stretched out in the distance, big and small, almost all of them with tall spires stretching up into the cloudless, cobalt sky.

It was almost unbearably hot, even for a donkey. Harry's eyes were drawn to pools of sweat dripping off the faces of the human members of the pirate crew. Already thirsty, he was tempted to run over and lick it off their faces. Harry hoped the race would be at a cooler time of day.

Kitt gestured at Spiner with a rare expletive, then pointed over at the side of the ship. Following their gazes, Harry saw the fueling tube from Dillbilly's was still attached. They quickly excused themselves to get a closer look.

Redbeard was too preoccupied with swearing and swiping at his face with an open hand, trying to keep the sweat out of his eyes. "Ewww, blimey, arse! Keep away from me hands!"

Harry stepped back from Redbeard's hand. *Humans are salty,* he observed to Buddy as he licked his lips. *We're even thirstier now, aren't we?*

A few paces forward from the rest of the group, Captain Cass conversed with a strangely garbed man who didn't appear to be the least bit affected by the sweltering heat. The only parts of his body not covered by white sheets were his face, hands, and slippered feet.

They both paused at Redbeard's outburst and glanced over.

"Sorry," Harry mumbled.

The man in white sheets gave Harry a quizzical look, then returned his attention to the captain.

Harry couldn't hear what they were saying, so he decided to drift closer….

"Have you completed the registration forms?" the man asked the captain.

"I have," Captain Cass replied. She reached out with some sort of square device, and the man did the same.

Then the man pulled his device back, and tapped at its surface, as if it were a console on the ship's bridge. "Everything looks in order." He extended his device back to the captain. "Here's a schedule, as well as the patterns you'll need for the showmanship portion of the event."

Captain Cass looked down at her device, biting her lip. "The showmanship portion?"

The man nodded. "Yes, yes. Very important, you understand."

The captain stared at the man in a way that suggested that she didn't, in fact, understand.

"We don't let just any donkey participate in the actual run," he explained. "All finalists must conform to standard, and being appropriately garbed is a necessary first step."

"Very well," the captain replied, after glancing down at her device again.

Harry was pretty excited. *We're going to get to wear clothes, Buddy! How cool is that?*

"You can find accommodations in a nearby hostel," the man said. "Or, if you prefer, you may come and go from your ship as you please during your authorized stay."

"We'll stay on our ship, thank you."

The man smiled and bent at the waist with a flourish of his hands. "Very good. Enjoy your stay and best of luck with the contest tomorrow."

The captain and Harry watched the man turn and walk away.

Redbeard stepped forward to join them. "Arrr we all good, Cap'n?"

Captain Cass stared back down at her device. "Tomorrow," she said quietly. "The event is tomorrow. And we're supposed to dress all the donkeys in special garments."

"Garments?" Redbeard repeated, scratching his beard. "Well, tha' won't be a problem, will it? Can jus' use the replicators."

. . .

"The replicators only work if you provide a pattern *and* precise measurements for the donkeys," Node explained.

"Precise measurements?" Captain Cass repeated.

Node's tone shifted from one of boredom to something edgier. "Yes. Would you like me to define those words for you?"

"Don't test my patience," the captain snapped. "I know what those words mean."

"What does he mean, Captain?" Spiner asked.

"Hah. Hah hah—"

"*Node.*"

The laughter stopped.

Node said, "Will that be all? Or can I pretend to go do something else now?"

The captain ignored the comment. "Listen up, crew. You heard the computer. We need to get precise measurements from the donkeys. I've registered all of us as contest participants to up our odds of winning, so that's five donkeys for each of us, twenty donkeys in all. Pick the best looking ones to measure. Kitt, Spiner, Redbeard, get to it."

Redbeard protested. "Arrr, c'mon, Cap'n … I don' wanna be touchin' those shite machines!"

"Can I help?" Harry asked, eager to have something to do.

"I don't think so," Captain Cass replied. "Unless you can grow a set of hands."

Harry lowered his head. "I don't think I can do that. Oh well..."

"Captain," said Kitt. "Taking measurements is only useful if we know what we're supposed to be measuring."

"She raises a valid point, Captain," Spiner offered.

"See?" asked Redbeard. "We don't even know wha' we're s'posed to be doin', then."

Node's pixelated face popped onto the viewscreen. "Look, I'd love to watch you morons struggle with this. But if you don't win this contest, I get the feeling I'm going to be stuck with you for a long time. So … how about I speed things along and help you find some instructional videos?"

The crew stood in front of the viewscreen on the bridge, which Node had made opaque and designated a rectangle of for playing back the instructional videos. They stood in a line, even Harry, heads tilted to the right as they studied what they were supposed to do.

Captain Cass straightened her head and rolled it around on her shoulders. "Ugh, Node, can't you find any of these damn things that are horizontal?!"

"Negative," Node replied. "It seems the morons who made these videos did not realize vertical videos were a bad idea."

"Blimey," Redbeard muttered. He, too, straightened to rub at his neck. "I don' understand anything they're talkin' about, especially with not bein' able to see it properly!"

The captain released a heavy sigh. "Well, we're just going to have to do the best we can. Node, can you adjust the video and play it back horizontally? My neck is killing me."

"I can adjust it, sure," Node replied. "But it won't help."

The video shifted from vertical to horizontal, but then the images stretched so horrifically even Harry blinked, snapping out of the trance of watching so many videos to shake his head. "Well, now it just looks like a bunch of blurry colors," he said.

Redbeard growled curses.

"Yeah, that makes it worse." Captain Cass rubbed at her eyes. "Okay, fine, put it back the way it was, Node."

The computer complied.

They went back to watching a man wrapped in white robes attempt to coerce a donkey draped in bright colors to trot toward a woman, who was the judge in this particular situation. But, because of the vertical nature of the video, they couldn't see both the entire donkey and the entire man —much less the whole arena in which this contest was taking place—at the same time.

"Blast it all!" Rebeard burst out. "'Ow we supposed to know what tha hell we're doin'? You can't see tha pattern when they're zoomed in."

"Node, stop the videos," the captain ordered.

The computer complied.

"Just ... just put up the schematics of the showmanship patterns on the screen, please." She sounded resigned and weary.

"Will do."

The video disappeared, and a white-and-black image took its place, all a series of circles, solid lines and dotted lines. It made Harry's eyes cross.

He lowered himself down to the floor once more, giving Buddy's feet another rest. *Whew. Preparing for this contest sure is hard work! I didn't know it would be this complicated. But we gotta figure it out, Buddy. We can do this! We have to win!*

"Well I don't understand this, neither," Redbeard scowled.

"Captain," Spiner spoke up from his station, having slipped away unnoticed. "I've found an article on the Running of the Donkey contest that explains what each of those lines represents. Would you like me to put it on screen?"

"Yes please."

Spiner did so.

Harry blinked again. The text was endless, and reading wasn't exactly his best talent. Oh boy.

"Bollocks," Redbeard said, and meandered over to fall heavily into his chair. "This is gonna take *hours*."

"Most likely," the captain agreed. "But what else can we do? If knowing all of this is how we win this contest, then that's what we have to do. So." She clapped her hands together, seeming to draw Kitt out of a trance-like state. "Node, we at least have the specifications for the garments now. Prep the replicators to comply."

She turned to Spiner, Kitt, and Redbeard in turn. "You three, start measuring the donkeys, then input the measurements into the replicators when you have them. I want this done in…" she checked the nearest chronometer, "two hours tops. Meanwhile, I'll go over all this."

She waved back at the pattern displayed on the screen behind her. "When the two hours are up, all hands meet me in the hold and we'll go over this showmanship thing."

"What about me?" Harry asked again, a hopeful note in his voice.

Captain Cass turned precisely on her booted heel to face him. "For now, I want you to rest up. If you really want to be in that contest, you need to be in tip-top shape."

Harry lurched to his feet, locking down on Buddy to hide the grimace. "Aye, aye, Captain!"

"Meet the rest of us in the hold in two hours to go over the patterns as well. Got it?"

Harry nodded vigorously. Well, at least he wasn't going to be left out this time!

"Okay, crew." She looked to all of them and straightened her shoulders, chin high. "Let's do this."

20

Harry was all for new experiences, so when the stern human male in colorful scarves circled around him in the staging pens, the momentary panic and shock of having Buddy's dangly bits groped and explored was only temporary.

"Woah," Harry exclaimed out loud, craning his head back. "Is that why gods have hands?"

The man leaned to the side, making eye contact with Harry. If he seemed put off by a talking donkey, he didn't show it. "If you please, try to hold still, and it will be over soon."

"Let the good man do 'is work, will ya?" Redbeard stood a few short paces away with his arms folded across his chest. When the captain had asked him what he was doing, he'd mentioned something about "Keeping a close eye on the arse ta' make sure he don' mess anything up."

Following that, Redbeard had been full of personal commentary on Harry's garments, which consisted of a sheer white material worn as a vest with straps and buckles across the chest. A matching wrap adorned his hips, with small, hollow metallic balls that jingled and clinked whenever he took a step.

"You may call me Al-Qadi," the man corrected.

"What?" Redbeard asked.

Al-Qadi's hands continued to probe. "I have a name. On my world, it is polite to use a man's name when referring to him."

Harry nuzzled into his host's spine and managed to impede Buddy's desire to wiggle and pull away.

"There, you see?" Al-Qadi stepped back and walked around to face Harry. He pulled out a tablet and tapped on its surface.

"Can I move now?" Harry asked.

Al-Qadi inclined his head and continued to work at his device.

Harry shook his body out, releasing the tension, creating a chorus of jingling bells. Then, he lifted his head and tried to peer at the tablet. "What are you doing?"

Al-Qadi grunted and tapped a couple more times, the final movement with an exaggerated flourish. "I'm judging you."

"Judging me?"

"He's not the only one judging ya, donkey," Redbeard helpfully added.

"Yes. I get to decide if you are worthy."

Harry took a moment to think it over, tilting his head to the right, then to the left, then back again.

Buddy, we don't like being judged, do we? Last time someone said they were judging me, they "passed judgment." Now I don't have a tribe. But, at least I still have you.

Buddy answered by drawing attention to a growing gas bubble in his stomach. An overwhelming sensation of pain flooded the nervous system, causing Harry's little tick body to recoil—his control over his host nearly slipping in the process.

"You can relax now," said Al-Qadi. "I'm done here."

The captain stood over with the other donkeys. She looked up as the judge approached.

Redbeard and Harry looked on for a moment as the captain and Al-Qadi exchanged words out of earshot of the others. Well, at least they'd managed to pass the showmanship part of the contest, which Harry was sure was the hardest part.

"Has anyone ever judged *you*, Redbeard?" Harry asked.

Redbeard grunted and peered down at him. "What?"

"You know. Has anyone ever grabbed your dangly bits before?"

Redbeard's face darkened to something approaching crimson as he squinted at Harry so hard that Harry thought his eyes might burst from the pressure.

Harry returned his gaze with an innocent expression. He'd say anything, or talk to anyone right now, just to think about something other than the stomach pains, or his aching feet. No matter what, he was going to participate in this race … unless the judging man in scarves didn't let him, of course. The thought of not being selected was almost too much to bear.

"No," replied Redbeard.

"What?" Harry replied with a start.

"What do ye mean, 'what?' I answered yer silly question. *No*," Redbeard said with unexpected enunciation.

Harry bared his teeth in a smile. "Oh, okay. It feels kind of funny. You should try it sometime."

Redbeard snorted. "Yer pretty funny, fer an arse."

"Oh look," Harry said. "He's judging again."

They resumed watching Al-Qadi as he walked around the

herd, groping here and there. Not all of the donkeys maintained their composure.

Redbeard chortled when a jennie turned around and tried to bite her assailant. The man took a practiced step back, avoiding her snapping teeth with apparent ease.

"Know what, 'Arry?" Redbeard asked. "If it weren't fer tha' prize, I'd a paid money to see you bite 'im."

Harry noted the giant man had addressed him by name for once. At least, he was fairly certain that was what Redbeard meant. Arry and Harry were pretty dang close to the same.

The judge returned to the captain, who promptly looked over in their direction and waved them over.

"C'mon, arse," Redbeard said.

Harry followed, doing his best to appear capable and pain-free as he trotted over.

"Congratulations," said Al-Qadi. "This donkey here gets to move on to the final contest."

Harry felt a thrill of excitement, almost strong enough to make him forget about the cramping stomach. "Yay!" he shouted. He would have pranced about, too, but he knew he needed to go easy on his host's feet until the big race.

Captain Cass asked, "What about the rest of our donkeys?"

The judge shook his head. "I'm sorry. Only one of your donkeys met our exacting specifications … and that's this one here."

Redbeard followed the judge's gaze to Harry. "Wha', tha' talking arse? Surely, yer pullin' us by the bits?"

"This is the one. If you wanted more candidates to move forward, you should have fed them all as well as you did this one."

"You're joking," Captain Cass said flatly.

"Wha'?" Redbeard exclaimed. "The race is fer fat arses

only, then?" He began to laugh. "This I gotta see with me own eyes!"

Al-Qadi put on a patient smile and nodded. "Just so. And now, I must finish judging the rest of the entries. Good luck to you."

Captain Cass and Redbeard watched the judge walk away, then exchanged glances.

"Cap'n," Redbeard began, "I've done some crazy things in me piratin' days, but this one takes tha cake."

Harry groaned as the next wave of stomach pain rolled over his host.

The captain knelt down next to him, her soft brown gaze sweeping over him head to tail. "You look like shit, Harold. I hope you can do this, because if you don't win, I don't think we can afford to leave."

"No pressure," Redbeard added.

The roar of the crowd vibrated in the bones of Harry's host as he and the other race participants made their way through the dark, cool tunnel toward the racetrack.

Harry had to hang on tight to his control, as Buddy wanted nothing more than to turn around and bolt back the way they had come. He dug down deep into Buddy's spinal cord.

Hang in there, Buddy! When we win this race, we're gonna be famous! You'll see!

Buddy did not seem convinced. He quivered with nerves.

Harry himself was feeling rather nervous, especially given that neither his feet nor his stomach were feeling any better.

But Captain Cass walked beside him, leading him along like any other donkey in a colorful halter bedecked with tassels along the forehead and cheeks.

Harry felt rather fancy in all his gear, and honored that

Captain Cass herself had opted to escort him, but it seemed the other donkeys in this contest did not share this appreciation of their garb nor their escorts.

He and the captain had to side-step more than a few gnashing teeth and flying hooves as they went, the captain swearing as one small hoof clanged against the power armor protecting her thigh.

Harry laid his ears back at the troublesome jack and bared his teeth, swinging his rear around in warning.

"Hey, watch it!" he snapped. "Touch her again and I'll wallop you one! You won't wake up for a week!" *Or at least a good thirty minutes*, he thought, remembering Dillbilly.

The man leading that particular jack did a double-take at hearing Harry's voice. Then he stared, eyes bulging, going from Harry to the captain to Harry again.

"That's right," Harry said, turning frontward toward the man again and putting on his best mean face. "I said, *watch it.*"

The man recoiled, still struggling to control his own donkey. But, to Harry's satisfaction, he moved hurriedly away through the crowd to put a safe distance between him and the donkey who could talk.

Harry grinned up proudly at Captain Cass, and was thrilled to find her already looking down at him, a faint smile on her face.

His heart swelled. Despite the shooting pains racing up his legs, he stood a little taller and stepped a little higher.

At last, they emerged from the tunnel into the dazzling sunlight, and Harry squinted. He blinked rapidly, trying to clear his vision as the crowds' cheering reached a crescendo.

Again, Buddy tried to bolt, and Harry almost didn't react fast enough to stop him. The result was a little sideways hop, which caused Captain Cass to glance at him quizzically.

"You okay?" she asked.

"Yes," Harry squawked out. It was hard to speak and

maintain such rigid control of his host at the same time. "Fine. I'm fine."

"Good."

They reached the track, which was nothing more than a large, rectangular expanse of dirt with straight lines marked from end to end with colored paint upon the ground. The dirt area was surrounded by a whitewashed wall, about the height of Harry's head, with stacks of seats rising beyond the wall high up into the sky.

Harry's mouth dropped open at the sight of so many gods —*humans*—in one place. He had never, ever seen so many people at once.

There must be thousands of them!

The gods came in every color, dressed in all manner of garb. They shouted and hollered, whistled and whooped, and some waved hats, banners, scarves, or flags.

Harry almost tripped over himself as he gaped at the crowd. He absently followed the gentle tug of the leadrope, the captain steering him toward the starting line.

"*Welcome*," a big voice suddenly boomed from the sky, seeming to come from everywhere and nowhere at once, "to the galaxy-famous Irrakeen Running of the Donkey!"

The crowd went wild, screaming and chanting.

The donkeys went wild too, some managing to escape the grips of their escorts and running off to who-knows-where, their humans yelling curses as they gave futile chase.

Harry tried to ignore the chaos as best he could. *Focus! Focus, Harry! Focus, Buddy! We can do this!*

Captain Cass watched the mayhem with an amused gleam in her eye. She looked down to Harry, who was the only donkey not running amok or trying to run amok.

"Well," she drawled, "I never thought I'd say this, but for once I'm glad you are the way you are."

The compliment sent a shiver of pride through Harry's

little tick body, which was echoed in a shiver from Buddy. He beamed. "I'm going to win this race, Captain."

She lifted an eyebrow, once more scanning the gathering of rebellious donkeys. "Yes, yes, I think you might be right."

"Race participants!" the big voice boomed again. "Take your places at the starting line!"

And they did. Or at least, Harry and the captain did. Then, they waited while the rest of the participants struggled to get their donkeys in place. Harry hoped they would hurry up. All this standing and walking was really making his feet hurt.

He leaned backward to put more weight on his hind feet and relieve some of the pressure up front.

The crowd eventually quieted, until the noise was a mere buzz of conversation.

At last, everyone who still had a donkey in hand was more or less lined up, along the thick white line painted in the dirt.

"Race participants!" the announcer yelled again.

Harry put his ears back. Did the guy have to shout so loud?

"Mount up now!"

Harry wasn't sure what exactly that meant, but he understood once he saw the other humans clamber clumsily onto their donkeys' backs. He sighed, head drooping. He'd wanted Captain Cass to ride him, too, even if it was only a crude, ungainly kind of riding, but the crew had been against it.

They'd claimed it would only slow Harry down, and they were probably right. Besides, as the captain had told him, the other donkeys were only being ridden in order to control their path from one end of the arena to the other.

Self-aware and in full comprehension of what he was supposed to do, Harry had little need for the extra burden of a rider. He'd have to wait for some other opportunity to have the captain ride him … or him to ride her.

Instead, Captain Cass removed his halter, looping it over her shoulder and smiling at him. "Okay, Harold. This is it. All you have to do is beat the rest of these bastards to the opposite end of the track. Think you can do that?"

He nodded, shifting on his sore feet. *Come on, Buddy. Don't let me down now!* "Absolutely, Captain! You can count on me!"

"Good." Captain Cass glanced up to the thousands of people in the stands, then up to the cloudless sky, so blue it almost hurt to look at. "Because otherwise … we might be stuck here a very long time."

Buddy slipped past Harry's imposed control, shaking his head. As interesting as this new city had been, it was far too hot here for his host's comfort. "Don't worry, Captain. We'll be off this ball of sand in no time!"

The captain's smile grew wider, and she patted his neck, now damp with sweat and covered with sand and dust. So much for his bath.

"That's what I like to hear," she said. "Good luck."

With that, she stepped away, taking a place along the wall.

A murmur rippled through the crowd at her action, and Harry saw the other riders nearest to him staring again. A dark-skinned woman beside him was squinting at him as she wrestled with her own mount, a pretty brown jenny.

The jenny tossed her head and brayed loudly.

Buddy's attention strayed toward his female neighbor, but Harry quickly reasserted control. Now was no time to be distracted! He swallowed hard and focused on the painted lines in front of him.

Just make it to the other end as fast as you can, okay, Buddy?

"Citizens of Irrakeen," the booming voice echoed out over the stands, "visitors from around the planet and across the galaxy … you're in for a treat. Held only once every twenty years, the moment we've all been waiting for is finally here! Are you ready?"

The cheering surged, deafening. Flags and banners and scarves waved wildly, filling the layers of seats with motion and color.

The donkeys startled, throwing up their heads, pawing, braying. Some reared or bucked, tossing their hapless riders to the dirt. But the announcer didn't wait for those participants to recover.

"Then let the *Running of the Donkey* begin!" he cried. "Race participants, on your mark!"

Harry found his mark, his front hooves directly on the white line. He set his legs, prepared to jump forward at the sound of the cannon as they'd rehearsed on the *SS Bray*.

"Get set!"

Harry laid his ears back, his full focus on the stretch of lined dirt before him. Even the thunderous noise of the crowd seemed far away.

This is it. My chance to prove myself. My chance to win. My chance to become a real space pirate and find a new tribe!

The boom of the cannon was much louder than Harry had expected. Buddy shot forward of his own accord, scared out of his wits. Harry let him go, adrenaline propelling his short legs on faster than they'd ever moved before.

Go, Buddy, go!

But then Buddy veered off to the left, wild-eyed and panicked.

No, no! No, Buddy, wrong way!

Harry reasserted control and brought Buddy back into his lane, barely dodging around another shaggy gray jack, who was cutting a hard horizontal line across the track, completely ignoring his swearing rider.

Harry bent his focus back to the finish line, but it was getting hard to tell where it was. Donkeys were everywhere, not even remotely staying in their lanes. Their scrambling hooves kicked up dust, marring the painted lines and obscuring the far end of the track.

Harry squinted through the rising dust cloud and coughed, all the while keeping Buddy's legs pumping forward. Gradually at first, the pain from his feet penetrated his focus. He fought back against Buddy's overwhelming urge to stop and take the weight off his hooves.

We can't stop now, Buddy! Come on! We're so close!

At least, he suspected they were close. Probably.

The dust haze was getting thicker. Were any of the other donkeys going in the right direction? Harry couldn't tell. He had no idea where he was in relation to any of the other contestants.

Another jenny came rocketing out of the cloud of dust directly in front of him, riderless, and Harry sat back on his haunches to avoid a head-on collision. The jenny laid her ears back and delivered a shocking bite to his shoulder before tearing off again out of sight.

"*Ouch,*" he yelled after her. "That was not nice at all!"

But she was already gone, and there was a race to win, so he shook it off and forced Buddy to pick up into a gallop, racing what he hoped was straight ahead and not backward.

He kept his eyes glued to the white lines in the dirt, using them to guide him length by length as he tore down the track.

Chaos and pandemonium surrounded him. Donkeys without humans, humans without donkeys, and a few humans still hanging onto their donkeys. Riding all over the place, running into each other, yelling at each other. Frantic braying and shouts of desperation filled the spaces around him.

All the while, the crowd beyond the curtain of dust roared and chanted with glee.

Somewhere in that crowd stood members of his crew, watching the race. His pirate tribe, if only he could be the first to reach the finish line. Redbeard. Kitt. Spiner. Back on the ship, even Node was probably tuned in to the local coverage of the event. Captain Cass was back at the starting line, too, likely covered head-to-toe in dirt by now.

They were all watching him. They were all counting on him.

His host really, *really* wanted to stop running, but Harry pressed him onward.

You can do it, Buddy! Come on, we have to do this!

His legs were burning, coat lathered with sweat. Dust choked him with every gasping inhale, his front hooves screaming in pain. His stretching gallop became short and choppy. It was all he could do to keep going.

Almost! Almost, Buddy ... come on, hang in there...

Harry's host had never been in such bad shape before. The arena blurred, his field of vision narrowing, and he realized it probably wasn't from the dust this time.

His control over Buddy was slipping. Buddy was reaching his physical limit, despite Harry's cajoling.

No, Buddy, you listen to me—we've got this! You are the best damn donkey in the galaxy, and we're gonna show 'em! We will *win this race!*

Buddy's gallop slowed to a stumbling trot, and the arena grew darker still.

That's when Harry saw it, through the dimness, tantalizingly close. A few paces ahead, a fat red line in the dirt. The area appeared devoid of donkeys. The finish line.

His heart soared. *This is it, Buddy! We got this!*

Hoof beats sounded behind him, drawing closer, and fast.

His excitement warred against a surge of desperate terror. He couldn't lose the race now, not after he'd put Buddy through so much to get this close!

"Buddy," he gasped out. *"Please. GO!"*

He buried himself deep into a nerve bundle and gave the poor creature one last burst of strength. Buddy staggered toward the red line, his legs tumbling forward.

The crowd thundered with approval, the ground vibrating, as host and tick crossed the threshold first.

"We did it!" Harry screamed, elation flooding through him. "We did it! We won! Buddy, we won!"

His words were lost in the cheers of the crowd.

Impervious to Harry's elation, Buddy fell to his knees in the dirt, panting hard.

"Congratulations to Captain Cass and the crew of the *SS Bray!*" the announcer's voice shouted cheerfully over the noise of the spectators. "Your donkey, Harold, has won the Irrakeen *Running of the Donkey!*"

Harry wanted to celebrate. He wanted to dance around. He wanted to jump for joy. He wanted to run to Captain Cass and see the look on her face.

But Buddy wouldn't move, no matter how hard Harry attempted to nudge him.

His vision was nearly black, and Harry suddenly noticed how fast his host's heart was beating. Concern dampened the thrill of winning the race.

"Whoa, Buddy, are you all—"

He never got the chance to finish his sentence.

21

For a long time, there was only blackness.

Despite Harry's best efforts, Buddy would not wake up. Even more concerned now, Harry withdrew his efforts to bring his host back to consciousness and instead turned his attention to Buddy's bodily functions.

The jack was alive, definitely, but it seemed he'd reached a point of physical exertion beyond Harry's ability to help.

His heart rate was gradually slowing, so that was good, and his breathing, too, had become slower and deeper. His digestive tract was still upset … that would need tending to when he woke up again. And his feet, especially his front hooves, were throbbing.

That's weird. That's never happened before.

Harry made a mental note to investigate more when Buddy woke up. But, for now, there was little Harry could do other than wait for Buddy to rest.

With a mental sigh, Harry settled in to do just that—wait. *Geez, Buddy. Way to put a downer on our awesome race win....*

Harry jerked awake some time later, hearing the drone of

voices in the background. He blinked groggily, and then snapped fully alert. *I can see again! I can hear again!*

Buddy was awake! He lay on the back of what appeared to be a small flatbed truck, legs folded beneath him, ears drooping.

Harry found himself staring directly into the face of Redbeard. "Hi," Harry said.

Redbeard leapt an impressive height for such a big man, spittle flying from his mouth as he spat a colorful string of expletives. "Blimey!" he roared as he regained his composure. "Don't be doin' tha' to people!"

"Doing what?" Harry asked.

Captain Cass was there too, covering her mouth with a hand, though Harry could still see part of her grin around her fingers.

Kitt and Spiner stood to Redbeard's other side, Spiner wearing his usual impassive expression, and Kitt's frazzled white fur now shining brown in the sun.

"Doin' *tha*'!" Redbeard shouted, gesturing wildly. "Turnin' into a regular ol' donkey an' then blurtin' out words when we least expect it!"

Harry blinked. "Oh. I'm sorry. I feel asleep while I was waiting for Buddy to wake up."

Redbeard just stared at him.

"But hey, I won, didn't I?" Harry jumped to his feet, then winced and laid back down. "I won, I won! Did ya see that? Huh? Did ya see it?"

"Yes, Harry," Captain Cass replied, still grinning. "We saw."

"'Twas one of the funniest damn things I've ever seen in me life," Redbeard supplied. "All those fat arses runnin' wild round the place, and their riders, too." He chuckled as his eyes grew unfocused, probably reliving the memory of the race.

"Yes, hilarious," came Kitt's dry tone as she stepped closer to the edge of the flatbed. "Now, can we please get our money and get out of here? This place is filthy." She looked to her dust-coated fur in dismay.

"Soon as the doc is done with Harold," Captain Cass said.

Harry cocked his head. "Doc?" He looked around at his surroundings consciously for the first time since waking up. He realized with a start he was no longer at the arena.

Instead, the truck was parked on a narrow street, the pavement partially obscured by small sand drifts here and there, and rows of white buildings on either side.

Tall, skinny trees with tufts of leaves at the top broke the colorless scenery, and crowds of onlookers were gathered in the spaces between the buildings and at either end of the street.

They jostled for better viewpoints and muttered amongst themselves, held at bay by a line of men in white robes. Each robed man held a staff of black wood, with a golden circlet around their brows.

Harry perked up his ears. Who were those people? They looked fancy. And, the pressing crowds heeded their quiet warnings with alarming deference.

"We were … worried about you, Harold," Captain Cass said, snapping Harry's attention back to her. "When the race ended and we realized you'd passed out. The crowd was worried about you, too." She nodded toward the spectators clustered in every open space between buildings and trees. "Turns out you're pretty popular after winning that race."

Harry looked back out to the crowds, causing murmurs to sweep across them like ripples on water. He did his best to smile, puffing out his chest.

The murmur grew louder.

"A doctor was summoned," the captain went on, "and she examined you while you were asleep. She's inside getting the results of her scans now." This time she waved toward the nearest building, a short, square edifice with a single door and few windows.

"Oh." Harry replied. "No need, really. I did my own check-up on Buddy, and he was just tired, that's all."

And his feet really hurt. For some reason. He didn't mention that part yet. He'd figure it out, eventually. No need to report on something he didn't have all the answers to yet, right?

"Yes, the doctor mentioned something about exhaustion," Captain Cass said.

Spiner stepped up beside the captain. "The condition the doctor specifically referenced was…"

Harry stopped listening. He was too busy replaying the part of the conversation where the captain had said she was worried about him.

"Yes, that." The captain rolled her eyes. "Anyway, as soon as we're done here, we'll be off to the winner's ceremony, and a parade, apparently."

Harry's attention focused again, and his eyes widened. "Wow! A parade? Just for me?"

"Yes," Spiner said before the captain could answer. "According to the historical data I've been researching, it is customary during the Irrakeen Running of the Donkey to hold a victory parade for the champion donkey. It is also customary for the accompanying festival afterward to last for a full seven days."

"Wow!" Harry said again.

"But we're not staying," Kitt said, then looked to Captain Cass. "Right, Captain?"

"No." The captain shook her head.

"Aye, arrr, soon as we be collectin' our prize, we be blastin' off this sandball!" Redbeard added, then tugged uncomfortably at the crotch of his pants. "I got sand all up in me bits."

Harry took a cursory check of Buddy's bits, but it seemed his host's physiology was better suited to sandy conditions, for his bits were mercifully sand-free.

Before he could say anything further on the matter, a stout woman emerged from the nearest building, a flat, square device in one hand. Her smooth skin was the color of honey, and her black hair shone almost blue in the afternoon sun. She, too, wore white, but not a robe. Instead, a loose-fitting tunic and pants adorned her bustling figure, with colorful scarves wound around her neck that trailed behind her as she approached the captain.

"Ah, here," the woman said, and Harry could only assume she must be the doctor. Her words were thick with some kind of accent, but one much different than Redbeard's. "Here, you see? And, here." She held the device up under the captain's nose, pointing.

Captain Cass squinted. "What exactly am I looking at?"

"X-rays," the doctor said. "X-rays of your donkey's feet. Front feet." She pointed toward the aforementioned appendages as she spoke.

"Ah, I think I see it now."

Redbeard, Kitt, and Spiner crowded around the captain to peer at whatever was on the device.

Harry thought about getting up to join them so he could see, too, but his feet were still really sore. Instead, he contented himself by craning his neck as far as he could—which was still not nearly far enough to see anything—and listening intently.

"See this bone here?" the doctor jabbed a finger toward a spot on the screen. "And here? These are bones of donkey's front feet. They are shifting down."

She held her flat hand horizontal, then tilted it downward to demonstrate.

Harry jolted and looked down at his front feet. They looked fine to him. But, shifting bones sounded rather scary...

"Wait, what now?" the captain asked.

"Blimey," Redbeard muttered.

"I believe in Galactic Standard, this condition is called *laminitis*," Spiner suggested.

The doctor nodded vigorously. "Yes, yes, that is it, precisely. Laminitis. Your donkey has laminitis."

Harry looked to his feet again. What in the heck was that? Shifting bones and laminitis? Buddy's heart picked up again, sensing Harry's agitation.

Oh man, Buddy. Are we in trouble? This sounds serious.

"Sooo ... what does that mean?" Captain Cass asked.

The watching crowd had gone deathly silent. A slight breeze cooled Harry's sweaty hide and rustled the scant leaves high above their heads.

"It means your donkey is truly incredible!" the doctor exclaimed.

She released the device into the captain's hands and turned to face Buddy, folding her hands before her chest as she gave a deep bow.

Harry watched her in amazement.

"I am in awe of your donkey," the doctor said as she straightened. "He is truly a worthy beast. Truly a champion of Irrakis!" At these last words she flung her hands up toward the sky, and the robed men watching the spectators did the same.

The crowd itself broke out into raucous cheering.

Harry's skin prickled at such praise and recognition. For once, he didn't know what to say.

"Um, okay." Captain Cass's voice was nearly lost beneath the cheers.

"Many of our champions end up in a similar state," the doctor continued as the crowd noise gradually died down again. "This is partly due to our exacting standards for our competitors. But your donkey ... your donkey is in advancing stages of laminitis. It is a wonder he could run at all, much less win. As I said, a truly worthy champion." She gave a bow again, this time to the captain.

Redbeard shifted on his feet, looking profoundly uncomfortable.

"Uh, yes, well of course he is," Captain Cass said. "That's us ... purveyors of champion donkeys. But, um, what do we need to do about this ... lamin-whats-iss? Do we need to treat him?"

The doctor waved a dismissive hand and took her device back from the captain. "Yes, yes, we have treatment. As I said, most of our champions end up this way. Leave it in our hands. We'll take care of your donkey after the ceremonies, no worries there."

The captain seemed to relax a bit. "Oh good. Great. So what do we need to do now?"

"Attend the winner's ceremony!" the doctor exclaimed, throwing up her hands again. "Join the parade. Collect your winnings!"

The crowd erupted into cheers again.

"Well, I like tha sound of tha' last part," Redbeard mumbled.

"That's good," Captain Cass said, almost yelling to be heard above the onlookers. "Very good!" Her gaze met Harry's.

He inhaled sharply at her expression. He'd never seen her look quite like that before, at least not when she had been looking at him. Was that actual happiness he saw? Pride?

Harry gulped, and despite the throbbing in his hooves, he clambered to his feet, standing tall on the back of the truck.

The crowd cheered louder.

He turned and dipped his head in a semblance of a bow, and their thunderous applause filled his heart with song.

They went then to the city square, and to Harry's relief, he was allowed to ride on the back of the truck the whole way. The pirates rode with him, and Harry couldn't stop the smile that pulled at his lips.

He'd won the race! And, for the first time in a long time, he felt as if he had a tribe.

A burgeoning crowd followed behind the truck, and as they pulled up behind a wooden platform erected at one side of the city square, the swarm of people spread out across the pale flagstones. More people trickled in from the surrounding streets, until they stretched back as far as Harry could see.

The grand marshal of the race awaited them on the stage, beaming down at Harry as he carefully stepped down a ramp extending from the truck. Gingerly, he ascended another ramp, up onto the stage, as the crowd's cheering surged, echoing among the surrounding buildings.

The pirates followed him up the ramp, arraying themselves behind him as the marshal, bedecked in a sash of gold, green and crimson, stepped up to the podium.

"Citizens of Irrakeen," he said into a microphone, his words blaring out across the square, "visitors from around the galaxy, I present to you our Champion of the Irrakeen *Running of the Donkey!*"

The screaming people nearly overwhelmed Buddy's sensitive ears.

The marshal accepted a large golden trophy from a lean

young woman standing to his left. He held it up before the crowd, so that it glinted blindingly in the sunlight. "I now present to the captain of the *SS Bray*, registered owner of the winning donkey, this trophy, in recognition of your part in the conditioning and training of such a magnificent specimen."

The grand marshal reached the trophy out toward Captain Cass.

Tight-lipped, she accepted it, but not before glancing down at Harry.

Wait, what does that mean? Conditioning and training? I mean, I guess I practiced … is that what that means?

The captain thanked the marshal before passing the trophy to Redbeard, whose eyes were huge as saucers as he stared at his reflection in the shiny gold surface. Harry didn't think he'd ever seen the man look so happy.

The marshal left the microphone and leaned in to heartily shake the captain's hand. "You may collect your winnings at the palace at the conclusion of the parade."

"Thank you," Captain Cass replied, with a sideways glance at Redbeard.

The marshal returned to the microphone, holding out his hands to quiet the crowd. After several long moments, the crowd complied.

"Good people, please join us in a celebratory parade to the palace!"

The raucous crowd erupted into cheers once more, waving their scarves and banners in the air.

Harry couldn't help but feel elated. Even with the soreness in Buddy's hooves, this was the best day ever.

The grand marshal stepped down from the podium and gave Harry a pat on the neck before sweeping an arm out toward the truck. "If you all will climb aboard, the parade can commence!"

They did so, Harry gratefully laying down once more as soon as he could. His muscles were starting to feel a little sore from the exertion of the race, and his feet hadn't stopped throbbing.

The truck revved up and started to move slowly forward, easing through the crowd, which reluctantly parted to let it through. The people pressed in close around the sides of the truck, reaching out their hands in attempts to touch Harry.

He let them, enjoying the attention.

They muttered awed words of appreciation in many languages, and some of them seemed to be praying.

Harry hoped the doctor would be able to fix him up after the parade. This experience of hardly being able to walk or stand was hardly convenient. Especially now that he was so famous.

How could he tend to all of his adoring fans if he could hardly stand up?

Captain Cass was less appreciative of the attention, her hand dropping down toward the pistol on her hip whenever any of the outstretched hands got too close to her person.

Spiner scanned the crowd with a tablet, and a distressed Kitt pressed herself between the captain and Redbeard.

Redbeard, on the other hand, seemed oblivious, cradling the trophy in his lap and staring at it.

A robed man stumbled alongside the truck. "What is your donkey's name?" he asked.

"Harold," the captain answered, before Harry had a chance to respond.

"Harold," the man repeated, and then he repeated it over and over again to the people around him, who then repeated it to the people around them, until Harry heard his name rippling back through the far reaches of the crowd.

His ears perked.

"Harold!" the chant began. "*Harold! Harold! Harold!*"

He blinked, stunned at the display of people chanting his name. *They should be chanting* your *name too, Buddy.*

The chant grew louder, stronger. The truck crawled through the streets of Irrakeen, swarms of people chanting his name the entire way. And the grand marshal trotted before the truck upon a massive white horse, yelling again and again to "make room for the champion donkey of Irrakeen!"

Harry wished this moment could last forever.

22

"Wha'!?" Redbeard roared. "Wha' the blazes is tha' supposed to mean!?"

Harry startled at Redbeard's outburst. He'd been nearly dozing on the back of the parked truck, the steady strokes of soft brushes along his neck and back lulling him into a relaxed trance.

He looked out between the arms of the white-robed men who surrounded him to see his crew standing with a small, nervous man bedecked in an embroidered tunic and pants.

The man wore gold sandals and bowed deeply in Redbeard's direction. "I am sorry, good sir, but he had all the proper credentials!"

Behind him, a palace rose high into the gathering twilight, the golden roofs of its multiple spires a dull copper in the fading sunlight. The sultan's palace, according to the grand marshal.

Redbeard was still holding the trophy, its large bulk seeming inconsequential as he tucked it beneath an arm and took a step toward the small man, who scrambled backward with a squawk.

Captain Cass stopped the big pirate's advance, placing a restraining hand on his arm. "What do you mean, the *proper credentials?*"

The small man wrung his hands together. "I mean, good lady, he presented valid identification as a member of your crew!"

Harry cocked his head at this information, his eyes darting from the nervous man to the captain, to Redbeard, to Spiner, and lastly to Kitt, whose tail lashed in irritation. Aside from Node, who was still aboard the *Bray*, the pirate crew was all here.

This was the part where the pirates were supposed to be collecting their winnings. From this very man. But, it seemed that something had gone wrong. Very wrong, to judge by the reactions of his companions.

Harry wondered if he should do something, but he was still so tired from the race. And his feet hurt. And the brushing felt *sooo* good. He'd never been brushed before…

"It was a man?" the captain asked.

"Yes, of course!"

"Wha' did tha swine look like?" Redbeard bellowed. "I'll hunt 'im down and break 'im in half!"

The much smaller man wrung his hands even tighter, with an audible gulp. "Well, good sir, he … he had dark hair. Fell over his face a bit, nearly to his eyes. And fair skin, like yourself. About this tall," he held up a hand near Redbeard's shoulder, level with the captain.

Harry frowned. That didn't sound like anyone he knew from the *SS Bray*.

Redbeard spat curses.

The grand marshal was with them, too, a proper mean face darkening his expression as he held his hands on his hips. He seemed nearly as upset about this development as the pirates.

Spiner lifted a hand. "Captain, if I may, based upon the description and present circumstances, I can only conclude that the individual in question must be ... Djerke."

"My thought as well," the captain agreed.

"I'll rip tha' bastard's arms clean off," growled Redbeard, who had begun pacing in a tight circle.

White-robed men scattered to avoid his path.

Harry had no idea who they were talking about. "Who's Jerk?"

The rest of his crew startled at his question and turned around in surprise, as if they'd almost forgotten he was still there.

The robed men brushing Harry murmured to themselves —possibly because they'd never been around a talking donkey before—but they continued with their careful ministrations.

"A dead man walkin', tha's who!" Redbeard snarled.

"He's one of us," Kitt offered. Her yellow eyes were narrowed to slits, and the fur around her neck stood on end. "He *was* one of us. Right up until he went and stole our winnings."

"*What?*" Harry couldn't believe it. Who would steal from his own crew? "Why would he do that?"

"Because he's a jerk," the captain muttered. She heaved a sigh. "He must have followed us here, and we never even noticed."

"In a cloaked ship, Captain?" Kitt asked.

Spiner stiffened and stared off into space. "Ah, of course. That would explain..." His unfocused gaze sharpened, and he looked abruptly to the captain. "Captain! You don't think..."

But she was already looking angrier than Harry had ever seen her. "He's our tail," she growled through clenched teeth. "He's working for the bloody Feds!"

Now it was Harry's turn to stare wide-eyed at his crew. *The spy!* So the spy was never even aboard the *SS Bray…*

Redbeard spat on the ground, almost striking the foot of an alarmed-looking grand marshal. Then he uttered a long string of profanities, hardly pausing to draw breath.

The robed men around them watched with wide eyes, waiting to see what they would do next.

"Feds?" the grand marshal squawked, glancing worriedly to the palace steward. "Did you say Feds? Are you all in some sort of trouble we should know about…?"

"Course not!" Redbeard hastily replied.

"Just a little misunderstanding," Captain Cass assured the marshal. She shook her head and let out a little growl, beginning to pace. "I always knew there was something slimy about him…" Her right hand went to the pistol at her hip, fingers tapping at it restlessly. "But who dares violate the pirate code so completely? He must be out of his mind!"

"Pirates?" muttered the man in gold sandals to the grand marshal.

The captain turned and caught his enlarged eyes. "Don't worry. It's a colloquial term where we come from…"

"Ah, but of course," replied the grand marshal, hefting an eyebrow at his men.

Captain Cass faced Redbeard, and Harry gulped at the look on her face. "Djerke is a thief *and* a traitor," she hissed. Her fingers tightened around the grip of her weapon. "And as his captain, I hereby sentence him to face pirate justice for his crimes. *When* we catch up to him, you leave him to me. Understand?" Her eyes went to every other member of her crew, who nodded gravely in agreement, even Harry.

Harry gulped again, feeling scared for this Jerk fellow. Captain Cass looked *really* pissed.

Abruptly, she turned to the palace steward, who flinched

as her glare fell upon him. "You," she said. "How long ago did this man come by? How long since he left with our money?"

"Not too long," the man insisted, backing away slowly. "He left maybe thirty Galactic Standard minutes before you arrived."

"Arrr, we still have time to get 'im!" Redbeard stared hard at the captain.

"Thirty minutes," she repeated. She gave the truck a speculative look. "How quickly can we get back to the docks?"

The grand marshal stepped forward, glancing about nervously. "Dear Captain, please forgive our error. If only you'd updated your crew manifest..."

Captain Cass waved him off. "Yeah, yeah. Forget it. Mind if we borrow the truck?"

The grand marshal glanced around at his men, eyes wide, then shrugged. "Sure, why not."

The pirates moved hastily toward the vehicle.

Harry peered over the edge of it. "Oh, yes! Are we going to go catch the spy now?"

"Ah ah ah," the grand marshal chided, suddenly running up alongside the back of the truck, next to Harry. "I'm afraid you're still required for the, uh, final ceremony."

"But—"

"'Arry," Redbeard called out, "it's better if you be stayin' 'ere. This ain't gonna be pretty."

A stabbing pang of alarm ran down his spine. Surely his new tribe wasn't going to abandon him *already*?

The captain paused before climbing into the vehicle and looked up at him. "Harold, don't worry. We'll be back for you when it's all over."

The grand marshal bit his lip, then nodded. "Of course. Don't worry, my champion. We'll take excellent care of you while your friends are gone."

Spiner stepped up beside the grand marshal. "See, Harry?

There's nothing to worry about. One more ceremony and then you can relax while we deal with Djerke."

The grand marshal snapped his fingers, and several robed men approached the truck with a litter. Two of the larger men jumped onto the back of the truck and went to wrap their arms around Harry, who promptly yelped in surprise.

"It's okay," said the grand marshal. "They're going to help you off the truck. Try to relax."

Harry bit back a sigh and let the handlers lift him and place him on the litter, a soft, cushioned platform carried by two poles laid across the shoulders of several people. It was going to be a shame to miss out on all the adventure of tracking down the spy. Hopefully, his friends would also be able to retrieve the prize money.

Meanwhile, he supposed being tended to by all of these nice men in robes wouldn't be all that bad.

Would it?

23

The ornate palace interior was quite the spectacle for any mortal being to behold, let alone a lone donkey from the planet Cern.

"This is amazing," Harry blurted. "You built this with your *hands?*"

The grand marshal led the way down a long corridor, followed by Harry on his litter, carried by a new small retinue of garbed humans.

Whereas the people outside had donned robes of white, these new attendants wore sheer, ankle-length emerald sheets. Lengthy wraps the color of lavender lay over their shoulders and snaked down and around the waists of their wearers.

"Make way," boomed the grand marshal, "make way for our champion ... *the Ass That Runs.*"

Golden-oak wooden doors lined the clay corridor, with pairs of men—similarly garbed in emerald sheets—standing at attention outside each.

The men carrying Harry murmured, reciting the words

back in Harry's direction. "Our champion. The Ass That Runs."

"Wow," said Harry. "You guys sure know how to make a donkey feel welcome."

The party emerged into a rectangular, musty-smelling chamber. The room was crowded with furniture—chairs, couches, desks, and other things.

Harry was so taken with the furniture that he almost failed to notice the large swaths of throw rugs.

"Oh, uh, those almost look like fur," Harry commented, wide-eyed, as his gaze swept the room.

The grand marshal inclined his head, his lips settling into a thin smile.

"And, oh!" Harry took in the walls and the still objects hanging absurdly into thin air. "Is it normal for donkeys to hang out here?"

He rolled off the litter, almost taking out one of the men carrying it. With a small apology, he clambered to his feet and approached the nearest wall, craning his head up to inspect one. It didn't react.

"Uh, hello there, I'm Harold. Friends call me Harry." He paused and looked back at the grand marshal. "Why isn't he answering? Is he hard of hearing?"

The grand marshal tilted his head to the side. "You might say that." He gestured with his hands at two of the nearest men in the party. "Come, let us not get distracted, my champion."

The men stepped up to Harry, flanking him on both sides. One of them leaned inward. "You'll have plenty of time to get acquainted later," he said. "Come along now."

Harry peered up at the man, then back to the grand marshal, whose smile was more menacing than friendly. "Is everything okay? You guys don't look very happy."

The grand marshal took a step closer. "Oh, we're quite

thrilled to have you. You are The Ass That Runs. You run so that we don't have to."

"Huh?" Harry chewed on the cryptic phrase, turning it about in his head. "Does that mean you have sore feet, too?"

"Come along, now. Enough chit-chat." The grand marshal's expression was decidedly mean-faced. He glanced up at the men flanking Harry. "Let's get on with it, before his companions get back."

Harry looked back and forth between the grand marshal and his entourage. "Wait a minute. What's going on? I thought there was a final ceremony?"

The grand marshal smirked. "Oh, there is, yes. It's very final."

Harry didn't like the sound of that. Not one bit. He glanced around. The men flanking him stepped closer, now definitely appearing quite menacing.

Buddy, I think it's time to run, one more time. Okay?

His host got the message. He bolted back in the direction they'd come from, narrowly avoiding grasping hands. They made it as far as the first rug, where Buddy's front hoof slipped as soon as it made contact. He collapsed in an undignified heap.

Harry looked up only to find that he was surrounded.

The grand marshal loomed over him, shaking his head. "Ah, see boys, behold *The Ass That Runs.*"

"*The Ass That Runs,*" the men repeated again.

Harry no longer felt flattered.

"*This* is why we make sure our champion is in such poor shape," the grand marshal said. "It would be a shame if you were to escape, now, wouldn't it?"

This time it wasn't just Harry's hooves hurting that made him balk. It was the terrifying change in attitude from his attendants, now surrounding him closely and ensuring he had no further opportunities for escape.

It didn't help that the deeper he was led into the palace, the darker the corridors seemed to get. The lamps along the walls were spaced further and further apart, with long stretches of dimness between.

And, the group had now been joined by four more green and lavender swathed men, only these four held staffs tipped with blades.

Very sharp-looking blades, which they pointed in his direction whenever he hesitated to take another step.

Harry grudgingly kept moving forward, if only to keep from being pricked. His ears laid back and his head hung low as he limped along.

He thought back to his tick tribe on Cern, who had been taught that they were the chosen of the Gods. If these humans were gods, they were decidedly not nice. Being among "the chosen" was overrated.

What's going to happen to us, Buddy? This doesn't look good. Why did we let the captain and the others leave without us?!

The further he went into the sultan's palace, the more trapped he felt.

Even if they come back now, how will they find us in here?

Escape seemed impossible. The palace corridors were like a maze. His entourage watched him closely. And, there were spears with sharp points involved.

He heaved a sigh.

Maybe we shouldn't have eaten all that peetz-a, Buddy. Maybe if we hadn't, our feet wouldn't hurt so much, and we'd be able to run fast enough to get out of here!

The thought only depressed him further.

The men led him through a set of guarded gilded doors, into a cool, circular chamber.

This chamber had lanterns set at regular intervals along

the walls, and a large stone slab on the floor at the far end. To each side of the large stone slab were two smaller slabs. The floor was richly carpeted and the adobe walls painted in vivid colors.

For a moment, Harry forgot his dread and depression, head lifting as he picked out the shapes of other donkeys in the wall paintings. They all looked very happy, frolicking and dancing across verdant green fields.

Hey, that kind of looks like Cern!

In the midst of them all looked to be a young man. He rode a donkey also, and his hands were outstretched towards the others dancing around him. Light seemed to stream from his palms and the top of his head, and eventually those painted lines turned into other things. Trees and plants and all kinds of other animals. Even some other humans.

Harry gawked. "Hey, who's that?" he asked. "He looks pretty cool. And it looks like he really likes donkeys!"

"He does," the grand marshal stated mildly. "You will get to meet him soon enough."

"Wow, really?"

Some of Harry's concern faded. Maybe this final ceremony wouldn't be so bad, after all. Those painted donkeys sure looked happy.

"Step up here, if you would," the marshal instructed, gesturing to the largest slab.

Harry did so, still staring around at the painting.

He did not notice the mysterious dark stains that marred the stone beneath his hooves, nor the carefully carved groove around the edge of the slab and finely decorated clay bowl positioned beneath the groove's spill point.

The entourage that had accompanied him surrounded him once more, taking their places along the edge of the stone block.

The grand marshal stood near Harry's head. "Now, lay down, with your head there."

Harry glanced down at the spot where the marshal pointed, but hesitated. "That doesn't look very comfortable."

"Do it." The grand marshal reached inside his robes and pulled out a long, jagged blade.

"Uh," Harry said, gulping as he settled onto the slab, then rolled over onto his side. "What's that for?"

24

Captain Cass and her crew climbed out of the truck, already exhausted from the effort of driving through the crowded streets of Irrakeen.

No one had bothered to move when Captain Cass had laid on the horn, but the locals had been more responsive to the angry ravings of Redbeard, who'd leaned out of the passenger window, snarling and salivating like a madman.

The docks were quiet. In fact, the SS *Bray* was the only ship left. A lone figure emerged from one of the squat buildings that served as an operations center.

Unlike the rest of the locals, this man wore a simple jumpsuit with a large utility belt. Several of the items looked innocuous enough, except for a current generation wide-arc laser pistol and stun stick. As he approached the group, he held his hands at his hips. "Are you the crew of this ship?" he asked, tilting his head in the direction of the SS *Bray*.

Redbeard stepped up alongside the captain and set his feet wide, scowling as he folded his arms across his chest. "Who be askin'?"

Cass glanced to Redbeard, but decided to let the moment

play out. If she needed to act quickly, better to let her second-in-command provide a distraction.

The man in the jumpsuit stood his ground. If he was intimidated by Redbeard's act, he didn't show it.

A professional, then.

"I'm Inspector Mufatish. Will you do me the courtesy of identifying yourselves, or shall I assume that you are the wanted criminal known as Redbeard?" He nodded to the ginger giant, then flicked his gaze to Captain Cass. "And you, the declared captain of this vessel?" He ignored Kitt and Spiner, standing a few paces behind her.

"Arrr, a wanted criminal?" Redbeard started.

Cass cut him off, staring back at the inspector. "What you should be concerning yourself with instead is the thief who stole our winnings."

Mufatish hardly blinked. "A thief, you say? Well, there was a man here a few minutes ago. As you can see, he's no longer on this planet … and no longer my concern. You, however…"

Several figures stepped into view then, out of the shadows, each of them holding long rifles.

"Hey," Harry tried again. The marshal was ignoring him. "You're not going to cut me with that, are you? I've never been cut before. I'm afraid."

The grand marshal waved his blade in the air over his head, chanting. "Lord of the Light, we call upon you on this, the One-hundred-sixtieth anniversary of your ascension to *The Golden Fields*."

"The Golden Fields? Lord of the Light? You don't mean my homeworld, Cern, do you? Because my friends have a ship. We could take you there, if you like. Seriously. There's no need for a ceremony. You can just ask for a ride."

The grand marshal paused and frowned down at Harry.

"There is only *one way* to access The Golden Fields ... and that is via sacrifice."

Harry chewed on his lip, thinking. "Oh, that must be inconvenient, then."

Droplets of blood from the grand marshal's wrist plopped onto the surface next to Harry's ear.

"Wait, no, no no! What are you doing? Are you okay?" Harry asked, feeling more than a little faint at the sight of blood. "That had to hurt."

The grand marshal swapped the dagger over to his other hand, and repeated the process on his other wrist.

"No, please don't—" Harry began, hearing the rush of his own blood in his ears, his heart pounding. More droplets of blood fell from the space above his head, landing with a sickening pitter-patter against the stone.

Harry promptly passed out.

"This doesn't have to come to violence," Captain Cass said, trying to keep her voice level even as she felt her heartbeat elevating in her chest. How long had it been since she'd been in an even fight?

Mufatish looked smug as the figures drew closer, standing in a loose semi-circle around the pirate crew.

Cass ran some quick mental calculations. If they moved quickly, they could probably avoid the first round of fire. It was good that they'd left their own rifles behind, and only carried their sidearms. Quicker on the draw, and more accurate at this range.

"You're right," Mufatish replied. "It doesn't. You can lay down your arms and put your hands over your heads."

Cass heard Kitt mewl softly. Of all of her crew, Kitt would be the most likely to draw first blood.

"Captain, I calculate our odds of escaping this encounter without injury at one-to-five," Spiner said, his voice flat of emotion.

Spiner wasn't much of one for joking, but Cass couldn't help but appreciate the irony of the statement. After all, he'd never specified *who* might escape the encounter without injury.

Mufatish lifted an eyebrow. "See, this will go better if you do as I say."

"Pah," Redbeard spat. "We've seen worse odds, 'aven't we, Cap'n?"

Well, that much was certain.

The chanting continued, penetrating Harry's subconscious as he drifted in and out of a dream-like state. He was back home with Buddy, roaming the green grassy fields of Cern with the rest of the donkey herd.

"Who would've thought the Gods could be so cruel, Buddy?" Harry mused, as his host trotted behind a cluster of jennies. "And bloody."

Buddy ignored his symbiont tag-along, consumed with a more basic desire to catch up with one of the females who was starting to fall behind the others.

"We shouldn't have let ourselves be separated from our friends." Harry continued his monolog, permitting himself space to acknowledge and accept his fate. "I don't want to die alone."

Buddy stumbled, his hooves still sore. The jennies ran off, hee-hawing at the poor jack as they did so.

"It's okay, Buddy. None of us are perfect, are we?" *Certainly not me. No matter the tribe, I've always been left behind.*

Harry wondered what it must feel like to be loved. To be unconditionally accepted. To never be abandoned.

A tear trickled down his snout.

For a brief moment, Harry considered letting go of his control of his host. Even jumping off, and experiencing the feeling of grass and dirt one more time before he died.

"What's that, Buddy?"

Maybe it was his own imagination, but Harry thought he sensed the flicker of a thought from his host.

Don't leave me.

Harry paused. "Oh, Buddy, I'm so sorry for even thinking of abandoning you like that. You're right … we're both going to die. And as long as I'm here, we'll be together."

Harry felt a surge of warmth from within as Buddy picked himself up off the grassy ground.

I'm not alone … I'm NOT alone!

"Buddy! I've been thinking I've been alone all this time, but you've always been here with me. How could I have been so blind to the obvious?"

Buddy took a cautious step forward. It didn't hurt. So, he took another step. Then another. His feet didn't hurt anymore!

"Wow, it's a miracle, Buddy. You're cured!"

Buddy ran. He caught up with the herd of jennies, to one who was especially responsive to his renewed advances. She didn't run away from him. She didn't even try to kick or bite him.

"I love you, Buddy!" Harry nuzzled into his host's spine, fully committed to riding things out with his lifetime friend.

Meanwhile, his host proceeded to ride things out with the jenny.

Nothing like a bright moment in this dark, cruel world, Harry mused.

. . .

"Yes, Red," Cass drawled. "We've seen worse odds. Now and then." She eyed Mufatish, but his smirk stayed in place. Ballsy bastard. Obviously, he was confident—to the point of arrogance—in the ability of him and his men to deal with her crew. And he struck her as just bored enough to enjoy a violent means to an end.

So be it. She had a traitor to deal with, and no dockyard watch dog was going to get in her way. Not today.

Cass slowly lifted her hands, splayed out to the sides, but only to about hip level. She watched Mufatish closely, a plan forming quickly in her mind. "But maybe this fight's not worth it," she said. "Just like that time on Aresh Five. Remember what happened there?"

"Arrr, aye," Redbeard muttered. "How could I forget, Cap'n?"

Kitt hissed in acknowledgement.

"I remember well, Captain," Spiner said.

Cass kept the smile from her face with difficulty. Good. They remembered. They knew what to do. She raised her hands higher. "We surrender," she said.

Mufatish's dark eyes gleamed. "Wise choice, Captain. Now, throw down your weapons and kick them towards me. Slowly, mind you. My crew has itchy trigger fingers. Don't give them a reason to shoot."

His companions did indeed look eager for a reason to shoot. That would up the challenge a bit.

Redbeard grumbled. She knew he always hated this part.

Obediently, Cass and her crew slid their pistols from holsters and tossed them to the pavement, then kicked them toward Mufatish. The sound of so many weapons skittering across the concrete was loud in the tense silence.

Mufatish smiled in self-satisfaction, then tilted his chin up and gestured for his people—men and women both, Cass realized as they drew closer—to move in for the arrest.

Just as they'd done on Aresh Five, she and her crew put their hands on their heads and waited. They stood quiet and motionless as the Irrakeen customs officers approached.

It wasn't until the man aiming to arrest her reached for the manacles on his belt that she finally reacted.

At precisely the moment one of his hands left his rifle to retrieve them, his steady gaze shifting from her for just a second, she smashed her armored knee into his groin, both hands locked around his rifle and wrenching it from his grip.

She spun the weapon as he doubled over, brought the butt of it hard into his temple, and whipped around to face Mufatish before the other man had even hit the ground.

Mufatish's mouth was agape, face as white as his jumpsuit as his hand scrambled for his own pistol.

Cass fired.

The laser bolt blackened a hole in his chest.

He staggered backward, hand falling limp from his holster. He stared blankly at her for a moment, then toppled to the pavement.

Cass turned a quarter step to her right, already sighting down the barrel at her next target; the poor sap who'd chosen to go after Redbeard.

The large pirate had the much smaller man by the throat, suspended in the air. Redbeard's other hand held the man's rifle.

That one was taken care of, then.

Cass executed another quarter turn to Kitt, only to find the *Homo lyncis sapius* bounding after her would-be arresting officer, the woman already fleeing, limping and screaming, a trail of blood in her wake from a large gash on her leg.

Spiner filled her sight, and she quickly lowered the rifle.

The android gazed at her impassively, the woman who'd attempted to arrest him lying unconscious at his feet. His large black eyes blinked once, and the electrodes protruding from his fingertips withdrew.

Shouts echoed across the docking area, and Cass whirled again to see another group of customs officers running toward them, rifles at the ready. They fired, fast and sloppy. Not troops, then … just bureaucrats with guns. Laser bolts flew wide as Cass and her crew crouched and ran for cover.

Redbeard emptied his hands—tossing both the man he'd been strangling and the man's rifle to the ground—and scooped up his own pistol, then hastened toward the *Bray*'s boarding ramp.

Cass and the others did the same, though Cass held onto her borrowed rifle. She tucked it under one arm and fired both weapons at the new group of officers, felling two with practiced ease.

Beside her, Kitt let out a horrific, hair-raising roar, her fully automatic pistol mowing down another three.

Cass swore under her breath and ducked another shower of incoming fire. She'd forgotten how ferocious Kitt could get when her bloodlust was stoked. They needed to end this fight, and fast, or the seemingly passive engineer would go into full predator mode … and no one wanted to see that.

Cass still had the occasional nightmare from the last time Kitt had lost control.

She threw herself behind one of the *Bray*'s landing struts, pressing her back against it, then leaned out to squeeze off a few more shots.

Redbeard had taken cover behind another strut, off to her left, and Kitt and Spiner huddled behind the one to her right.

Cass glanced to Redbeard, but he was in full battle mode, too, gleefully mindful to nothing but destroying their opposition. His battle cry mingled with Kitt's second roar as he swung around his cover to fire unhindered.

"Red!" Cass barked, but he paid her no mind. "Red, get your ass back—"

An incoming laser bolt chewed into his shoulder and he roared in pain, spinning back behind his cover.

Cass swore again, louder this time. She looked to Kitt and Spiner. Only Spiner seemed unaffected by the heat of the moment.

The approaching officers were getting nearer now, their shooting more precise. But their numbers had already drastically thinned.

Bureaucrats or not, these were dedicated—if overmanned —professionals. Of course, Kitt hadn't launched into a rampage of rage yet, either.

Ballsy bastards.

"Spiner!" Cass yelled. "We need to end this! Now!"

"Affirmative, Captain." Spiner's voice was completely calm. He reached down to a false pocket on his thigh and opened the flap. Then opened a small compartment built into his leg and removed three small spheres that resembled silver marbles. Touching a fingertip to each one, he leaned around the landing strut to toss them at the feet of the dock-yard officers.

They didn't react.

Well, not until the marbles exploded, releasing a charge strong enough to knock out beings twice as large as Redbeard for a full twelve hours.

Those were an upgrade from the ones Spiner had used to get them out of the mess on Aresh Five, and Cass greatly appreciated *not* being in proximity to their blast this time.

The officers collapsed mid-run, some skidding to a rest, the rest flopping onto the ground, their bodies rolling several feet from their momentum.

The dockyard was silent.

"Arrr!" Redbeard frowned at Spiner. "Why'd ye do tha'! Took all tha fun outta it!"

Kitt growled low in her throat, tail lashing, seemingly in agreement.

"We don't have time for this!" Cass snapped. "We have a traitor to catch, remember?"

Redbeard sobered, then winced. He cradled his right arm gingerly to his side. The laser burn in his shoulder looked pretty bad. "Arrr, right," he said.

"Everyone on board before more of those bastards show up!" Cass ordered. Fear tried to push up her throat, concern for Redbeard's injury, but she clamped down on it. Now wasn't the time.

The lot of them pounded up the boarding ramp, and Cass slapped the button to close it. The *Bray* would protect them from any late arrivals who might try to arrest their departure.

They raced to the bridge and hurriedly took their stations.

"Node!" Cass barked. "Get this boat in the air!"

"Oh, hello," Node's lazy voice filled the bridge. "Wasn't expecting you all back so early. The ceremony isn't even finished yet."

"Effin' thief stole arrrr winnings!" Redbeard yelled.

"Node, can you hack the dockyard system's departure roster and find out if there was a ship that left about forty minutes ago, Corvette class, registered as *Girlboss*?" Cass barely paused to breathe. "If so, I want you to calculate its heading and set a vector to pursue!"

"Um, okay. Scanning now."

There was a moment of ringing silence.

Cass drummed her fingers against the arm of her chair.

Beside her, Redbeard prodded at the charred hole in his shoulder, face tight with pain.

"Stop touching it," Cass barked, causing Redbeard to jump in his seat. "You'll just make it worse."

"I found a ship matching your description, Captain," Node spoke up at last. "It departed forty-five minutes ago. I have plotted its most likely trajectory. Engines are warming now. Are you sure you'd like to follow it?"

"Of course I would," Cass replied, biting off the words.

"What about Harry? It'd be a shame to leave him now."

"He's fine," Cass retorted quickly, struggling to bite back her frustration at the surly computer. "He's getting pampered. We'll come back for him. We have a more pressing matter to attend to for now. The man piloting the *Girlboss* has been reporting our location to the Feds this whole time. That's why we haven't been able to shake them. *And* he stole our prize money. And *my* ship."

"Well, okay," Node said, after a small pause. "But … well, you might want to see something first. About Harry. It's kind of important, I think."

"We don't really have time for this, Node." Cass rubbed at her forehead, peering anxiously out the viewpoint, waiting for more customs officers to arrive at any moment.

"This will only take a moment," Node said, and then her view of the dockyard changed to a display of a local news broadcast.

"As I am obviously unable to partake in the festivities myself," Node said, "I've been watching the local feeds to keep apprised of events."

The video feed showed footage of the parade, with people swarming around their truck and the crowd chanting Harold's name.

Cass rolled her eyes, muscles tense with impatience. "Yes, Node, we were there."

"Hang with me for a sec," Node said. "While watching the broadcast, I learned something quite distressing, and from your eagerness to depart the planet, I'm thinking you may be unaware."

"What are you talking about?" Cass threw out her hands in exasperation. "Node, the longer we sit here, the further away *Girlboss* gets, and the greater the chance more customs officers will come and try to arrest us!"

"Nearly there now," was all Node said in reply.

The broadcast was given in the native tongue of Irrakis, which Cass did not understand. But, Node had helpfully put subtitles on the display, which she skimmed quickly as the view changed to a shot of Harold being carried into the palace on a litter by an escort of purple and green-clad men.

"THE NEWEST CHAMPION DONKEY OF IRRA-KEEN," the screen read, "IS QUITE A SPECIMEN INDEED. TRULY, THE LORD OF LIGHT WILL BE PLEASED BY THIS OFFERING. THE GRAND MARSHAL IS CERTAIN TO RECEIVE A SEAT AT THE LORD'S RIGHT HAND, WHEN THE SACRIFICE IS COMPLETED AT TONIGHT'S ZENITH OF THE FULL MOON."

A pained gasp escaped from Redbeard.

Cass came up out of her chair, hands balled into fists. "*What!?*"

"Presumably you understand what a sacrifice is?" Node asked.

"Blimey," Redbeard muttered.

"THE BLOOD OF THE CHAMPION DONKEY WILL WET THE ALTAR OF THE LORD OF LIGHT ONCE MORE." The words scrolled across the bottom of the screen. "AND HIS BODY BE ENSHRINED IN THE HALL OF CHAMPIONS FOREVERMORE."

"Yes, yes, I get it," Cass choked out. "Turn it off!"

Node complied.

Cass stood stock-still, staring out into the stillness of the dockyard, the bodies of dead and otherwise incapacitated officers littering the pavement. Her breath came hard and fast.

For a long moment, no one spoke.

"Captain," Spiner said in a hushed tone. "Upon further cross-referencing with local records, I can confirm that according to tradition, the Irrakeen grand marshal does indeed intend to sacrifice Harry to their local deity."

"Why didn't you tell us this before?" Cass demanded, turning to glare at the android.

He seemed to shrink back in his chair. "I-I did not have reason at the time to cross-reference the cultural traditions," he offered weakly. "The initial research on the ceremony says nothing about a sacrifice."

"It does, actually," Node interjected, his voice as chilly as Cass had ever heard it. "The ceremony is clearly implied via the liberal use of euphemism, which it seems you are not programmed to interpret."

Spiner slumped in his seat. "I am sorry, Captain."

"*Fuck!*" Cass looked out the viewport again. "When is this supposed to happen?"

"Tonight," Node said. "When the full moon reaches its zenith in the night sky. Which I calculate to be right at midnight, local time."

Her mind raced, balancing odds and possibilities, weighing priorities. Go after the traitorous thief Djerke and get their desperately needed winnings back, not to mention *her ship*, possibly ending the dogged pursuit by the Feds at the same time ... or risk another run-in with more customs officers—and who knows what else—in an effort to save Harold, the strange little talking donkey who had, surprisingly, turned out to be almost as useful as he was annoying.

She chewed at her lip. "Node, is it possible for us to intercept the *Girlboss* and still get back before midnight?"

A red hourglass briefly lit up on the viewport, rotating as Node stayed silent.

Kitt growled, stepping out from behind her console to stare at the screen.

"I'm afraid not," Node replied at last, his disembodied voice somber. "With Redbeard's ugly mug being plastered all over the galaxy on the Federation's Most-Wanted list, it'll be difficult to re-dock. Not without a fire fight. And let me remind you, the *Bray* is not equipped for space combat."

"*Bollocks,*" Redbeard said.

Kitt let out a displeased mewl.

Cass paced a tight line in front of her captain's chair, mind racing. She lifted her gaze and met Redbeard's stare.

"Wha' do we do, Cap'n?" he asked quietly.

25

Harry felt himself rising back to consciousness and debated fighting it. It was so nice here in this dreamland, where he and Buddy could be together, romping through the green fields of Cern with feet that didn't hurt, and pretty jennies as far as the eye could see.

And, he could reflect fondly upon his time as a pirate intern. Sure, it had involved cleaning up a lot of shit, and feeling his body turn inside-out every time the ship jumped to hyperspace, but there had also been so much *adventure*.

There was the time he'd gotten to check out a gas station and a store. And see a nebulae and an asteroid field. And there was the time they'd nearly gotten assimilated by the Borg—or, er, the Feds. And the time he'd gotten to meet that interesting character Beiber. Not to mention that time Redbeard had *thanked him* for the Zoomels.

How could he forget all his hours of watching *DS9* with Node, or that time Spiner had cooked him some protein cubes? Oh, and that time Redbeard had stepped in puke! That had been pretty funny.

Harry smiled at the memories. He'd had more adventure in his brief time with a pirate crew than he'd ever had back home.

If it had to end this way, it was worth it, wasn't it? At least he'd been accepted as a part of a tribe again for a short little while before he died.

They couldn't have known that his winning the race would end this way. Could they? Surely not. Surely they wouldn't have left him if they'd known … right?

A little snake of worry slithered its way through Buddy's unconscious brain, waking him up a little more.

He'd been a good pirate intern, hadn't he? Maybe one day, he would have made a good pirate. Maybe one day, he could have even captained his own ship, like Captain Cass. She was so badass.

Harry had proven that he could be a good pirate, too. Or he thought he'd done a pretty good job of it. After all, beyond being a prize-winning champion, he'd done his part at Dill-billy's store.

I could have been a great pirate, I know it...

I could have been … or am I, already?

How long exactly did a pirate internship last? He'd been an intern for awhile now. He'd seen them fight. He'd seen Redbeard's best mean-face, Kitt's quiet competence, Spiner's helpful nature, and the captain's calm and collected leadership during high-stress situations.

Wait. Buddy, I already know how to be a pirate! Why can't I be a pirate now?!

The thought jolted him fully awake.

Harry opened his eyes and found himself laying on his side, on the stone slab, looking directly up at the grand marshal, who was still chanting some nonsensical words.

His hands were lifted toward the chamber's ceiling. Blood

ran down his arms from his wrists, soaking his sleeves and dripping slowly onto the slab near Harry's head. The man clutched the dagger loosely in one of his hands, the blade glinting orange in the light of the lanterns.

Harry realized with a start that he could now see open sky, too. A small, circular portion of the ceiling had opened somehow. Outside, the darkening sky of dusk was visible, the first stars twinkling faintly into existence.

Wow. It's so beautiful!

For a moment he was distracted by the sight, but then he remembered what he was supposed to do.

Act like a pirate, Harry!

He put on his best mean face and heaved himself to his feet. Too bad the grand marshal and his companions were too busy looking at the sky and chanting to notice. Oh well. Just like Dillbilly, they were distracted. Which meant he could do *this*—

Harry kicked out with both hind feet, nailing one of the men behind him in the kneecaps. There was a terrible cracking sound and the man screamed shrilly and fell, clutching at his legs.

The other men stopped chanting, frozen for a confused moment as they stared down at the injured man.

Harry ignored the shooting pains in his hooves, let out a grunt, and spun his hindquarters toward the next man, kicking again.

His rear hooves made solid contact with the second man's chest. An audible whoosh of air escaped his lungs as he was flung across the chamber, hitting the floor in an unmoving heap.

By now the grand marshal and the other lone remaining man had come to their senses.

"*Bad donkey*," the grand marshal hissed, his face livid. To the other men, he shouted, "Get this *bad ass* under control!"

Harry laid his ears back and sunk his teeth into the marshal's right arm. The man shrieked and took a wobbly step backward in response, the curved dagger falling from his bloodied fingers.

In the back of his mind, Harry replayed the grand marshal's words. *Buddy, did you hear what he called us? We're badass, just like Captain Cass!*

The lone uninjured man was scrambling for something on a nearby shelf.

Harry flung his head sideways, teeth still clamped on the marshal's arm, and tossed the bleeding man out of the way. Head lowered and teeth bared, he charged at his next target.

The man was white as a sheet. With one last desperate grasp, he finally gathered up what he'd been searching for and pointed a short gray rod toward Harry.

Harry didn't slow.

He was a pirate—*a real pirate*—and he was going to kick ass, just like Captain Cass. *Wait until my friends find out what I've done. Wait til they see—*

A bright blue flash shot from the end of the rod, and every muscle in Buddy's body locked up in shock.

Harry nearly released control of his host, recoiling in pain as the jolt extended into his own tick form. He crashed into a pile at the man's feet, helpless and twitching.

Oh no! Buddy, what happened? We were doing so good...

The screaming from the man with the broken legs was suddenly overwhelming. If only Harry had a way to cover his ears…

The grand marshal staggered to Harry's side, cradling his torn arm. His face was pale.

"Dagger!" he gasped, holding out his left hand, blood still seeping from his wrist.

The man with the rod hastened to comply, though his hand shook as he handed the weapon over.

"All right, *you*," the marshal growled, glaring down at Harry. "I've had quite enough of this. The Lord of Light can deal with you now!"

"But … but, sir," the remaining man interrupted nervously, "the full moon hasn't fully risen yet. You *know* what the Scriptures say! We must wait, for surely that is the path to green fields returning to our barren lands."

The marshal hesitated, then glanced up to the circle of exposed sky. It had grown darker, the stars brighter. He ground his teeth in indecision.

The sounds of shouting, screaming, and weapons fire from beyond the chamber door interrupted further contemplation.

The marshal's eyes grew wide, and both men turned to face the closed door.

"Who *dares* to interrupt our sacred ceremony!?" He hissed so vehemently that spittle flew from his lips.

Harry wished he could look where they were looking, but Buddy's body was completely unresponsive. Whatever that blue flash had been, it had a paralyzing effect. Given how he had landed, he was stuck looking up at the small circle of sky. Not an unpleasant view, but it sounded like something much more exciting was happening out beyond the chamber's door.

A moment of panic gripped him.

What if he was permanently paralyzed? *How can I be a badass pirate if I can't move?!* This was even worse than having sore hooves.

"Whatever it is, they won't get past the palace guard," the second man stated, but his tone sounded anything but confident.

The grand marshal didn't seem overly convinced, either. He gestured toward his standing companion with a blood-drenched hand, dagger and all. "Get the stun baton. Quick!"

The man did as he was told, then the two of them stood ready, brandishing their weapons in the direction of the incoming threat.

Behind Harry, the man with the broken legs continued to wail.

"Fadel, by the Lord's mercy, shut up!" The marshal groaned, then wobbled again on his feet. He reached out to his companion to steady himself.

"My legs!" Fadel cried. "My legs!"

"Yes, we know," the marshal muttered. "It is very clear your legs are broken. But what does it matter? You will not need your legs when you join the Lord of Light in his Kingdom above!"

For that, Fadel had no answer. But he continued to whimper.

Harry tried with all his might to move. The noises from outside grew louder. But it was useless. Buddy's muscles wouldn't comply with his commands to get up.

Then, through the thick wooden doors and adobe walls sounded a bellow Harry would have recognized anywhere.

Redbeard, it's Redbeard! And the others must be with him, too. They came back for me. They're here to save me. My heroes ... my friends!

A warmth like he'd never felt before suffused his numb body, and Harry thought he might burst from overwhelming relief and happiness. He made a hard effort and managed to move his eyes just a little, allowing him to leverage Buddy's nearly 180-degree field of vision.

He looked toward the door.

And then, just like his happy heart, the chamber's wooden door swelled outward. Until at last it exploded—unlike his happy heart, thankfully—throwing a shower of splintered wood into the chamber.

The grand marshal and his upright companion ducked, shielding their faces from the shrapnel.

The pirate crew poured into the room like a maelstrom, and Harry's mouth would have dropped open in awe if he could have moved it. He watched them with the one eye not stuck gazing at the floor.

The man next to the marshal fired his rod, and Harry's heart dropped as Captain Cass, who had charged ahead in the lead, was struck in the chest by it.

But, to his shock, the blue flash only arced over the surface of her armor, leaving her unaffected. She gave a grim smile and fired the rifle held at her shoulder.

The man with the rod blew backward, hit the wall, and crumpled to the floor.

Faster than Harry's eye could track, the grand marshal stepped to Harry's side and shakily put the edge of the dagger to Buddy's throat.

"Stop!" the man shouted.

Harry quailed. *Oh no, Buddy! This is it! We're going to die! I love you, Buddy ... just remember, I love you. We did good, didn't we? I certainly think so!*

The pirates froze where they stood, just inside the ruined door, maintaining their deadly combat stances.

Only then did Harry notice the rather gruesome blood splatter adorning their clothes and armor, and the bandage wrapped around Redbeard's right shoulder and chest.

Whoa. So badass. Do you think they'll let me wear a wrap, Buddy?

"How dare you interrupt this sacred ceremony!" the grand marshal screamed. "No outsiders are allowed in here, you *blasphemers*. The Lord of Light shall smite you where you stand!"

There was a brief silence as the pirates peered around the chamber with expectant expressions.

"Eh, well," Redbeard muttered at last, "seems the Lord o' Light don't mind arrr tresspassin' so much?"

The marshal's face grew slack, the hand holding the dagger trembling against Harry's shaggy neck. "Turn around and leave, now," he croaked, "or I swear by the Lord's mighty hand, you will not escape this palace alive."

The captain raised her eyebrows and looked back over her shoulder, to the trail of carnage they'd left in their wake. Then she faced the marshal again and shrugged. "I don't know. We weren't supposed to get this far, either."

"An' yet, 'ere we arrrr," Redbeard supplied. A feral grin split his bushy red beard. "Give us tha arse, and we'll be quietly on arr way, see. Don't give us tha arse, an' I'm bettin' you'll be the one who be regrettin' it."

"You don't understand what you're meddling with," the marshal hissed. "You signed the forms to enter your donkey into the race. You agreed to the terms and conditions. Interfering now is not only blasphemous, it's *illegal*."

"I feel your forms should have been more clear," Captain Cass said evenly. "I'll be filing a formal complaint with the Galactic Contractual Office, certainly."

The marshal's face was ghostly white. "If you do not allow me to complete the ceremony, I will cut his throat right now. Either way, you will be losing your donkey."

The dagger's edge pressed a little harder against Buddy's neck, and Harry could hardly bear to watch. He buried deep into the donkey's spine and hung on tight.

Be brave, Buddy. It's okay. The captain will get us out of this, somehow...

"I would advise against any rash action, Grand Marshal." It was Spiner who spoke up this time. "As you well know, in your Scriptures—penned by *the mighty hand of the Lord of Light himself*—it is explicitly commanded that the champion donkey be sacrificed at the precise moment the full moon reaches the zenith of the sky. If you sacrifice Harry now, you will be committing blasphemy yourself."

Redbeard and the captain both stared at Spiner, mouths agape.

Spiner continued, "We are merely heathens, and as such, blasphemy is expected of us. But you? According to your rather lengthy biography in the local newspaper, *The Irrakeen Word*, you have spent your entire life in service to the Lord of the Light. If you botch this ceremony, do you think the Lord of the Light will offer you forgiveness? Or will he condemn you to eternity in the Barren Land of In-Between?"

The marshal stared at the android, and Harry felt the pressure of the knife against Buddy's throat ease.

"On the other hand," Captain Cass said, "you could give us Harold now, and then you can find another donkey to sacrifice at the correct time. Or, you know, just wait another twenty years to ascend, or whatever."

Spiner nodded. "The captain is correct. You still have a couple hours left to find a substitute."

The grand marshal was shaking all over now, his skin ashen.

Harry realized with a start the man was still dripping blood from the small cuts on his wrists, and then there was the large chunk of his arm Harry himself had mauled.

The grand marshal crouched there, silent, as if contemplating his next action or his next threat, drops of blood continuing to drip off his hands onto the floor.

And then, abruptly, he collapsed to the floor face-first, the dagger clattering away from his still, limp hand.

The pirate crew didn't move, but stood staring down at the body, expressions of confusion flitting across their faces.

"Er, I suppose that's one way to go," the captain said after a pause.

"Very anticlimactic," Kitt commented mildly.

"Arrr, no one wants to see ya rip out another throat, me kitten," Redbeard muttered, glancing sideways at the cat-like alien as she moved further into the chamber.

Kitt only mewled innocently in reply.

Captain Cass crossed the room quickly and knelt by Harry's side. "Harold, are you all right?"

Harry tried his best to speak. Wanted to shout. Wanted to say, *"Yes, I'm fine. I'm so glad you came back! You missed the best part ... when I was kicking their asses!"*

But all that came out was a small puff of breath from his nostrils.

Spiner stepped up alongside Harry and pulled out his tablet. "Ah, his nervous system has been paralyzed by some kind of electrical charge. Probably the same charge they fired at you, Captain." He leaned down and pulled a small pen-like device from his belt, then jabbed it into Harry's neck. "There."

Harry had neither the time nor ability to protest.

"He should regain use of his limbs in a few minutes."

"Thank you, Spiner." The captain stood up and gestured at Redbeard. "Red, are you up to carrying him with that shoulder?"

Redbeard slung his weapon over his back and grunted in response. He ambled over and lifted Harry with one arm. "Not a problem, Cap'n."

"Good," Captain Cass replied. "Then let's get out of here before someone else shows up."

All Harry could do was silently cheer. *Buddy, we did it, we survived! No one can stop us now.*

And indeed, the pirates met no resistance on the way out of the palace. The truck was waiting outside for them. Captain Cass and Kitt got in up front, and Redbeard climbed onto the back with Harry, with Spiner following.

"We should hide Harry," Spiner said.

Redbeard grunted again and laid Harry down on the truck bed, then threw a tarp over him.

The sounds of celebration continued to fill the streets as throngs of parade-goers partied in clusters. But no one bothered the unremarkable truck as it made its way back to the dockyard.

Finally, the truck came to a halt and the engine switched off.

The starry sky returned to Harry's view when the tarp was yanked off, looking even more beautiful than before.

The pirates clambered out of the truck, and Redbeard picked Harry up again. Aside from the lone silhouette of the *Bray*, the dockyard appeared empty.

By this point, Harry was feeling somewhat capable of movement, if groggy. Still, it felt nice to be pampered, so he relaxed and let his ginger giant of a friend carry him around for a while longer.

"That was too easy," Captain Cass said as they walked toward the *Bray*. She glanced around the yard, weapon at the ready as if she expected an ambush at any moment. "There should have been reinforcements here by now."

"Arrr, Cap'n. Guess we won't be needin' tha hostages, after all."

Spiner said, "Captain, shall I remove our prisoners from the hold?"

"I'll help," Kitt offered.

"Alright," the captain conceded. She still looked uneasy. "Let's get on with it and get the hell out of here." She stepped up to the ship and opened a panel, revealing a button, which she promptly pressed. The doors to the cargo hold opened, and a ramp lowered to the ground.

At the top of the ramp, a familiar uniformed woman stood at stiff attention, a pistol leveled at the pirate crew.

A moment later, several more figures emerged from the hold, fanning out behind her. She took a step forward, a cold smile forming upon her lips. "Ah, Captain Bambi. We were starting to get worried about you."

26

"Woah, the mean-faced lady is back," Harry said, craning his neck past Redbeard's shoulder to get a better view. Whatever Spiner had injected him with was working. He was able to move his head and lick his teeth. It was a start.

Redbeard, for once, spoke quietly, his voice a harsh whisper in Harry's ear. "Wha? Stop mumblin' an' stay quiet."

Captain Cass stepped up to the base of the ramp, her rifle hanging loosely from her hands. "What are you doing on my ship?"

The mean lady, who Harry remembered as being called Commodore Something, took a matching set of steps forward, the metal of the ramp clanging as her boots made contact. "*Your* ship? Let's give up any pretenses, shall we? You are a pirate and a deserter, and I am a commodore in the Federation Navy. You and your crew are going to surrender now, or I promise you will regret it."

The captain squinted up at Commodore Something. "I thought we had a week?"

The mean lady in blue practically spat out her reply.

"*Rear* Admiral Hawke is my superior, yes, but that doesn't mean he gets to make up the rules. When it comes to *deserters*, Federation policy is clear. Hawke may have a soft spot for you, Bambi, but rest assured that I do not."

Captain Cass took another few steps forward, her own metallic boots causing the entire ramp to vibrate. She paused just paces in front of her pursuer. "So tell me something, Commodore. Since when does the Federation Navy work with pirates and thieves?"

The mean lady frowned. "What are you talking about?"

"The tail you had on us. He's a pirate."

"Informants are not my department."

Harry lifted his muzzle to Redbeard's ear and tried to whisper. "What are we going to do? Blast them?"

Redbeard made a grunting noise, but didn't reply. Though Harry thought he could make out an upward curve of the man's lips.

To the ginger giant's side, Kitt and Spiner appeared frozen in place, maintaining an almost unnatural level of stillness.

Harry put on a smile for their benefit, but no one showed any sign of noticing.

"Did you damage the computer?" Captain Cass asked, gazing past the Federation officer into the hold.

The commodore's shoulders moved fractionally. "Why would I bother? I entered the Federation override code. All *properly* registered ships are programmed to comply."

"Ah," the captain nodded. "But do you know the override code for the holding pens? It'd be a shame if the livestock were to accidentally get loose or stampede about…"

The Federation woman's stern composure cracked, her forehead wrinkling as her nostrils flared. "That's irrelevant. Quit stalling and—"

Captain Cass cut her off with a shout. "*Node*, if you're listening, I *know* you can read between the lines!"

The commodore sneered and leveled her pistol at the captain. "That's *quite* enough."

Then, two things happened at once. First, a loud series of snarls and roars erupted from the hold, sounding like the lions Harry had once learned about from his tribe's elders. At the same time, the Federation officer squeezed off a shot, a tight laser beam slicing into the captain's midsection.

"*Noooo!*" Redbeard shouted.

"No!" Harry echoed.

Captain Cass crumpled to the ramp with a dull thud.

The commodore bared her teeth in a savage grin. An alarmed shout from her men wiped the smug look off her face just as quickly. A chorus of moos erupted from the hold, followed closely by a growing rumble and the startled protesting of chickens.

"Look out, Commodore!" one of the men shouted.

"*Ahhhh!*" shouted another as a hefty bull knocked him to the ground, instantly trampling him.

The Federation boarding party tried to scramble out of the way as a herd of cattle fled from the cargo hold, quickly followed by Harry's herd of donkeys. A pair of officers grabbed a protesting commodore by the arms as they hustled down the ramp.

"Hang on, 'arry!" Redbeard pivoted and rushed to get away from the oncoming Feds and livestock.

Kitt and Spiner were also on the move, taking cover at the base of the ship beneath the ramp. They held their own weapons at the ready, taking shots at blue uniforms as the Feds ran.

Redbeard noticed his companions and altered course. Huffing, he set Harry down on the ground and leaned against the frame of the ship. "Arrr, I've got to get tha cap'n before she gets trampled!"

The predatory roars from the cargo hold upped in intensity, and a moment later feathers were flying around everywhere as chickens trailed the donkeys out of the hold, half-flying, half-running.

Spiner fired off a couple more shots, then replied, "I'll cover you. Try to hurry."

Kitt mewled, her pupils fully dilated as her gaze flicked back and forth between blue uniforms and frenzied livestock.

Harry tried to sit up. "I can help," he mumbled.

Redbeard reached out to restrain Harry, then winced. "Stay 'ere." He scanned the chaos as he crouched, licking his lips. A cow ran past, a hen clutching at its back. As soon as it was out of the way, Redbeard sprinted forward.

Spiner took a few steps forward himself, risking partial exposure to the livestock, and laid down covering fire.

Kitt had gone prone, her stomach inches above the ground as she crawled forward on all fours.

"What are you doing?" Harry asked.

"Shhh," she hissed. A moment later, she paused and wiggled her posterior from side to side.

Harry tilted his head in confusion at her antics. *What is she doing? Is that a dance? Does she have to pee?*

Then, without warning, she sprang into action, bolting out into the chaos, a flash of white fur that moved faster than Harry's eyes could track.

He was so distracted by watching Kitt that he didn't notice when the commodore crept up alongside the ship, closing in on Spiner.

"Don't move," she said, her pistol pressing into the back of the android's head.

Harry's stomach clenched at the sound of her voice. He

turned his head only to realize his green friend was in peril. He tested his limbs, attempting to stand. He resisted the urge to let out an "ugh" as they wobbled, then collapsed beneath his unsteady frame.

With her off-hand, the commodore reached up behind Spiner's right ear and began to poke and prod. After a moment, she paused and pressed. A section of his skull appeared to peel back, revealing circuitry and a couple of small buttons.

"If I may?" Spiner began.

"No, you may not," the mean lady replied, then pressed one of the buttons.

Spiner collapsed to the ground.

At that moment, Redbeard appeared around the ramp, an unmoving Cass slung over his shoulder. His mouth opened in shock to find himself suddenly at the business end of a Federation-issue pistol.

The commodore regarded him coolly. "Set her down and put your hands up. Or don't." She leveled the pistol at his face. "It would bring me great pleasure to end you."

Redbeard opened and closed his mouth, sweat running down his face, which was quickly draining of color. "Blimey," was as much as he chose to say.

Oh, no! C'mon, Buddy, we've got to do something. Harry tested his limbs again, slowly scooting his body around to face the backside of the mean Federation officer.

Redbeard knelt and gently laid Captain Cass down on the ground. His hand lingered on her face, cupping her cheek, his eyes filled with tears. "I'm sorry I failed you, Cap'n," he whispered.

Awww, I think he loves her, Buddy. Harry resisted the urge to whimper in sympathy. Instead, he dragged his body forward. *Just a little further.*

The commodore stiffened as a white blur flashed across the ground a couple dozen feet away.

A uniformed officer leapt out of the way, just dodging Kitt's outstretched claws. She skidded along the ground, then flipped back onto her feet, never noticing the dire situation facing her fellow crew members as she bolted off in pursuit of another cluster of livestock and uniforms.

The commodore shook her head. "You are a pathetic lot." She gestured with the pistol at Redbeard. "Now, stand up and place your hands over your head. Good … now, turn around."

"Arrr you gonna shoot me in tha back, then?" Redbeard asked.

"Shut up and get on with it."

Redbeard turned around as ordered.

The mean Federation lady took a step forward, her pistol still outstretched. She aimed it at the base of Redbeard's skull. "Do you have any family you'd like to pass a message along to?"

Harry closed the remaining distance. All he needed to do now was get up and kick her. *If* he could stand up. His legs were beginning to itch, and a sensation of pin-pricks ran from shoulder to hoof.

"Arrr, ya. Me little girl," Redbeard muttered.

The Federation officer smiled at that, sending a chill down Harry's back. She was an awful, evil human, he decided.

"I didn't realize you had children."

I didn't, either. Wonder why he's never talked about them?

"All the more tragic … for you," the mean lady said.

"Oh, I don' have children," Redbeard said.

Harry blinked. *Huh?*

The commodore seemed equally confused. "Excuse me?"

Redbeard turned his head to the side and spat. "I was jus' stallin' so's 'Arry could get his feet workin'."

Ohhh. Oh!

The commodore snarled. "What are you talking about?"

Come on, Buddy! That's us! Harry clambered to his feet and twisted around, hopeful that he had his legs lined up. With no time to waste, he'd have to hope for the best.

"You know what? Nevermind," the mean lady snapped. "I'm done with the lot of you. Prepare to die!"

Harry felt his front legs wavering. He kicked back quickly, before he could fall over. "*Oomph!*" he groaned.

"Argh!" another voice answered.

"Ha!" a third voice called out.

Harry collapsed, but not before he'd managed to fully extend his hind legs right into the side of the commodore's knee. As he craned his head around to judge his handiwork, he saw her tumbling over the inert form of Spiner, then Cass, losing her balance and her pistol as she toppled to the ground.

Redbeard spun around and pounced on the evil Federation lady's back, yanking on her arms and pinning them behind her back.

"*Ouch!*" came her muffled shout, her face pressed into the ground. "Get *off me!*"

Redbeard busted out his best mean-face and pulled her up to her feet, nearly yanking her arms out of their sockets.

"You been bested by arrr secret weapon," he snarled.

The commodore winced, whether at the words or from her rough handling, Harry couldn't tell.

Her eyes widened at the sight of Harry. "Wait, I was assaulted by a *donkey?*"

Harry rolled his legs under him and struggled his way up to standing. *Okay, let's give her our best mean face ever, Buddy!*

The woman's brows lowered over her eyes. "Is it *smiling* at me?"

Redbeard grinned at Harry. "Cute fer an arse, ain't he? Fierce, too."

"That's right," Harry said. "Get a good look at me. *I'm* the one who bested you." He paused to puff out his chest. "*Pirate intern* Harold, the meanest, most badass donkey in the galaxy!"

It took some time, but after reactivating Spiner, Redbeard was able to calm Kitt down. Together, they tied up the remaining Federation officers—those who had not fled or been trampled or mauled to death—and rounded up the wayward livestock.

Spiner remained with Captain Cass in the captain's quarters, where she'd been tucked into the bed. He scanned her with his tablet as Harry paced around them on his tender hooves.

"Is she going to be okay?" Harry asked.

Spiner reached down and jabbed her with a cylindrical object.

"Is that what you used on me?"

Spiner scanned the captain again, then paused to look up at Harry. "It is similar to what I used on you, yes. The captain is stable. She'll be okay as long as we're able to get her to a medical facility in the next twenty-four hours."

"Oh, good!" Harry cheered, then lowered his voice. "You know what, Spiner?"

"What?"

"Learning disability or not, you're pretty badass."

Spiner stared at Harry for a long, silent moment, then returned his attention to the captain.

. . .

Harry let out a sigh of relief as Redbeard punched a button on the inside of the cargo hold, causing the ramp to slowly close shut. "Phew. I don't think I can take any more excitement today," he said.

Redbeard turned around and fixed Harry with a level gaze. "Arrr, tha's fer certain. You done good, 'Arry."

Did you hear that, Buddy? We've done good. Harry's ears straightened and he smiled proudly at Redbeard. "Thank you. What can I do to help now?"

Redbeard shook his head. "Take a break, 'Arry. Ye've earned it."

"Oh, I guess I can do that." His feet still aching, Harry settled his butt down on the cool surface of the hold. He thought about saying something about the pain in his hooves ... but if they were going to Haven to fix up the captain, surely they'd be able to do the same for him?

Redbeard turned to regard the other pirates. "Spiner, get tha captain secured in her bunk so she don't be fallin' out when we jump, then meet me an' Kitt on tha bridge."

Spiner nodded. "Affirmative."

"Redbeard?"

"Yes, 'Arry?"

"What did you do with the Feds, after you tied them up?"

Redbeard leaned in toward Harry, with a squint that almost looked like a wink, and laid his accent on thick. "We stowed 'em away in *carrr*-go cubes an' left 'em on tha *tarrr*-mac, along with some other riff-raff we bested and tied up earlier. That'll learn 'em."

Harry's ears drooped as he considered their fate. Sure, they'd almost killed his friends, but some of them hadn't seemed so bad. "Aren't you worried they'll starve?"

Redbeard drew back, his lips twisting sideways. Notably, he dialed his accent back to intelligible levels. "Arrr, yer no fun, 'Arry. If it be botherin' you, we can send some sorta message to tha planet, once we clear orbit."

Harry perked up, satisfied with that answer. They might be pirates, but that didn't mean they had to be cruel to their enemies. Captain Cass had taught him that even in the short time he'd been a member of her crew. And if she wasn't around right now to keep the others in line, well, Harry figured it was up to him. "Yes, please. That would be the nice thing to do."

Redbeard slowly shook his head. "Tha *nice* thing to do? Blimey."

He turned away from Harry. "Kitt, yer with me."

Kitt looked up from where she sat on the ground, licking her forearms and claws clean. "*Meow.*"

Redbeard tilted his head. "Kitt?"

She had resumed licking her fur.

Harry looked at her, confused. He'd never seen her like this. In fact, before he'd been abducted off of Cern by the Gods and then kidnapped by space pirates, he'd never seen anything like her. Was this normal? Judging from Redbeard's expression of concern, it wasn't. "Is she okay, Redbeard?"

Redbeard stepped up to Kitt and knelt down to scoop her up off the floor with his good arm.

"*Meow!*" Kitt said in protest, but didn't attempt to resist as Redbeard placed her on his shoulders, careful of the bloodied bandage that still covered the right one.

"Don't worry. I know wha' to do. Kitt, ye've earned yer kibble."

Kitt's ears stood at attention. "Kibble?"

"Aye."

She began to purr audibly, then nestled in atop her human perch. "I like kibble."

Redbeard reached up and scratched her underneath her chin. "C'mon."

Harry suddenly remembered something. "Wait, Redbeard! What about the jerk? He still has all our prize money! Are we even going to be able to leave?" Captain Cass had said without the prize money, they might be stuck on Irrakis for a long time. And Harry most definitely did not want to stay on this planet for even one more minute.

Redbeard paused and scowled. "When I get tha chance, I'll blast 'im to pieces! But tha Cap'n comes first. She needs medical attention, an' I ain't gonna risk her life by delayin' it, not even to go after a good-fer-nothin' traitor. We'll go to Haven first, get 'er tha care she needs. Then we'll deal with tha jerk. And as fer leavin' this ball o' sand ... let's jus' say our hostages were more than willin' to make a few *contributions* to our coffers in exchange fer their lives." He grinned widely.

Harry exhaled in relief. "Whew! I'm so glad. That was really nice of them."

Redbeard frowned and blinked. "Err. Right."

"I've always wanted to go to Heaven."

Redbeard got a funny look on his face, then broke out into another grin. "Heaven? Hah! Yer pretty funny, fer an arse."

Harry watched as Redbeard turned away, shaking his head, and carried Kitt out of the cargo hold. Spiner had already left to secure Captain Cass in her bunk, leaving Harry alone with the rest of the livestock.

"Totally a cat."

"Node?" Harry looked up and around, trying to find the familiar red eye.

It was on the wall right in front of him. It blinked, then expanded into a large, dancing smiley face.

"Node!"

The digitized face paused its dancing. "Hey, friend. How was your day?"

Harry beamed at the wall. "Amazing. Crazy. Terrifying. I've got so much to tell you!"

"Let me guess. A sacrificial ceremony?"

"Yes! How did you—"

"And an improbable victory over Federation forces?"

"Yes! That too! How did you—"

"Know?"

Harry bobbed his head. "Yes!"

"I'm Node. I know everything."

Harry laughed, gleeful.

Node rewarded him by performing a happy dance across the wall. Good thing Kitt was no longer in the hold.

"Say," Harry ventured. "What was all that noise earlier? It sounded awfully scary."

"Oh, I put on some video clips from an old Earth TV station called *Animal Planet*. Lions. Tigers. Bears. That kind of thing. Worked even better than I thought it would."

Harry surveyed the holding pens with all their frazzled animals. His herd still milled around nervously, and the cows ignored their hay to peer around the hold with bright, wary eyes. The chickens' feathers were all ruffled as they indignantly picked around their pens, seeming more offended by the excitement than scared by it.

"You really scared the shit out of them," Harry observed. "I should probably clean that up."

Node winked in response. "Probably, but you heard Redbeard. You earned a break."

"I guess so. So, now what?"

"Want to watch the second season of *Deep Space Nine*?"

Harry almost leapt off the floor in excitement. "What? There's even *more* episodes?"

"Oh yes. One-hundred and seventy-six in all. We're just getting started."

"Well, then, what are we waiting for? Put it on!"

"Of course."

Harry tilted his head, suddenly remembering their dramatic escape from the gas station and the giant rifle. The cannon. "Wait!"

"Yes?"

"How are we getting out of here? Won't someone be trying to stop us?"

Node chuckled. "Hah. I don't think so. Not only did your captain incapacitate most of the dockyard staff already, but I planted a worm in the planetary government's network. Anyone who tries to access the defense grid is going to be in for a big surprise."

"Oh?"

"You ever hear of anyone being rickrolled?"

"Umm…"

"Never mind, of course you haven't. Basically, once they try to perform an action within their systems, a really awful music video will play instead."

"A music video? Is that like a TV show?"

"Yes."

"Oh, well that's not so bad."

Node's pixelated face smirked. "Oh, it is, trust me. *Trust me*. You ready to watch your show now?"

Harry thought about it for a moment. He was still worried about the captain, but then, Spiner and Redbeard both had said she'd be okay once they reached Haven, and they were going to go straight there.

Satisfied that they were out of danger, then, and no one else was going to get hurt, Harry let himself relax. "Yes," he sighed, "I'm ready. Bring on the second season of *Deep Space Nine!*"

"As you wish, my friend. Enjoy."

Node winked, then blinked out of existence, replaced by a giant viewscreen and a thematic music score.

Harry laid down on the floor, resting his chin upon his folded front legs. "Ahh, I love this show."

—The End

Did you enjoy this book? Reviews are the lifeblood of our business. When you leave your honest review, you help us find more readers, and we get to put out more books (like the one on the next page!).

GRAB BOOK TWO TODAY!

ABOUT THE AUTHOR: ETHAN FRECKLETON

Whether I'm writing self-help books, songs, or absurdist low-brow comedies, my works embody the authentic and sometimes irreverent perspectives of a person who has tried to live in two worlds at once: one of professional and technical excellence, and another of romantic abandon, in search of a world that values love over fear.

ABOUT THE AUTHOR: J. R. FRONTERA

J. R. Frontera has been telling stories in some form or another since she could hold a crayon and draw. Her love of science fiction and fantasy originated with her early exposure to the worlds of *Star Wars*, *Star Trek*, *Lord of the Rings*, and *Dune*. When she's not writing, momming, podcasting, or working at her full-time job, she's often horseback riding, playing videogames, or cosplaying. Find out more about J. R. Frontera at jrfrontera.com.

KEEP IN TOUCH

For more information on the authors, or to sign up for a mailing list, please visit:

https://www.ethanfreckleton.com
https://jrfrontera.com